HOLLY GARDEN, PI: RED IS FOR R OKIE

Book #1
Handcuffed In Texas Series

ANNE GREENE

Elk Lake Publishing
Holly Garden, PI: Red Is for Rookie
(Book 1 in Handcuffed in Texas Series)
Copyright © 2015 by Anne Greene

Requests for information should be addressed to:
Elk Lake Publishing, Atlanta, GA 30024
Create Space ISBN-13 NUMBER: 978-1-942513-38-4

Cover and graphics design: Anna O'Brien
Editing: Deb Haggerty and Kathi Macias
Published in association with Joyce Hart, Hartline Literary Agency

I dedicate this book to my precious Lord Jesus,

my dear husband, Larry,

and my darling children,
Michelle, Shaun, Michael, and Geoffrey.

"Let your light so shine before men that they may see your good works and glorify your Father in heaven." **(Matthew 5:16, NKJV).**

CHAPTER ONE

"Ever notice that Cupid rhymes with stupid?" Hands jammed on my hips, I surveyed the five-star hotel ballroom decorated with porcelain cupids and scarlet hearts.

Here I was, Hollyhock Garden, clad in strappy, spiked heels, Valentine-red dress, diamond earrings, and shaking knees…working undercover security. Hired by my mother, the same dear lady who saddled me with my name.

My friend Temple Taylor grinned at me, twin dimples in her milk-chocolate cheeks. "Only you would rhyme Cupid with stupid."

My heart stuttered. "Yeah, with me being stupid." We moved to the ballroom's center to watch the first trickle of invitees enter. To perk up my mind from my lost love, I quipped, "If only my fourth-grade Sunday-school students could see their teacher now. They picture private investigating as dangerous."

Amusement flashed across Temple's exotic face. "That is *sooo* you! Your mom spins the world to make this Meet-A-Thon happen…" Temple swept her arm to encompass the softly-lit ballroom filled with white-clothed tables. "…melt-in-your-mouth chocolate hearts, glittery Valentine cards, tables assigned according to professions for the eligible bachelors, and you want more excitement."

My left eye twitched like it does when I'm stressed. "Who'd have guessed Dallas had so many lonely executives? Thus the need for tight security."

"Right. Not even the rich want to be dateless on Valentine's."

My stomach flip-flopped. Dateless. "Rub it in."

To help me forget my own lack of a male love-of-my-life, I roved around the room reading a few of the designated professions etched on placards above centerpieces of roses and candles flagging each table. Temple kept me company on my rounds. "This sign reads 'Attorneys.' This one 'Physicians.'" I pointed. "That one's for architects. And—"

"Honey, you can bet your white bod that this dinner-bash beats a dating service."

"Yeah, for lonesome work-a-holics who don't have time to look for dates." I buried my nose in the sweet fragrance of a velvet-textured rose. "It's sad."

My friend gave a throaty laugh. "Sad, nothing. Your mom's created a meet-market. We can shop 'til we drop."

I gave Temple a "yeah-right" look. "Shop all you want. Tonight's strictly business for me."

Temple smiled with the same dimpled sincerity that gained her more friends than she could text in a single lunch hour. "You don't have to buy. Window-shop. You look smashing in that red dress. It's time you stop languishing. This holiday's created for love. Make a new start."

I rolled my eyes. "New *risk*, more like." Hugging myself to hide feelings of rejection still clinging to me from my last romantic venture, I shifted to the next table. "I'm here to work. Garden Investigations doesn't need any more bad publicity. A splashy robbery pulled off under our noses tonight would close our doors."

Temple tapped one of the table placards with a coral-tipped nail.

"Hey, girl, I noticed your mom didn't invite any of your new spy-buddies from work."

"Just Matt. He's my backup tonight."

Matt Murdock, my next-door neighbor and lifelong pal, had worked for Uncle Robert at Garden Investigations a year longer than I. After Dad's murder, Matt hovered over me like a too-protective brother. I liked working with the sweet nerd, but hated him butting his nose into my non-existent date life.

Holding up my black sequined evening bag with its noticeable bulge, I joked, "What we don't need tonight is someone besides Matt and me packing weapons."

Temple's almond-shaped eyes twinkled. "What you need in that purse is lip gloss and Tommy Girl perfume."

I snorted. Even Temple wanted me to date. I shook my head until the few strands of hair framing my face tickled. I had yet to succeed in love, but I had high hopes for my shiny new career of detecting.

"What I need is a real client. Someone other than my mom. I need a case."

The seven-piece orchestra climbed the stairs to the small stage, settled behind their instruments, and began to warm up. With the first bars of a romantic song, a few smartly-dressed men sauntered inside. They passed us and tossed Temple and me appraising glances. As several women in designer gowns glided in, their evening Jimmy Choos shimmering against the blue carpet, I squirmed in my high heels. *And these women are also dateless?* I made a wry face and scanned the growing crowd. Diamonds everywhere. They sparkled on long feminine necks, elegant wrists, and tiny ears. Gold barged in second. This gala offered an open treasure chest. The only thing missing? A sign inviting pirates.

More and more men roamed into the room. Along with expensive aftershave, I almost smelled testosterone. Some wore tuxes, some dark suits. Most ambled toward their assigned tables, trying for the cool look, but appeared as uneasy as trapped lions. Some resembled cuddly, tux-suited bunnies with rounded tummies, and others penguins with polished heads. A few simulated antelopes about to flee the watering hole. No warthogs to be seen.

I glanced toward the door. "Looks as if everyone's here. I better get with it." I sucked in my lack of theatrical presence and headed toward the stage.

Silently praying I wouldn't break my neck, I tottered up the three steps, crossed the strip of floor in front of the musicians, and clutched the hard sides of the glass lectern. Most days I wore jeans and tees, so I felt exposed in the short dress. Knees pasted together, I produced a smile and spoke into the microphone.

"Good evening."

My soft words boomed over the elegant crowd. I swallowed and prayed my voice wouldn't tremble. "Welcome. The Dallas Ladies Auxiliary is so pleased you accepted their invitation to this evening's Valentine Meet-A-Thon." I wiped a clammy hand on my velvet-covered thigh and watched numerous men slink through the rose-scented room like robbers casing a glamorous bank.

"If the rest of you gentlemen will kindly find your seats, the ladies can start making rounds." I took another breath and hurried through the rest of Mom's ridiculous instructions.

"Each lady will choose a seat next to a gentleman of her choice. Dinner will be served, and if an interest sparks on either side, business cards will be exchanged." I pried one hand loose from the glass and waved it in what I hoped was a graceful, welcoming gesture. "Now relax and enjoy your evening."

I again navigated the steps in my short dress and tricky shoes.

Feeling inadequate to begin my first field job, I hit level ground and bee-lined to the pillar Temple stood beside. "How was that?"

"You did good." Temple's smile looked encouraging.

I nodded then blurted out what was uppermost in my mind. "You know what?" I scanned the crowd for problems and tried to erase the uncertainty from my face. "Sometimes I think I'm crazy to become a private detective. How can I be a light while working in the sinful underbelly of society?"

Temple snorted. "Come on, Holly. Don't look so upset. I believe in you."

"Yeah, but... I've agonized about this job. Sometimes dirt rubs off."

"If a place is dark, even a flickering candle sheds a lot of light."

"You don't think the dark will douse the candle?"

"Not your candle."

"But what if I don't have what it takes?"

"Trust me. You do. Now I'm off to dig for gold. You're on your own." Temple blew me an air-kiss, waved a finger, and slipped past me to undulate, like a sun-blessed wave, among the tables. Her '50s--style shimmering gold sheath caught every male eye. Men's faces acquired that stunned, slack-jawed look they got when they first gawked at Temple, no matter what outfit she wore. My friend wafted irresistible female pheromones. Males dug into tux pockets for business cards, stood, and flaunted them at her.

I leaned against the column. *Lord, please let something more exciting than singles finding mates happen tonight.* My matchmaking-mother finagled this evening to get me out of Uncle Robert's hair. But knowing Mom, she had a dual purpose going here. Mom wanted her adventure-loving daughter married. I wished she'd cut me some slack. My new career demanded all my attention.

Matt waltzed over, a grin on his intelligent, computer-geek face.

"See anything suspicious, Garden?"

For the nth time, I eyed the room from end to end. "Not yet." The atmosphere had taken on a texture of intimacy, with the candlelight, scent of roses, and romantic music doing their number on the senses. Men eased into their personalities-on-display roles as ladies slipped into empty seats next to them. Business cards appeared like snow on the Alps. "You spot any trouble?"

"Nope." My old friend locked his gaze on one particular young lady.

I'd often thought he preferred blondes, and this one looked stunning in a black strapless, above-the-knee Vera Wang creation.

I gave Matt's arm a friendly poke. "I'm guessing you want to police her side of the room." A sisterly type of happiness made me wink. "Just keep your mind on business."

"Right." He straightened his tie. "You're always looking out for other people. Why not bat those eyelashes at me and catch yourself a gent?"

Amusement gleamed in his eyes, revealing the teasing boy still strong inside the man he'd grown into, so I lapsed into one of the pretend voices we'd shared through the years. "Get on with ye."

"Somebody's got to keep ye out of trouble." He grinned, one eye on security, the other on the blonde, and took off.

After he left, I surveyed the guests and tried not to fall under the room's romantic spell. Some nifty red sports-car types revved their engines among the black-BMW guys parked at the tables. Glittering, perfume-scented women surrounded them, intent on test-driving. Drivers had all evening to check out the offerings.

So I glided into the effervescent scene, praying I knew what I was doing.

I kept both eyes wide, searching for sticky-fingered men or women seeking treasure more tangible than a relationship. I prowled my half of the bustling room, eye-frisking each guest for a concealed weapon.

Soon waiters removed empty salad plates and began serving the prime rib. The room crackled with barely controlled hormones. Women glowed. Men preened. Peacocks performing a mating dance.

Looking for trouble, I wove around the full "Engineers" table and passed the glittering-women-double-seated "Physicians" table. Everything appeared to be going without a hitch until—

A delightful breeze of suspicion flitted through me, interrupting my thoughts. Hair rose on the nape of my neck. Something wacky at the back of the room. I glanced over to see if Matt, working security on the ballroom's other side, noticed. He looked busy separating two gentlemen from commandeering one apparently special lady.

As I approached the rear table where four burly men, dressed in matching black tuxes, red bow ties, and red cummerbunds, long hair flicking their shoulders, sat glowering, my tickle of wariness itched. Temple must have picked up on the men too because she sashayed to my side.

I whispered in her ear, "Mom didn't arrange that table. Get a load of their placard: 'Champion Wrestlers.' It's not professionally lettered." A creepy sensation crawled over my skin. "Mom has zero interest in athletes. She absolutely wouldn't invite wrestlers." What was happening here?

"Mmm. Maybe she missed a good thing."

Excited goosebumps stood at attention on my bare arm. "No socialite tire-kickers are shopping among those musclemen." Their table of pretty-faced wrestlers with juiced-up muscles remained an island of loneliness in the crowded room. "Wonder why they came."

"They each paid their five-hundred bucks, or they wouldn't be inside." Temple took a step toward them.

I put a hand on her arm. "Don't." Tugging Temple with me, I backed away from their table. "Look at those scowls. Those guys need an attitude adjustment."

"Spoilsport."

I smiled. "I might find a client there—after they chill. They're the kind of semi-shady guys who hire surveillance." My smile grew to a grin. "Or protection."

Temple pushed her generous lips into a mock pout. "I can just see little ol' you protecting those mountains of muscle."

I huffed and tried to toss my hair, forgetting I wore an upsweep. "Gatecrashers or not, those wrestlers aren't causing any trouble. I'll keep them high on my radar screen and check with Mom when she arrives. She's doing her usual late dramatic entrance."

"Since I'm not prospecting for muscles, I'll get back to my mining." Temple winked and sauntered toward more promising tables.

As I turned away to retrace my surveillance route, my gaze swept across a man I hadn't noticed before. He stood near the ballroom door with his back to me. I did a double-take. An off-duty cop. I could spot one a mile away. The way he walked, stood, and observed his surroundings. A cop couldn't disguise his identity. Calm, professional, strong, he looked as though he controlled the world. With legs braced wide, right foot behind, he kept his piece away from the crowd. Even from the rear the guy looked cocky.

Someone touched my shoulder. I jumped. While I'd been eyeing the cop, Matt had crossed to my side of the room.

"Who invited the police?" Matt jabbed a thumb toward the ballroom door.

"My question exactly. Maybe one of the rich types demanding extra protection. Or maybe the cop's moonlighting as a bodyguard."

Matt rubbed his clean-shaven chin. "Maybe. Don't know."

"Whatever. I'll find out."

"You do that." Matt sauntered back to his side of the ballroom.

I planned to check the cop out but didn't want to meet him this way. I had an image to project. I was an investigator. A professional. Strong. Independent. Cool. Granted, I had a lot to learn, but I sure didn't want to be seen on Valentine's night appearing to shop for a man. In a town as closely connected as Dallas, if we met in the line of fire—and I had no doubt we would—he'd never take me seriously. Sometime tonight I'd inform him I was actually working.

I policed my half of the room then headed back toward the champion-wrestler table.

Big warm fingers grasped my arm with just enough pressure to make me brake and take notice. The dark-haired, fine-looking man extended his other hand. A sense of recognition nagged me. But I didn't know him.

He sat with his back to the wall at the attorney table catty-corner to the wrestlers' enclave. I shook his waiting hand, feeling warmth and solid strength I hadn't expected to find in a lawyer's grip. He wore his dark suit like other men wore uniforms. Daring. Proud. Indomitable. Candlelight reflected mystery in his brown eyes. With the kind of smile you see on a man given an unexpected dish of ice cream, he stood and offered me the empty chair his polished wingtips had guarded. With the chair now free, a bevy of females flew over from different tables and circled him.

"Sit a while."

His compelling expression excluded everyone in the room but me. I didn't want the invitation, but my feet, aching from the unaccustomed spiked heels, did. So I slid into the seat.

"Thanks, but just for a minute."

Sophisticated women glared, shoppers vying for the attorney's attention. He flashed them a smile and motioned to the nearby wrestler table. "Those men want to meet you."

"I'll be back." One woman, wearing heavy eyeliner, trailed her hand along the top of the attorney's chair and threw him a seductive glance before she moved away. The other ladies stepped over to the strong-men's den.

"Thanks, man." One wrestler nodded, his long blond hair falling into his square-jawed face.

I turned to the attorney, a real James-Bond type. Unwanted sparks ignited my insides. Too intense to be handsome and too electric to be ignored, he was big, tense, and concentrated. I'd never met a man who looked so ready for adventure.

Here was trouble masquerading as charm.

"They're gonna love this at the office," Bond drawled.

I blinked. The heat in his eyes warmed me like sun-melted chocolate. The challenge in his steady gaze stiffened my backbone.

"The office?" I noticed the bulge under his armpit not quite hidden by his well-fitting dark suit-jacket. Tingles thrilled my spine.

"Stryker Black. You're Holly Garden."

Recognition hit me. The out-of-uniform cop I'd spotted standing in the foyer with his back to me. How had he settled in so quickly? His proximity caused my eyelid to do its thing. Most people never see my twitch. I hoped Stryker didn't. The quivers make me look unprofessional.

"How do you know my name?"

"Looked up your file at our office."

Suspicion brought sudden anger biting into me like the Genesis serpent. To keep my temper in check, I whispered, "You're a police officer?"

"Used to be. Now a PI. Ace Investigations."

14

I shot to my feet, snagged a four-inch stiletto on the chair rung, and lurched forward, catching the table's edge to keep from landing in his lap.

"I knew it!" Mom again.

With my nose inches from his ear, his masculine scent broke through my protective aura. Trying not to breathe in his woodsy, nautical aroma, I scooted away.

Because I wasn't breathing freely, my whisper sounded weird and nasal. "I want you to leave. At once."

"Why should I?"

I stared and forgot to lower my voice. "You're not needed."

The four lawyers seated around Stryker perked up. Fat and thin, they gazed at me like I was a valuable bequest in a contested will. One leaned so far forward on the table his French cuff dipped into his coffee.

Stryker remained cool. "I'm sure you're acquainted with a lady named Violet Garden."

My palms turned sweaty.

My own mother thought I couldn't fill Dad's shoes. She thought I didn't have the guts to be a detective. She thought I'd fail. Knees weak, I slid back into the chair and gazed down. My fingers itched to fiddle with the clasp on my glittery bag, but I held them still. I couldn't let the PI see how his words curdled my self-esteem.

"Security was the word Ms. Garden used."

I spoke low, not wanting anyone else to hear. "She didn't. She couldn't." I clamped my lips. He didn't need to know how his words upset me.

"Hard to believe?" He gave me a hard-boiled, tight-lipped Bogart smile.

Sitting so close, he didn't look like a cop. Or a PI for that matter.

More like a very, very sexy bad guy. Mafia or something. My throat closed. How could Mom do this to me?

"Mom asked for you? Personally?"

"She asked for Ace's top man." His dark eyes spoke of secrets, hinted of danger. Pulled me in even as they warned me off.

I whispered, "Luck of the draw?"

We'd been talking in hushed tones, but now the PI, a beguiling smirk on his face, spoke louder. "I won the lottery."

One lawyer said, "I've got to remember that line."

The other lawyers grunted agreement.

Their responses helped me regain my poise. I turned back to the PI.

"Okay, you work for our competition…and you're here?" I'd staked out Ace Investigations to see what I was up against, so why hadn't I laid eyes on him there? And he *was* an eyeful. Plus he was feeding me a line. And good at it. Too good.

I scooted my chair away from him. Not that long ago I'd been dumped by another charmer. I wasn't about to nibble this bait.

Even if I'd wanted to chance another romance, God had laid out other plans for me. I had a new vocation. I had Dad's murder to solve and his reputation to sanitize. I needed to prove to the city of Dallas and the entire police force that Dad hadn't been a dirty private investigator. If I failed, our investigative firm would dribble on down the drain. I lifted my chin. Even if I had time to spend with a man, I'd never choose this smoothie. But I did need to size up the competition.

Investigator Rule #1: Know Your Enemy.

So I did an about-face and turned on the sugar. "Stryker, is it?" I smiled sweetly. "I thought I had every PI in Dallas pegged. Glad to meet you."

Stryker's focused expression didn't change. "Likewise." He laid a strong hand on my bare arm, raising the hair with a single light touch.

"Stay a minute more. Tell me about yourself."

A male voice interrupted Stryker. "Let's be judicious here. Fair's fair. There are four attorneys at this table and one lovely woman. Time to share. My name's Jeff Davidson of Davidson, Hillyer & Greene. I'm sure you've heard of my firm. And this is…"

While Jeff introduced the other three suits, Stryker leaned back and scanned the room, doing his security thing. With me quickly shaking hands around the table, the trio of women who'd huddled around Stryker earlier made their move. Rising from the nearby wrestler table as if directed by an unseen choreographer, they mobbed Stryker.

I sucked in a breath. His mouth hanging ajar, Stryker looked stunned. Three wrestlers stood too, pushed aside their chairs, and towered over Stryker. I glimpsed Matt striding across the ballroom toward us, security face on.

The big blond wrestler, who seemed to be their leader, rasped, "We wasn't just twiddling our thumbs over here. We was talking with these ladies." His expression looked downright testy. He raised a fist, looking about to deck Stryker.

The three glamor girls stepped away from Stryker and melted into the crowd.

Prepared to intervene, I grabbed my purse and wriggled to the edge of my seat, curious to see what Stryker would do. This scene was plain screwy. Were the wrestlers *trying* to pick a fight?

Stryker's face grew leaner, showing clear bone definition. A paper-thin scar slicing through his cleft chin whitened. He stood and faced the three muscled men, their crimson cummerbunds flashing.

"So?"

"So we want our ladies back."

"Take them."

"Cool it, you guys." I unclasped my purse, thinking I might need my gun.

The fourth wrestler jumped to his feet, tipping his chair backward. It landed with a thud on the carpeted floor. A solid wall of red cummerbunds circled Stryker. I shot off my chair. One mat-pounder grabbed my arm and hauled me toward his table.

"We want this one too."

I jerked my arm loose. My abrupt movement caused my ankle to turn in one of the tricky stilettos.

"Yeow!" I stumbled. Before I could catch my balance, I lost the shoe on my twisted foot and fell to my knees.

Events fast-forwarded. Two wrestlers pummeled Stryker. Someone kicked my evening bag. On hands and knees, I chased it under the attorney table to rescue my gun. I glimpsed Matt confronting the other two wrestlers, and attempted to squirm out from under the table to escort the muscle jocks to the nearest exit. Crouched on hands and knees, my dress tightened around me like shrink-wrap and stopped me cold.

A lawyer squatted beside me. "Let me help—"

One of the wrestlers slammed him backward with an open palm. With a crash and tinkle of broken glass, the table flipped onto its side. A white-and-silver rain of crockery and cutlery poured down. A plate of romaine lettuce and blue cheese dressing slapped against my thigh, releasing the odor of salad-splashed velvet. My vision slowed as if I starred in a surreal movie. Mind scanning possible actions, my skirt creeping higher above my knees, I crawled free.

Was this a diversion for a robbery? I had to take control. Still on hands and knees, I smelled something acrid and sulfuric. The lighted candle centerpiece smoldered at the edge of the tablecloth. With a soft whoosh, flames leapt to life. I grabbed the closest thing at hand, a large slab of prime rib, probably from the same uneaten place-setting as the salad, and beat the flames with the semi-rare meat until they died in wisps of smoke beneath charred beef. Smelling cooked steak mixed with scorched hair and fearful of what I'd find, I touched my eyebrows and bangs. Crispy but still there.

Gasps and murmurings told me the crowd grew around us. Heavy feet shuffled, and I jerked my hand back to keep it from getting trampled. Fists struck flesh, accompanied by grunts and colorful language. I couldn't believe such brouhaha erupted in our little corner of the big room with so little provocation. Something smelled fishy, and it wasn't the shrimp cocktail sauce dripping onto the carpet. I was about to spring to my feet when a body thudded to within an inch of me and lay still.

Stryker. One look at Stryker's bloody face and I all but keeled over him.

My pulse spiked, pushing me into unthinking mode. Okay, so I lost it here. Thoughts of my job flew out the window. But only for a few seconds.

Still on my knees, I fished in my clutch for my cell and dialed 9-1-1. Dead zone. Resisting the urge to throw the instrument at a wrestler, I dropped the useless thing back into my purse.

As quickly as the commotion started, it ended. The dull thud of fists on flesh died. Fingers and knees digging into the thick carpet, I lifted one hand and pressed two fingers against the carotid artery in Stryker's muscular neck. Warm skin. Steady pulsing.

Lord, please don't let him be badly hurt.

With all quiet above me, I assumed Matt held everything under control. I loosened Stryker's red power-tie and rubbed his big limp hand between both of mine. His lashes, fanned across those high cheekbones, looked longer than any man had a right to own. Other than being a little bloody and lying motionless, he looked fine. Too fine. But I didn't have to remind myself that Mom hired him. A twinge of joy pricked me that it was him and not Matt or me lying on the floor. Then an uncomfortable guilt squashed the relief. So I said another quick prayer for the competition PI.

He groaned, and his eyelids fluttered.

Men's polished dress shoes, accompanied by glittering high heels, moved close enough for me to touch. One wrestler squatted next to me. "Here, let me—"

"No. Don't touch him." I swatted the man's beefy hand away from Stryker.

Stryker opened his eyes, relieving my worry about him. But Mom would arrive any minute for her grand entrance, and I desperately wanted her to gawk at *her* security being carried away in an ambulance.

So I said to the wrestler, "I've got to call EMS."

Furor at the ballroom doors made me look up. "That was fast. Matt must have gotten through to them already." But doubt nagged my brain. Too fast. Way too fast.

Before I could follow up my hunch, the crowd opened up and two blue-uniformed men, carrying oxygen paraphernalia, a stretcher, and a medical kit, hustled to the table.

The EMS team ignored Stryker who lay concealed by a drooping tablecloth, with only his long legs and feet protruding. One medic knelt beside another stretched-out body. I struggled to my feet, red dress hiked almost mid-thigh, to identify the victim.

"Matt!" I rushed over in time to see the medic jab a syringe into my co-investigator's limp arm.

Electrical impulses spiked my nerves. I'd never seen an emergency team do that. The first medic finished a cursory check for broken bones, and then both men heaved Matt onto the stretcher and hustled him through the crowded ballroom.

Juggling on one four-inch heel and one bare foot, I elbowed my way through the crowd after them. "Which hospital?"

They mumbled something incoherent and disappeared through the hotel's exterior door.

Lord, please take care of Matt. He's a good friend. Keep him safe.

I started after them.

The blond wrestler clutched my arm, stopping me from following them out to the ambulance. Then he smiled crookedly, straightened his bowtie, and righted his cummerbund.

"Don't look so worried; the PI's in good hands."

I stiffened. "How do you know Matt's a PI?"

The wrestler frowned and clamped his lips.

Shivers snaked my spine. Something was very wrong.

CHAPTER TWO

With Matt gone and most of the Valentine crowd moving back to their tables, I returned to Stryker. He moaned, stirred, and shoved himself into a sitting position. His movement yanked the cloth draped across his shoulder off the table, smashing the remaining dishes.

The PI's fingers explored the blood clotting at the corner of his mouth. He cupped his hand under his jaw and carefully wiggled it. Then, avoiding the broken crockery, he grasped the adjoining upturned table for support, and jacked himself to his feet.

I figured he'd live, so I swiveled around to confront the blond wrestler.

He was gone.

I stood on tiptoes to search the crowded room—no easy feat in my remaining stiletto—and gazed over the heads of the few people still gaping at our mess. No hunk wrestler. I shrugged. No problem. I'd check Mom's guest list, phone the guy, and question him. Besides satisfying my suspicious nature, I could retrieve his personal information if Matt wanted to press charges.

Another groan from Stryker, and I relegated the wrestler to my mental waiting list.

The PI leaned against the ballroom wall, one hand massaging the back of his neck.

"Hey, beautiful brown-eyed Hollyhock, where'z everyone?" His words sounded slightly slurred. Since three guests remained staring at him, I assumed he meant Matt.

"EMS whisked him to the hospital." I wished I were as sure as I sounded. I rubbed the frown lines between my brows. "But that whole medic/wrestler scene was downright weird. I'll give the ambulance five minutes, then I'm phoning hospitals to find Matt and see how he is."

"Since the medics left me here, I must not look as bad as I feel," Stryker growled. "What do you think?" His sea-otter brown eyes had cleared, and he now looked ready for anything.

I breathed in his six-foot-something frame, disheveled suit dripping *au jus*, dark hair spilling over an eye rapidly turning purple, mouth puffed and pulled to one side, red tie hanging askew, and contemplated my answer.

Because of Dad's dirty death, my run-away fiancé, and my Christian faith, I recently vowed never, under any circumstances, would I tell one tiny lie, not even to shield someone's feelings. Was a partial truth a lie? Yes, possibly. So I decided truth offered as a joke was still truth. Physically he looked awful, but he was still a hunk.

I winked. "You look terrific."

Stryker twisted his battered face into a grin. "Ask a dumb question and get…" He shrugged and spread swollen hands, knuckles seeping blood.

"Yeah." I wasn't famous for my brilliant comebacks. Snappy answers popped into my mind hours later when I tossed on my pillow.

Stryker reached under the tablecloth and retrieved my shoe. "This yours? Too bad you didn't wear your glass one tonight."

"Are you pulling a Prince Charming on me? That routine won't work."

24

The musicians floated a few notes, and the romantic music lured the last gawkers watching us out onto the dance floor. Other couples wove through the tables to join them.

Glad Stryker seemed almost recovered, I slid my foot back inside my stiletto. "Too bad y—"

"Holly, sweetling, what on God's green earth happened?"

Recognizing the spun-sugar drawl, I turned. The ruckus had ruined Mom's grand entrance, and she'd arrived unnoticed. Since she already thought I was wildly dysfunctional, I purposefully underplayed my answer.

"A small security problem." I waved my purse toward Stryker. "Mom, this is Stryker Black…" I hesitated a beat for emphasis. "… *your* security."

Mom didn't even blink at my accusing tone. She just stood, hands on her slim hips, and glared.

"Ma'am." Stryker held out his hand. "Nice to meet you."

Whoops. Mom hated being called ma'am. Inwardly I did a Snoopy-dance. How did she like *her* security person now?

At Mom's frown, the disheveled PI dropped his unshaken hand, straightened his tie, and ran bruised fingers through his untamed hair. "Got to get back to work," he mumbled and staggered off toward the men's room.

"Holly!" Mom's raised voice stole my gaze from Stryker's retreating back.

I sucked in a breath and tried to hide my shock. Mom now had her hand tucked into the arm of a silver-haired gent who wore old money and suave as easily as his elegant black tux. Though a good inch shorter than Mom, they made a great-looking couple. In fact, they lit up the room.

She looked chic in a black lace dress I'd never seen. With

highlighted blonde hair fluffed into a youthful do, flawless complexion, and blue eyes with smoky lids, Mom passed for years younger than her lithe fifty-five. She didn't plan to let middle-age catch her without racing maturity to the finish line.

"Holly, your hair…your dress." Mom lifted a parsley stem from my sagging upsweep. Her silver-tipped nails glowed as she brushed a clinging baked potato skin from my red velvet skirt. Her voice pitched higher. "Why do these accidents always happen to you?"

My mom was a darling, but when I messed up, she still made me feel like an awkward teen. At least my younger twin sisters weren't with her. I didn't need their giggles to make my cheeks burn. Choosing to ignore her chiding and taking the offensive, I motioned to the aging Romeo.

"And this is?"

"J. C. Hogg." Mom's eyes twinkled Valentine hearts. "Not of *the* Hoggs of Houston, of course." She raised a perfect brow and turned to the sophisticated stallion. "Are you?"

Under the silver hair, the broad face reddened. "No, darlin'. That is, we are distantly related. We're in the same business. But my end's shipping, not drilling." J.C. smoothed his silver mustache then thrust his hand toward me. I caught a whiff of some exotic aftershave.

Mom's question hadn't been subtle, but she effectively flushed out the man's financial status. My chest tightened, but I forced myself to shake the offered hand. The contact felt squishy, but not because he had a weak grip.

"Sorry. That's sour cream. We had an incident." I swiped my fingers on a handy napkin then offered a clean one to J.C.

So Mom planned all along to make her own debut back into the dating game. I pasted on a smile and tried to enter the get-acquainted chatter, but my mind fuzzed.

HOLLY GARDEN PI, RED IS FOR ROOKIE

Mom dating? Dad had only been in his heavenly home for…

I narrowed my eyes against the painful memories. That first hazy year when my family barely managed to zone through life, that second six months when Grandma Garden moved in, then I had that ghastly experience with Preston. Yeah, a little over two years since Dad died on that stakeout-gone-bad and my nightmares started.

Mom dating? How had I not suspected? And I called myself a PI. As soon as I could make a getaway, I turned to interrogate the wrestlers, and then almost hyperventilated. Excitement zonked through my bloodstream, making the hair on my bare arms stand at attention like gravestones in a cemetery.

All four men had disappeared.

The cloth on their table hung crooked, plates teetered on the edge, chairs were scattered, and the food picked clean. They must have dashed off right after the disturbance.

Except for the two messy tables, the room appeared as if Mom waved a magic wand and restored order. Music drifted through the air as Cupid again shot arrows. The crowd, including the women who'd surrounded Stryker, had danced back into their search for love.

I needed to find and question those wrestlers. Everyone around me thought hearts and flowers. I thought mystery!

I examined the tables and the surrounding area to see if the mat-tumblers left any clues—business cards, match boxes…fortune cookies. Nothing. Except for one empty stemmed water glass, someone had picked the champion wrestler table as clean as an olive pit. Not only were plates of prime rib and chocolate mousse licked to the porcelain, but a waiter stood sandwiching the dirty dishes onto a stainless-steel utility cart. I hooked two fingertips around the lone remaining glass just before he whisked the dishes to the kitchen, and wrapped the seemingly innocuous thing inside a small paper bag to preserve fingerprints. I always carried at least one evidence bag for emergencies.

But where had the wrestlers hailed from? What had they wanted? Where had they gone? I hoped they actually appeared on Mom's guest list, but I could lay odds they didn't.

I was spit-cleaning my dress when I spied Stryker slipping through the crowd, headed my way. Hiding the paper bag in the crook of my arm and covering the bundle with my purse, I turned to face the PI from Ace Investigations. I didn't want Number-Two Detective to learn I'd copped a clue. When he stopped beside me, looking as cool as a man in his condition could, I pointed to the empty table.

"What do you know about all this?"

"Me?" He raised his dark brows. "Nothing."

He'd straightened his tie, combed his hair, and the scent of soap he'd used to wash his face and hands mingled with his manly aftershave. Except for his puffy left eye doing a slow close and the cut on his lip, he looked as in charge as before.

He kicked his smile up a notch. "Hit me with it. What did you find?"

How cute was that? Since I couldn't lie, I gave him a partial answer. "Spilled coffee on the tablecloth."

His chocolate melt-my-heart eyes darkened, and the smile crinkles disappeared. He searched my face, while I worked to keep my expression smooth and unreadable. I waved a vague hand toward the table.

"You can see the crime scene is clean."

His dark look said he didn't believe me. "Who were those guys?" The frown puckering Stryker's forehead didn't make him one red blood cell less attractive.

"No idea."

"Okay. Have it your way, princess. I'll finish tonight's security this side of the room." His frown smoothed, and he flashed me a look he no doubt used to charm any woman within a hundred yards. "You okay with the other side?"

His charisma was deadly, but I resisted. BP—Before Preston—I'd been naïve. Now I'd wised up to all to-die-for men and their charm. I shook my head.

"No. I'll police this side." I wasn't about to take orders from Tom Cruise Investigator. "You take the other."

Stryker grunted, narrowed his eyes, but nodded.

As soon as the room seemed under control, I dashed outside, darted to a nearby window, tugged out my cell, and speed-dialed Matt.

No answer.

Then I phoned all the local hospitals, but none had admitted him. Something was wrong.

I called Uncle Robert, and he assured me he'd find out what he could.

Meanwhile, I had to go back inside and continue surveillance.

Stryker patrolled the side of the room I designated while I prowled my half.

Anxious to solve the mystery of Matt's disappearance, I fidgeted out my security stint, keeping eagle-eyes on the romance-seekers. At last people began to leave. Mom stayed to settle with the management. Temple and I hugged her goodbye.

Stryker cruised toward the three of us, no doubt to collect his pay from Mom, so I waved to him. "It's been fun," I called.

As Stryker closed in, Temple murmured, "Wait a sec. Mmm. He's hot."

Stryker stopped close to her.

She grabbed his left hand and waved it. "Look! No wedding ring."

I made a face and grunted. "Temple." My shrug aspired to convey "who cares?"Stryker's dimples played around his mouth. "I can't believe that just happened."

I ignored him. "Come on, girlfriend, I'll drop you off. I've got work to do." I grabbed Temple's arm and propelled her out of the ballroom.

Fifteen minutes after leaving Temple at her front door, I drove my Jeep up the circular drive to the white-pillared three-story antebellum where my family and I live.

Grandma Garden hurried down the wide veranda steps and hugged me like I'd been gone for days. Enjoying the sensual tropical scent of Available she liked to wear, I let her take my hand and lead me up the stairs to the lighted wrap-around porch.

"Tell all! Where did you get those stains on your dress? What do you think? Should I wear my hair up like yours? Those strands falling down look real attractive. Did you bag a man?"

How like my hip Granny. Her sweet face reminded me of a wrinkled apple. A treasured one.

I laid on a Marilyn Monroe imitation and winked. "The most interesting man I met ended up at my feet."

"Fascinating." Granny clasped her hands as if praying. "I want to hear every juicy detail." Then her eyes widened. "Oh, I forgot. I ran out to let you know Bobby called."

"Does Uncle Robert know where Matt is?" I held my breath. Granny's youngest son now ran my late father's once-famous-but-now-infamous-as-well-as-unprofitable PI firm.

"Bobby said Matt Murdock's missing."

CHAPTER THREE

A chill sliced through me from scalp to toe. I almost dropped the paper evidence bag I'd coddled all the way home.

Granny dipped her head like a bobble-head doll. "And an orderly reported an ambulance missing from Parkland Hospital."

I thought I'd have to handcuff my heart to keep it from running away. Sweet, nerdy Matt missing, probably kidnapped.

And there it was. There really *was* a reason for my worry-niggle.

I leaned back against the veranda railing while the information seeped into me. My brain fogged. Only half aware, I set the bagged glass on the arm of the nearby glider and let my purse slide to the seat cushion. Granny's face fuzzed into soft focus.

"Give me a minute."

My mind revved from stalled to overdrive. Since our firm nosedived after the police accused Dad of abetting drug dealers, Matt moonlighted at other jobs. Was he working a case dangerous enough to get him kidnapped? A vision of the medic injecting Matt's bicep through his suit sleeve curled my toes. I grabbed a deep breath. I'd track down that missing Parkland ambulance, which was certain to have an automatic-vehicle-location-device aboard. If I was lucky, the hospital had equipped their ambulances with those helpful Fleet Eyes to give the staff real-time awareness of where each vehicle drove. Then I'd discover where the fake EMS guys had taken Matt.

Granny waved her thin arm, causing her robe to gap at the bottom, revealing a purple Teddy and still shapely legs. "There's more, Peach Tree. Bobby wants you to investigate."

My heart flipped into a cartwheel. After graduating college and getting my PI license, with Dad murdered, Uncle Robert became my new boss. Up until now, he'd given me nothing to do except warm a desk chair at the office, open junk-mail, and type other investigators' reports.

Bile rose in my throat and made my eyes smart. How awful that my first case involved my oldest friend!

I clutched Granny's shoulders and buried my nose in her soft, coconut-scented hair. "Lord, please keep Matt safe and calm me down."

"Amen." Granny's face tilted up, and she squeezed my hands. "God's in control, you know."

"But why Matt? First Dad. Now Matt." Helplessness tingled through my stomach and weakened my knees. I steadied the evidence bag and sank down on the glider. The cold cushion on my legs brought the grim reality into focus.

"Peach Tree, Matt needs you. I know you won't let him down." Granny sat on the glider beside me and patted my knee. "You were born to catch criminals. Before you drove up tonight, the Lord gave me a verse for you, one we memorized together last summer." She closed her eyes. "The Lord himself goes before you and will be with you; He will never leave you nor forsake you. Do not be afraid; do not be discouraged."

Yeah. Deuteronomy 31:8 had gotten me through oceans of heartbreak last summer. "You're right, Granny. Now's no time to wig out. Matt needs me." I wrapped an arm around Granny and hugged her. "Thanks. I've got to go."

I snatched the paper bag, sprinted inside, flew up the grand staircase—almost losing a shoe in the process—clicked over the inlaid floor into my bedroom, and flipped on the light. After lifting the pink hollyhocks from the flowerpot on the sill above my plaid window seat, I retrieved Dad's *Dallas Private Investigator* badge. I opened my sequined purse, pushed my Glock to one side, slid Dad's badge in next to my own, and snapped the clutch shut. Then I shoved the fake flowers back on top of the terra cotta pot.

I wanted to carry Dad's badge on my first investigation. I clattered into Mom's bedroom and snatched up her Valentine Meet-A-Thon guest list. Not taking time to change, I beat feet for my Jeep.

Twenty minutes later, Uncle Robert glared across his untidy desk at me. "Your grandma jumped to the wrong conclusion, Holly. You're not on this case. Too dicey."

"Dicey?" Back rigid, I clutched the arms of the padded client chair as my uncle tried to explain his reasoning.

"Matt's missing. More than likely kidnapped. This isn't your regular PI-type job. Let me remind you that PIs have no special powers. We're not police officers. Probably the kidnapper's an armed crazy." Concern pinched Uncle Robert's guard-dog expression. He ran a hand through his iron-gray hair, his fingers like a lawnmower that zigzagged through the rough on a golf course. "How will you react?"

I made my voice hard. "I'll handle it."

Uncle Robert's shrewd eyes looked kind enough at the moment, but I knew they could shoot sparks. I wanted this case more than I feared those fireworks. Matt lived next door and had been a friend since kindergarten. If anyone could find him, I could. I turned the full force of my big hazel eyes on my uncle.

"I was the last person to see Matt. I can I.D. the wrestlers and the medics." For a wild second, I wondered if the blonde in the Vera Wang dress belonged to the gang and had acted as a diversion. "This case is rightfully mine."

Uncle Robert's gaze hardened. Without looking down, he shuffled through the stacks of manila folders and loose papers pyramiding his desk.

I seized the chair arms. "Let me find Matt!"

Uncle Robert leaned back in his leather chair and stared at the ceiling.

"I care about Matt. No one else has the same heart to search for him. I know him and what he's likely to do. How he'll respond in a desperate situation."

Uncle Robert assessed me. His lips puckered and thinned.

I pointed to the purse sparkling in my lap. "I've trained for this job, and I'm licensed to carry." Of course, we both knew PIs seldom bothered to carry their guns. Who needed a gun when tracking down an errant wife? "And look, I picked up this water glass for fingerprinting." While handing the paper evidence bag across the desk to him, I had to snatch my purse to keep the heavy thing from sliding off my lap. Wouldn't help my case at all for my gun to accidentally fire.

"I'll dust for prints and get AFIS involved in tracking any we find." Uncle Robert snapped on a pair of latex gloves, examined the stemmed glass, then cleared a spot on the desk and set it down.

I leaned forward, hoping to take advantage of his slight relenting. "I'm on this." When I nodded for emphasis, strands of gooey hair tickled my eyes.

"Email me a detailed report of what you know, along with descriptions. I've filed a Missing-Persons Report with the police, and they want to take your statement." A crease appeared between Uncle Robert's dark, gray-streaked brows. He leaned forward, arms flat on the desk. "So you think you inherited your dad's detective genius?"

"You got it!" I flashed what I prayed looked like a confident smile.

Uncle Robert snapped his chair upright. "This office can't afford any more bad publicity." He heaved a long sigh. "And Matt's a good man. I don't want to take any chances with his life."

"Neither do I."

"Okay. Give the police your statement tonight, and then you've got twenty-four hours before I call in Jake." He shook his head, reminding me of a sad Sharpei. "Your mother's going to have my neck."

"I'll take care of Mom." I bolted around Uncle Robert's big desk. My progress caused a small tornado. Papers flew off Uncle's desk and slithered across his hardwood floor. He scowled, swiveled his chair toward the mess, and began to heap the papers back on his desktop.

I kissed the top of his head. "Thanks. I'll find Matt. I know I will."

While he retrieved his papers, I scoped out his floor-to-ceiling bookshelves filled with cameras, video equipment, night-vision goggles, a book whose spine advertised *One Hundred Ways to Disarm an Adversary,* and various other items I couldn't imagine how to use.

Investigator Rule #2 popped into my mind: *Be Armed and Ready.*

"I need a pair of handcuffs."

My uncle took a minute to scan his collection then dug a new pair from the pile of older cuffs. "Pretty sure of yourself, aren't you? Just like your father."

I grabbed the cuffs, but he held onto one metal circle. "See you don't end up like he did."

A shiver skipped down my spine. "Right."

"Twenty-four hours." He dropped his end of the cuffs.

"I'll find Matt. I called Parkland on my way here. Their AVL had finally located the missing ambulance only six miles from the hotel. The kidnappers had taped a metal pie tin over the GPS antenna so the vehicle would disappear from Parkland's monitoring screens. And they'd turned off the rig's radio."

"But Parkland's security tracked the vehicle?"

"Yep. The pie tin dislodged, and the AVL went back online." I shrugged. "The kidnappers must have moved Matt to a different vehicle at that point. There's nothing there. Not a building in sight. Nothing but open fields. Not even tire tracks."

Bushy gray brows rose. The corners of Uncle's mouth tipped up. "You did good. Keep in contact."

One hand on the doorknob, I called over my shoulder, "Of course. And my cell's always on. I'm going to check out Matt's office while I'm here."

I scooted down the hall, entered Matt's dark office, and flipped on the lights. His desk looked forlorn and empty. I stopped to peer out his window. Far below, car lights zoomed in a continuous yellow river through all five levels of the US-75 and I-635 intersections.

"Where are you, Matt?" His sandalwood scent hung faintly in the air.

My gaze felt drawn west toward Fort Worth; northwest toward Preston Road caught my interest as well. But neither stirred the hair on the nape of my neck. Nothing.

I turned my attention to Matt's desk. Except for his green-shaded desk lamp, a laptop computer, and a printer, the top stood empty. I pulled the lamp chain, and the green glow added to the dim overhead light.

I opened the three desk drawers and found them populated with a stapler, paper clips, a flash-drive, letterheads and envelopes, rubber bands, and computer paper.

I moved over to the four-drawer gray file next to the window and started rummaging. The top drawer held index dividers with a few labeled manila folders behind them. All turned out to be closed cases. I jotted down the names and addresses in the event any looked promising, but nothing inside the closed cases seemed in any way menacing or even exciting. Matt's PI career appeared to be almost as skimpy as my own. No wonder he moonlighted other jobs. After perusing the files another twenty minutes, I slammed the last drawer closed.

Nothing.

I opened his laptop and hit the on button. The cases he'd entered mirrored the closed ones inside his metal file cabinet. I surfed his recent documents and spent another half-hour searching for some clue.

Nothing.

Maybe whoever Matt moonlighted with kept all the files they worked together. I'd have to find who his partner was and question him.

By the time I jumped up from Matt's desk chair, my back hurt and the only information I'd gathered seemed to be that Matt was far from making a living working for Uncle Robert.

I left Matt's office as dark and lonely as I found it, walked down the empty hall, and eased the main door—Garden Investigations etched on the window—shut behind me.

Though I'd discovered nothing, my adrenaline ratcheted high.

I would find Matt. I'd let nothing stop me. I had to find him. His absence left a huge hole in my life.

As I walked to the elevator, the tapping of my red stilettos on the marble floor echoed in the empty hallway. I pushed the down button to the lobby. Eerie, being at Uncle's this late at night. I touched my chest over my fast-beating heart and wondered how high my pulse soared. I'd have to develop some cool, or I'd suffer a heart-attack before I turned twenty-five.

The elevator door slid open, and I headed through the huge, empty lobby toward the front entrance. Even the normally lit five-story fountain inside the glass atrium was dark.

So who kidnapped Matt? Where was he? Why would they snatch him? Who was Matt's moonlighting partner?

Before I reached the exterior revolving door, the glass started moving. A dark shadow loomed toward me. I was about to dart out through the next revolving section when a tenor voice stopped me.

"'Lo, Holly. You're out late."

"Jake."

Uncle Robert's top investigator threw me a sharp look. My imagination always conjured up the nondescript man as wearing a fedora pulled down over his eyes and a trench coat, a cigarette hanging from his lips. He was the quintessential PI—average height, average weight, average looks, except for a thin, barely noticeable scar that slashed through his right eyebrow, giving his expression a slightly quizzical look. After meeting him, most people found him hard to recall. Really a plus in the investigative business.

Uncle Robert treasured him.

I didn't think about Jake much, except to feel annoyed that the man snapped up Uncle's few investigator jobs before I even caught a whiff of them.

Jake didn't know it yet, but tonight I'd edged him out, if only for a few hours.

I smiled sweetly.

His expression didn't change. "You up to no good?"

"Nope. See you around." I slipped out the revolving door and moved into the crisp air.

Jake's greeting flashed my mind back to the last time I'd seen him.

HOLLY GARDEN PI, RED IS FOR ROOKIE

I'd stepped inside the Dallas Athletic Club to rev up my disinclination to work out my muscles. Jake had been headed for a shower, and sweat coated the skin showing around the sleeveless T-shirt that ended just above his abs. My mouth fell open. The man was ripped from shoulders to sneakers—definitely not someone a crook would want to meet in a dark alley. Okay, so he had a brawny advantage over me, but I figured my brain worked as well as his or better.

As I walked into the dark Dallas night, the Bible verse Granny and I claimed for finding Matt ran through my head. *God himself goes before me. Don't be afraid.* Lifting my chin, I reminded myself that though meeting head-on with kidnappers wasn't part of my job description, I could do this. I had to. Matt would do the same for me.

The light at the far street corner barely illuminated the sidewalk in front of the fifteen-story glass-fronted building where Uncle barely hung on to two suites of offices. A chunk of melancholy hit me. I clenched my jaw. Once the entire seventh floor belonged to Dad.

I slid into my Jeep and locked the door. Not that locking did much. Any bad guy with a knife could slice through the canvas top and have his weapon at my throat before I could scream. I hadn't told Uncle Robert I'd be functioning on prayer and bravado. I had no real guts. Surely guts would come later. With experience.

Fishing inside my purse, I lugged out my Glock and laid the 9MM-gun, barrel towards the door, on the shadowy passenger seat. I laid yesterday's newspaper over the weapon, and the, as if the kidnapper already knew I sniffed his scent, checked my rearview mirror. Was he hot on my tail?

Seeing nothing, I flicked on the Jeep's dashboard light, glanced through Mom's guest list, then threw the steno-pad to the passenger-seat floor. Of course, no champion wrestlers listed. They'd crashed.

Then I bee-lined it to the police station.

Judging from the ringing phones and the harassed expression he wore, the young officer manning the desk seemed to be juggling a crisis. He shoved a statement form and a dental form across the desk and asked me to fill them out.

I had to leave the dental form blank. I only knew my best friend flashed a warm smile backed with white, straight teeth. I had no idea how many fillings he had.

Fifteen minutes later I'd written everything I could think of pertaining to Matt's description and kidnapping on the missing-persons form, signed it, and pushed the paper back across the desk toward the busy officer.

He nodded at me and held a hand over the mouthpiece of the receiver. "We'll get on this right away, Ma'am. Within four hours his description and picture will be posted on the National Crime Information Center database." He shuffled through a stack of papers on his desk and came up with the latest picture of Matt. I had an identical 5 x 7 on the end table in my bedroom that Matt gave me for Christmas.

I sucked in a breath. The photo so did *not* belong here on the busy police officer's messy desk.

"You just missed the victim's parents." The officer's frown didn't make him look any older or any more competent. He shuffled through more untidy stacks and came up with two sets of papers. I craned my neck and saw the Murdocks signed one, and the other contained the statement Uncle Robert phoned in. He stapled my forms to the bottom of the other two and laid the group on top of a stack of papers at his right hand. Then he turned back to the receiver in his hand and barked some more orders.

"You *will* make sure this gets to the Missing Persons Unit, right?" I asked when he paused to listen to the person on the other end.

He nodded and turned away.

I waved to his back and walked out the door. Experience told me those reports would end up in a file, a couple calls would be made, and if nothing showed up, that would be that. I had to find Matt myself.

Before heading home for a sleepless night whipping up what little I knew about Matt's case in my brain, I decided to call in help. My night-owl friend seldom went to bed before the wee hours.

Sliding my Blue Tooth headset over the shambles of my upsweep, I speed-dialed Temple's number.

"'Sup, Holly?"

My hands trembled on the steering wheel, but I fired up the Jeep and gunned into the street. "Did you see any of those wrestlers leave the Valentine's party?" I drove toward the freeway.

"You mean the ones who knocked that Mission-Impossible hunk out and sent Matt to the hospital?"

"Yeah, the four guys wearing matching red cummerbunds."

"Nope. Didn't see them leave." Temple's excited breathing came over the earpiece. "That scene was so cool! Just like a movie."

"Yeah? Well, Matt's disappeared. Kidnapped, I think. I'm on the case."

Temple gasped. "No!"

"Please pray for him."

"You don't have to ask. Of course I will. What happened?"

I filled in the blanks for her. Turning the Jeep onto US-75, I noted a lot of traffic still sped the freeway, though I estimated the time ranged long after midnight. I couldn't see my Seiko, and the Wrangler didn't have a clock.

Once I moved into the center lane on 75, Temple and I prayed over the cell for Matt. Since there was nothing else we could do for him at the moment, I tuned in on her life.

"Hey, girl, I didn't get a chance to ask earlier, but did you meet a lucky guy who made your pulse race?"

My friend shrieked then said, "I feel just like the matchmaker in *Fiddler on the Roof*. Remember the part in the movie where the three older daughters sang?" Temple belted, "'Matchmaker, matchmaker, make me a match.' Except I made the match for myself."

I yelped. "Someone finally snagged you! This *is* a first. Celebration time." Men gravitated to Temple, but she barely gave them a passing glance. "This guy's gotta be hot, so spill. Details!" I whipped up the high-level entrance ramp to 635, a.k.a. LBJ Freeway.

"No keeping my little secret. He's a cop. He didn't even carry his business card. Scribbled his name and number in that little notebook cops always carry, tore it out, and slipped it to me."

"Crazy!" I screwed up my face. "You with a cop. Hard to believe." Then my nape shivered like it does when I'm on to something. "What's his name?"

"Frank McCoy. He was at the party doing security with another guy." Temple paused, and I sensed her hesitation over the cell. "I thought *you* had security covered."

"Mom didn't think so."

"Oops. Gotcha." Her voice oozed sympathy. "Sorry she has so little faith."

I bit my lip. I was dying to ask Temple if her guy mentioned anything about a dark, mysterious private investigator named Stryker. I told myself I didn't care. Does never lying include not lying to yourself? I didn't want to go there. Instead, I asked, "Does your guy know Matt?"

"Like a Siamese twin. They moonlight together. But tonight Frank worked with a snoop named Black. Frank took off in a big hurry right after the fight."

"Yes!" I jabbed a fist into the air, and my knuckles almost punched through the Wrangler's canvas top. "Stryker's sidekick! I need Frank's number to help find Matt."

"Cool. I'll go get it." Temple's cell picked up the clack of her footsteps as she looked for the phone number.

I tapped my fingers on the floor gearshift. Where was my brain? I hadn't laid an I.D. on Frank or seen him leave. How had I missed spotting another cop? I'd been too busy with my vendetta against Stryker. Not good. I hoped nothing else important sneaked past me at the party.

"I'm back." Temple rattled off Frank's phone number.

I jotted the number on my wrist. "You're the greatest." I rang off. Guiding the steering wheel with my knees, I dialed Frank McCoy's number. I figured that after the trumped-up fight, Stryker sent Frank out to follow the ambulance. The sly competition was already a step ahead of me. The tension in my neck relaxed slightly. Maybe Frank saw Matt's transfer from the ambulance. Maybe he'd followed the vehicle and knew where the kidnappers took Matt.

On the first ring, a deep voice answered. Disappointment tightened my stomach. I deduced that since he answered so fast, Frank hadn't found much and probably had gone home.

But Temple's new guy sounded good. Steady, strong, and confident, with a reassuring resonance to his voice. I explained who I was and what I wanted, then I swung the Jeep onto the exit ramp that led to Preston Road.

"Yeah, at the last minute Stryker recruited me to help him stake out security."

"Is now a good time for you?"

After a short silence, Frank answered, "I'd meet with you now, but I'm following a lead. How 'bout we get together first thing in the morning? Say, Dolly's Donuts on Mockingbird?"

"Let me help track down that lead." I couldn't let Stryker find Matt before I did. Garden Investigations had to find our own kidnapped PI. If we didn't, the media would sling more mud at us. I visualized the front page of the *Dallas Morning News*: Rival Firm Rescues Private Investigator. After those headlines, even if people didn't know about Dad, few prospective clients would use us. My heart hammered loud enough to compete with the stereo that shook the car in the next lane. I screeched into a *U-ey* to head back toward Frank's precinct.

"Too late, Holly. I'm there. Gotta go. Tomorrow?"

"Wait, I want to—"

"Eight a.m., Dolly's." Frank clicked off.

I hit the steering wheel with my fist.

CHAPTER FOUR

Concealed carrying isn't frowned upon in Texas. Still, I didn't think I'd need my Glock this morning since Dallas considered the Mockingbird area high-class. The day awakened with the sun shining and the temperature perfect. In my daily Bible-reading God promised, "He calls His own sheep by name and leads them out. He goes before them and the sheep follow Him because they know His voice. A stranger they will not follow, because they do not know the voice of strangers."

So I took God at His Word that He'd guide my search for Matt. I expected to uncover an important lead today. With only sixteen hours left, I needed a clue that led directly to Matt.

I felt certain he was still alive.

Full of optimism, I parked the Jeep in the only free space across from Dolly's floor-to-ceiling plate-glass window then scooted out and entered the double-wide doorway. The aroma of fresh-baked pastries made my stomach rumble.

The place rocked. For a second, I thought I'd walked into a Starbucks by mistake. People filled the easy chairs clustered around small tables. The smell of vanilla-hazelnut coffee made me sniff the air like a blue tick-hound on point. Behind the counter, three women wearing latex gloves darted about, serving chocolate-sprinkled donuts, raspberry-filled scones, and other delicious-looking pastries. My mouth salivated like said canine.

Though I hadn't taken time for breakfast, I scurried past the calorie-laden showcase to the coffee urn and chose the dark roast. After all, even a broken-hearted girl must watch her waistline. I fumbled inside my oversized red shoulder-bag among my spy paraphernalia for cash and paid the girl behind the register.

Then I turned to the tables and gazed at the busy scene.

No uniformed cop in sight. Male and female business types, mothers carrying babies in slings or parked in strollers, and geeks engrossed in wireless laptops all slouched comfortably in every seat. I stood, coffee in cardboard container warming my hand, and switched on my radar. I can spot a cop a mile away.

I didn't see one. After my rush into jeans and turtleneck and dashing over on an almost empty tank, had Temple's cop stood me up? No. According to the still, small voice inside my head, he hadn't. Where was he then? I shifted from foot to foot and adjusted my gimmick-heavy shoulder-bag. If only I'd taken time to slap on makeup and TLC'd my hair. I'd been too excited to sleep last night, so I overslept this morning then convinced myself the faux-messy look was still in.

My friends say I look a twin to the '50s actress Audrey Hepburn, except for her pixie hairstyle. Mine is shoulder-length, and my eyes are hazel. But I personally think I have more curves. I usually wear black to make myself look more menacing.

Would the cop recognize me?

A slight, dark-haired man wearing horn-rimmed glasses sitting next to the front window lifted an index finger and crooked it at me. He looked more like he belonged on his knees sifting dirt at an archeological dig than wearing a police uniform busting criminals. Okay, so I couldn't always spot a cop a mile away.

I sipped hot coffee through the hole in the lid and sized him up. In a normal batch of guys, this one would be overlooked. I don't like drinking coffee through a hole, so I popped the lid off, threw it in the trash, and sauntered over.

"Holly?" He stood.

I recognized his deep voice. The smile he flashed morphed him from a dweeb into the type of cop I'd trust in any dark alley.

"Frank." I thrust out my hand, and the abrupt movement spilled dark roast over my coffee-toting arm.

Frank shifted into warp speed. He wiped my arm dry before the coffee had a chance to burn. Tremendous reflexes. He waved at the overstuffed chair he'd vacated. "Sit here."

I slid down into the cushions already warmed by his body and set my dripping paper cup on the tiny table. "Thanks." Stretching out my legs, I settled back. "So you're the brains, and Stryker's the brawn," I quipped.

"And you're the bloodhound." He swiped an unused straight chair from a newly vacant miniature table, dropped onto the seat, and looked me over. I got the impression that my five-foot-eight slender frame, though clad in working black, wasn't what he'd hoped for. Had he expected an Amazon? Obviously he hadn't ID'd me at the Meet-A-Thon last night either.

"What do you need from me?" He leaned an arm over the back of his chair.

I'd just like to understand how the male mind works was my first thought. I didn't think I needed to share that news-flash with this guy, so instead I asked the question burning in my brain. "Did you follow the ambulance last night?

When Frank didn't say anything, I changed to my best teasing voice. "Why did you leave the Valentine's party early? Temple's dying to know."

I could tell from the long silence, Frank hadn't fallen for my ploy. But why didn't he answer? What did he know? Why wouldn't he share?

I clamped my lips against a frustrated scream and spoke quietly. "We're in on this together."

Frank pursed his lips but finally answered. "Yeah. Okay. I chased the ambulance. They kept the siren blasting, and I stuck to their tailpipe."

"And?" My heart beat faster.

"I lost them."

I exploded. "What?"

"I'm not proud of it. The streets were clogged with Friday-night traffic. Cars opened up in front of the EMS siren, and their vehicle slipped through. After the ambulance passed, cars slammed back into their lanes. I got stopped dead. The ambulance headed west on 635. Whoever drove knew what he was doing. Even if he hadn't used a siren, I'd have had a tough time following. Smells like professionals."

I swallowed my disappointment. "So that's why you didn't want to tell me."

Frank grunted.

I slumped back into my chair. I'd had such high hopes. So where did we go from here? "Since Garden Investigations has so few cases these days, I know Matt did some moonlighting. Did he work with you very often? During your police off-time, do you freelance or work for a particular firm?"

"Freelance mostly when I'm off-duty. And yeah, Matt's been working with me quite a bit lately."

"What cases were you and Matt working? Why do you think he turned up missing? Did you know the wrestlers?" I guessed from Frank's disapproving look I needed to fine-tune my interviewing technique.

Frank took off his glasses and transformed from Clark Kent into Superman. Wow. Okay, Temple, way to go! He waved my questions aside. "So you're the rookie Strike told me about."

Stryker mentioned me! My face grew hot. I ignored it. When had Stryker talked with Frank about me? I decided to insert that question after my face cooled. "Before we delve into Matt's work, did your lead pan out last night?"

Frank made a zipping motion over his mouth. "Sorry. Can't share."

I glimpsed a flash of movement outside. My involuntary jerk made my eyelid twitch. "Speak of the devil! What's Stryker doing sprinting past the window?"

Frank lifted a brow.

Had I imagined seeing Stryker? Was the veteran PI affecting my mental health?

Frank glanced sidewise at the empty window, letting his gaze stray outside before pulling his attention back to me. "Okay. Let's discuss Matt's caseload. Nothing dangerous. He and I were working the Bridge—"

A crash shattered the window beside me. Frank knocked the table over and jerked me down behind it. Intending to see what happened, I sprang up. An inflexible hand forced me to my knees. People screamed.

Another splintering crash...then silence.

CHAPTER FIVE

Call me scared, but my first thought was, *I'm alive!*

Still on my knees behind the overturned table, my heartbeat mushroomed into manic mode. I gripped the table with both hands. Alone in a sea of upright tables, ours lay on its side, coffee spilled on green carpet, laptop miraculously safe on the floor and out of range of both coffee puddles. No doubt Frank rescued both of us—the laptop and me.

Shock blurred my vision. "What happened?"

I peeked out from behind the table barricade and took in the interior scene. At the far side of the room, a leggy blonde leaned over a stroller, trying to quiet a squalling baby. At the next table, two middle-aged women, eyes wide and mouths ajar, sat stiff as mannequins. All three serving ladies, only the tips of their heads visible, crouched behind the counter. Standing across from them, hands shaking, a pimply teen held a purple-haired girl against his skinny chest.

I grew aware of something warm and wet soaking my knees. Blood? Had Frank been shot? Had I? No. Black coffee seeped into my jeans.

Frank, .357-Magnum in hand, jumped to one side of the shattered window.

Now where in those tight jeans had he hidden that gun?

Murmurs around us grew like Dolby sound, louder and louder until they became shouts. Frank's shoes crunched on splintered glass as he searched the perimeter where we'd been sitting at the table closest to the window.

A new series of screeches, like a trolley careening off its tracks, thundered through the broken window. Chills, sharp as tinkling glass, slashed down my spine.

Frank pivoted from the window. His deep, steady voice addressed all Dolly's Donuts patrons. "Relax, folks. No problem. Excitement's all over now. A drive-by shooting." He offered a half-hearted grin. "And for those of us parked near the front door, there's been a hit-and-run in the lot." Cellphone in hand, he pointed outside. "Cars are bulldozed."

My heart jolted. "What about my Jeep?"

My question drowned in the noise and confusion of patrons stampeding for the door. A guy in snakeskin cowboy boots galloped outside shouting, "My truck! My truck!"

I stood on tiptoes behind Frank and stared out the broken window. Air, scented with oil and gasoline, hit my face. I expected to see Stryker outside searching for clues. But he wasn't there.

My head started to pound. Every time the man lurked in my vicinity, someone got hurt. The opposition PI caused fireworks. This time Frank's warp-speed reaction saved me. Did Stryker lug trouble around with him like Pilgrim's load of sin? Or was *he* trouble? Something told me both questions deserved a resounding yes. I swallowed. As if I needed that inner directive to steer clear of Stryker.

Frank knelt on one knee and slipped his weapon back into his ankle holster. I made a mental note to ask Uncle Robert to spring for one of those handy gadgets.

"Did the perp hit your car?" Frank darted a look in my direction.

With a sinking sensation souring my stomach, I threw my hands in the air then shrugged. "I can't tell from here."

Frank joined the other customers flooding the parking lot. I stood by the door and let the shop empty before I forced my black Nikes outside and onto the sidewalk. I sure didn't want to find my Jeep on the casualty list. Five vehicles parked across the pavement from the entrance had been pretty much demolished. I'd parked Bunny, my Jeep, in the sixth spot. I grabbed a happy breath and slapped a hand over my mouth so I wouldn't scream. Yay! My precious old friend sustained damage on the left fender, but appeared drivable.

The culprit vehicle must have been silver because a wide silver streak lay atop my camouflage paint job. "Had to have been a big jacked-up Texas truck or a Hummer to drive away from that mess of crumpled steel," I announced to no one in particular.

I dialed 9-1-1. No dead zone this time. I spit out the pertinent information. Stomach settling, my curiosity swelled.

Frank, gun hidden, horn rims replaced by Oakleys, laptop in hand, turned to me. "More cops coming?"

"Yeah." I suppressed a grin. He'd transformed to Clark Kent again. "Typical day for you, Frank?"

"Naw. I don't get shot at that much." He leaned a hand on the building's brick siding, heaved a deep sigh, and cranked out a dark look.

"What?" I smoothed my sweater down until the material met my low-slung jeans.

Frank pointed to a red car mashed between a beige Ford truck and a dark green SUV. "The '67 T-bird's mine."

"Oh." I didn't know what to say. I felt bad for the guy. A vintage car like that had to mean something special to Frank. I loved that model Thunderbird myself. That two-door hard-top sport-car in mint shape had been the sweetest thing to ever roll off the assembly line. "I'm really sorry."

Frank, muscles around his jaws stony, turned to the crowd standing three-deep around the crash scene. He flashed his cop badge. "Anyone see what happened?"

Heads shook.

Frank and I, followed by the owners of the other four damaged vehicles, tiptoed through the debris on the pavement and eyeballed the carnage. Frank's classic car wasn't going anywhere anytime soon. Maybe never. I glanced away from his pained look. Poor guy.

We searched the parking lot for ejected gun casings. Nothing.

Sirens shrieking, lights flashing, three patrol cars roared up from different directions. Two men sprung from each sedan and hustled over. All the officers knew Frank and joshed him about his "'Bird road-kill."

He worked to change his expression and pasted on a weak smile.

"I'll never understand how men think bad jokes help an agonizing situation. Has to be a man thing." I laid a sympathetic hand on Frank's tense arm.

The officers gave me dirty looks. Not because of what I'd just said, but because they recognized me. They hated my father because of his supposed betrayal. Perhaps Frank tolerated me because of Temple. Or maybe he just hadn't yet placed my name. No, he was too savvy for that. A ripple of warmth tingled through me. Best bet? Frank didn't believe my father was guilty.

He broke away from the cop brotherhood and inspected the bullet-shattered shop window. Crunching glass underfoot, I practically trod on his heels. With his eyes hidden behind dark glasses, I had no clue what he thought.

Wiping clammy hands on my black jeans, I kept my voice low. "This was no drive-by."

"Right. Not in this neighborhood. Someone made an intentional hit. Wish I had a camera."

I pulled my Android from my shoulder bag. "Will this do?"

Frank gave me a thumb's-up. "Got a copy machine in there too?" He eyed my roomy carry-all. "I'll need dupes."

"It'll cost you." I snapped a succession of window pictures then turned the camera phone to the wrecked cars.

"Information-sharing?" Frank gave me a real grin.

"You got it." I liked Temple's guy.

After the police finished questioning them, Dolly's uninvolved patrons melted away. We smash-up victims spent almost an hour supplying information and waiting for tow-trucks. The police canvassed the shopping area for witnesses, but no one had so much as glimpsed the vehicle that shot at us then rammed the cars. The perp had been fast.

I figured problems like shootings and crushed cars happened to Frank all the time. "I'll remember not to park anywhere near you again," I teased.

Frank, eyebrows pinched and thoughts hidden, scrutinized me.

My scalp tingled. "What?" I lifted his sunglasses and gazed into his narrowed eyes. "You think the perps targeted *my* Jeep?"

He lifted a bristling brow. "If you hadn't backed so far into that space, you'd be minus an engine."

My stomach did a flip-flop. "No. I refuse to buy into your theory. Yours is the totaled vehicle. But here's some brain-food to chew on. I really did spot Stryker slinking around just prior to the shooting."

Frank didn't say anything, but his nice full lips thinned.

I tried to sound professional. "How long have you and Stryker known each other?"

Frank shrugged. "Long enough."

For sure the cop wasn't going to disclose anything about his mysterious PI friend. But I'm nothing if not persistent. I opened my mouth to probe harder.

Frank suddenly found urgent business elsewhere and ducked into a pal's patrol car.

I stuck my head in through the open window. "You owe me."

"So we'll talk in my office." He motioned to the cop in the driver's seat, and the black-and-white roared off before dust could settle on my unasked questions.

I strolled over to my Jeep, did a walk-around, and snapped pictures for the insurance company. The front left bumper rubbed against the wheel. I rummaged through the pile of detective equipment I kept behind the backseat until I found the tire iron and pried the front quarter panel a hair's breadth out from the wheel. Then I stood in the sun among the tow-trucks and the window-glass truck already pulling into the parking lot and assessed my situation.

So far this morning, I'd learned a lot about Frank's character. Temple's cop had tremendous reflexes and kept a cool head in a crisis. Qualities I intended to cultivate as soon as possible. Both would come in handy in my chosen profession where the job description might include being shot at. But I'd learned next to zero about Matt's cases. Or about Stryker. That big, omnipresent man now walked his big feet onto my list of suspicious characters. He'd not be my pick in a line-up of the usual suspects, but he did manage to pop up at every crime scene. Why?

So now Frank was out-of-pocket, and I had no leads. The clock was ticking. Tonight or this time tomorrow, Uncle Robert would sic Jake onto Matt's case. And wherever Matt was, he could be hurting.

I needed to take the next step. Go into action. I needed to talk with Matt's parents and check out his personal computer.

I bowed my head. *Thank you, God, that the spray of bullets didn't hit anyone. And I'm so thankful my Jeep escaped serious damage. Please show me what to do next.*

Still hanging onto my early-morning optimism by a fingernail, I opened my scratched-up door, jumped inside good old Bunny, and settled against the cracked leather. I called my Jeep Bunny because sometimes, no matter how smoothly I put her into second gear, she hopped down the street like she had hiccups. The looks I got from other drivers kept my pride stomped down to a safe zero level.

Bunny's part of me. Dad gave her to me for my sixteenth birthday, and no amount of my hard-earned cash spent to keep her running could entice me to part with her. I invested in radial tires and had a new canvas top fitted to her roll bars. But her original olive green camouflage paint suited me. Because of the spot she held in my heart, I completely empathized with Frank's losing his beautiful T-bird. What make car did Stryker drive? I'd guess the tall, well-muscled PI owned a black Hummer with dark tinted windows.

A sinister thought wormed into my brain. Maybe Stryker drove one of those big silver Texas-type jacked-up trucks with enormous wheels. And a big patch of that silver paint decorated Bunny's front fender.

I blew out a long breath. I'd know soon enough. Frank had put in a word for me, and the Dallas Police promised to let me see the accident report from each vehicle. But they'd go only that far for Frank. They refused to keep me updated on Matt's investigation. I'd have to bug them. Plus I had a date at the police station to give my statement about Matt's disappearance ASAP.

I inserted Bunny's key and cranked up the engine. The motor

turned over slower than usual. After fastening my seatbelt, I drove out of the parking space, avoiding most of the glass and metal polluting the pavement. Already this morning I'd been a bull's-eye for someone's target practice and just missed getting my Jeep totaled. I didn't need to get a flat.

But God loved me. I still had Bunny. The day was sunny, the temperature hot for February, the air sweet, and the yellow winter grass didn't kick up my allergies. Now if I could just snag a lead.

On Central Expressway, traffic was deadly. Merging in, I zipped over to the fast lane, hair blowing, hand tweaking the radio for my station. Belting out my favorite tune, I passed under the bumper-to-bumper traffic clogging the High-Five interchange. Then Bunny gulped an ominous *klunk klunk*. I pressed hard on the gas pedal, and my Jeep slowed. As Bunny coasted, I steered across two lanes between honking cars until I eased onto the right shoulder. I gunned the engine, but the rabbit went paws up.

Traffic whizzed past, trailing fumes so thick I wanted a gasmask. Morning sun punched heat through the canvas top, almost knocking me out. Drivers slowed and rubbernecked. I snagged my cell and dialed Temple.

"I'm stuck just south of the High-Five on Central."

"Oh, Holly, not again! When are you going to get a car that runs?" Temple blurted. "Never. Bunny's family."

"Then fix the stupid thing! Permanently." She added under her breath, "In a chop-shop."

"I heard that."

"I'll Google a tow-truck."

I felt too hot for banter, so shouting over the traffic din, I brought Temple up to speed about the shooting, how Frank's vehicle got totaled and Bunny sideswiped.

"Was Frank hurt?" Temple didn't disguise her worried tone.

"No." I yakked about how Frank hadn't had time to help me yet, but left out the part about how thoughts of Stryker kept stealing my focus during the short time I chatted with Frank. And I didn't mention seeing Stryker wing it past the window just before the gunshots.

"I miss all the excitement." Temple paused. My mouth opened to ask again for a tow-truck when her voice turned all breathy with excitement. "So, Holly, what did you think of Frank?"

I grinned. "You bagged a prince." Perspiration began to soak my sweater. "Call a tow, will you? The temp's rising. Must be almost eighty, and I'm smack in the sun. Not a blade of shade. And no air-conditioning."

"Consider it done."

I clicked off and dialed the office. "Uncle Robert, have you heard anything about Matt?""Nothing. I rechecked every hospital in the Dallas/Fort Worth Metroplex. No Matt. Find out anything from that cop?"

"Our meeting was prematurely interrupted."

Uncle Robert cleared his throat. "I'm thinking of changing my Missing-Person Report to Kidnapped. But we have no ransom note."

Kidnapped! "Yeah. I'm thinking so too." I heaved a sigh. I had to get off the phone. Hearing the dreaded word almost freaked me out. "Uh, I'll check back later. Gotta go." Plus Uncle Robert didn't need to know about the shooting yet. I didn't want Mom exerting pressure to ax me off the job.

After my heart stopped tripping double-time, I waited, tapping my fingers on the steering wheel. Heavy traffic whizzed by, air pressure from their passing rocking my little Jeep. I speed-dialed Matt again. My call went directly to voicemail. I slumped in my seat.

A long fifteen minutes later, a tow-truck zoomed by, swerved onto the freeway shoulder, squealed to a halt, rammed into reverse, and backed up to Bunny. A young man, sculpted muscles displayed by a sleeveless tank and wearing jeans and a backward ball cap, climbed out. He took in my situation then strutted to my door. I gazed at him through my open window. He looked familiar, but I didn't know that many broad-shouldered guys with serious blue eyes and slightly crooked noses. My mind went *tickety-tick* through various wanted posters. Nothing.

Without even a nod, he bent over my front bumper and hooked up Bunny. Sweat left a dark streak down the back of his white tank-top. I slid over the four-on-the-floor, opened the passenger door, and jumped out, snagging the back of my sweater. By now my coffee-wet knees had dried, but I'd become soggy with perspiration and short-tempered.

"Hey, do I know you?" I stared at the interesting profile bent over Bunny's olive green-on-green fender. "I'm Holly."

He straightened and smiled. "Chuck." He launched himself into the cab, leaving the door open, maneuvered some levers, and started hoisting Bunny's front end into the air. Then he climbed back out, faced me, and pulled off his cap. Wavy blond hair tied back in a tail fell between his shoulder blades.

I slapped my forehead as I placed him. Duh. "You're the wrestler who helped me up from beneath the table last night."

He jumped back as if I'd slugged him and stared at me like an adrenaline junkie about to take his first skydive. Oh, he was scared. If Bunny hadn't been hooked to his tow-truck, he'd have taken off and left me flat-footed in the hot sun.

"Uh, yeah. That would be me." Big muscles turned back to hoisting Bunny until her front wheels dangled just below his shoulder. "You didn't set your brake?" he asked the gravel at my feet.

"No. I know enough not to burn my brakes up." I cocked my head.

"So do I hitch a ride with you, Chuck?" Just the man I was dying to grill. *Thank You, God.* I could hardly keep from jumping up and down.

"Yep." He scowled. His runner-on-the-mark posture yelled that he wanted to ditch me. But I was a paying customer.

I was already climbing the high step to his clean cab. I settled in, seatbelt tight. "Umm, smells like a brand new truck."

He scowled, fired up his engine, and barreled into traffic.

I braced against his crazy dodging through traffic. Driving one-handed, Chuck juiced up the air-conditioning, tossed me a clipboard with a form to fill out, and almost side-swiped a semi to get into the fast lane.

Before I tried to fill in the information on the clipboard bouncing on my knee, I slipped my smartphone from my trusty shoulder-bag. As nonchalantly as possible, I tapped in Chuck Eggleston's name, along with his address and phone number, all handily inscribed on the form's top. Then I tried chitchat laced with seemingly innocent questions.

"Is wrestling a part-time job?"

He kept his eyes focused on traffic. "Yeah. Brings in extra cash."

"Are you good?"

"The best."

"You wear a red cummerbund and bowtie when you wrestle?"

"How'd you guess?"

I didn't want to get sidetracked with a visual of him in wrestler's garb, so I concentrated.

"Who invited you to the Meet-A-Thon? You weren't on the guest list. I checked."

"So we crashed." An artery bulged in his neck. His large hands gripped the steering wheel so hard the knuckles actually turned white. He sped up, my Jeep weaving into the next lane and almost taking the paint off a blue minivan. "We like hot dates as much as the next guy."

"Umm." Wanting to arrive in one piece, I thought it prudent to wait until we parked at his shop to ask more questions.

Weaving in and out of traffic like a racecar driver on steroids, chest rising and falling, breath whistling through his teeth, he ignored me the rest of the drive to the repair shop. He pulled off the freeway, onto the service road, and careened into a large concrete parking area. A service station with three empty bays standing wide open looked recently built and spotless.

Chuck stopped the tow-truck and we climbed out.

I read aloud the neon sign blinking above the white stucco shop: "Arena Repair."

"Catchy name, right?" His pride seemed to exert a calming effect over his respiration.

"Yeah, like a place to wrestle. Looks totally new. You the owner?"

A sullen look. No answer. This wrestler-mechanic wasn't about to let me pin him to the mat.

I sighed. "Do you have a loaner car? I've got places to go."

"Yeah." He strode to a black beast parked near the curb, threw open the hood, fiddled with the interior, then slammed the lid. "Caddie's seen better days, but she runs." He tossed me the keys, raced to the tow-truck, jumped in like he had a championship match to win, and backed Bunny into the middle bay.

I gripped my shoulder bag with both hands. I wasn't sure I trusted Bunny with this madman.

"Wait." I trotted over to where he sat and leaned inside the open window. "I've got some stuff in the back I need to take with me."

Chuck hopped out of the tow's driver side and craned his neck to take in the Jeep's littered back seat. When he swiveled back around, a flame burned in his eyes. "Need a bag?" I could almost see horns spring up from his curly blond hair.

"That would help." I backed away from the door.

Chuck raced across the shop and into the office then returned a second later with an industrial-sized brown paper bag. "I'll hold it open for you."

"Oh, that won't be necess—"

"Come on, lady. I got work to do." He opened the rear door and spread the bag wide.

I sighed. "Just give me the bag."

"You got too much stuff."

Chuck's face had taken on the square-jawed, narrow-eyed look of a Pit Bull.

"Well, thanks." I bent inside and began retrieving my items. I handed Chuck my binoculars, night-vision scope, tape recorder, Slim Jim, extra AA batteries, duct tape, paper evidence bags, coil of rope, and my large four-cell flashlight. I left the ice chest. Fortunately I hadn't had time to add my cuffs and transponder, and I'd left my Glock at home, safe inside the terra cotta pot under the hollyhocks. As I handed out the items, we both knew his show of help really meant he insisted on seeing my detective tools. Round one goes to Chuck the Wrestler.

My face burned as I handed out my stuff and stood to face him. I mean, how many suspects got to see what the detective on their case used to trap them?

"Got anything under that seat?"

"Nope. What you see is what I've got."

The Pit Bull laughed and there, once again, was the nice guy who helped me up from the Valentine table last night.

"What I see is an eye full of woman." He winked.

Investigator Rule #3: Don't Let the Suspect Get the Upper Hand.

The words flashed through my mind, but I tried to look confident as I lugged my heavy bag to the Caddie and deposited my stuff on the cushioned backseat. Now I'd ask my questions.

I strolled through the auto shop toward the enclosed waiting area and tried to pinpoint clues beyond its obvious newness. Even the automotive portion didn't smell greasy. New tires were stacked to the ceiling, filling the air with their nauseating rubbery odor. Air wrenches, hoses, and belts lined the walls. Shiny new toolboxes waited on a metal rolling-cart. The whole place looked neat. Too peachy-clean.

No other mechanics appeared. Weird. Even in broad Texas daylight, being alone with the muscleman who probably kidnapped my friend Matt made my eye twitch. My stomach joined in. Why hadn't I brought my gun? I glanced around for a substitute weapon.

Meanwhile, Chuck backed the tow-truck out of the way and shoved Bunny onto the lift. Then he hopped out, pressed the button, and hoisted her into the air. Bunny looked helpless with her four wheels dangling. I knew exactly how she felt.

Stuck with a tight-mouthed suspect, no other leads, and a loaner car from the eighties, I shifted from foot to foot as I memorized the tow-truck's license plate. I'd run it as soon as I left. Then I'd call Frank and see if he could run an ID on a Chuck Eggleston.

Chuck hoofed it toward the tools hanging on the back wall.

Not the best interrogator, I'm nothing if not persistent. "Wait! Did you know the PI you kayoed?"

Chuck froze, air wrench raised in one hand. Slowly he lowered the expensive tool and grabbed a nearby tire iron. "What's it to you?"

I backed away. "Steady, boy. Matt's a friend. You know, he's the guy you kidnapped."

With a clatter that hurt my ears, Chuck threw the tire iron on the concrete floor.

He ignored my jump to a safer spot and strode past me toward the office adjoining the bay where I'd retreated. One foot on the doorstep, the other in midair, he spoke to the door. "You better leave."

"Have you seen Matt since last night?"

His back still toward me, Chuck shrugged.

"Where is he?"

"I'll call when your Jeep's ready." He dove from the shop into his office, slammed the door, flipped the open sign to closed, and jerked down the blind.

The direct approach hadn't snagged me any answers either. I definitely needed another course in interrogation. I shrugged. Okay, no problem. I knew Chuck's name. Using a fake scary voice like in those old horror flicks, I yelled to the closed office door, "I know where you live."

I slid into the Caddie's plush driver's seat, switched on the AC, and steered the black whale toward the street. First I'd do a background search on the shop. It hadn't been in business long. Maybe there were partners. Then I'd get a make on the tow truck's license plate. I'd sandwich in my appointment with the police, and then I'd interview Matt's parents.

I pressed hard on the Caddie's gas pedal. I had precious little time left of my twenty-four hours, and I couldn't get the memory of Matt's limp arm dangling from the stretcher out of my mind.

CHAPTER SIX

I was approaching the High-Five interchange over US-75 and I-635 when my cell rang. I clicked on my headset.

"Hey, Bloodhound, where are you?"

I appreciated Frank's sweetness in not calling me rookie. "On my way to the office. What's up?"

"New lead. I've been expecting it, but it's not good."

My heart did a bongo number. Excitement zipped through me from my phone to my toes. "I'll be right there."

The hard-boiled cop was clueing me in on the case. Yeah, he owed me, but this was bigger than his debt. Did his attraction to Temple have a lot to do with his opening up to a rank beginner? I didn't care. I'd grab whatever break God gave me.

"I'm at the North Dallas station. How soon can you get here?"

I knew the way like the back of my hand. I tagged along when Dad visited the place a hundred times.

"Fifteen minutes. Don't follow that lead without me." I took the first exit from US-75 west to I-635 then exited north to Preston Road. My heart used to sink when I drove Preston Road because my ex-fiancé's name was Preston. But that downer finally passed. These days I felt barely a twinge. Okay, so I can't lie even to myself—no more than a spasm…or two.

Trying to park the luxury car at the station was not a fun trip. I had to hop out and check to make certain I backed the behemoth inside the white stripes. No big shock why little old ladies drove these buses so slowly.

I trotted inside. Entering the station always kicked up my pulse. Exciting things happened here.

The burly middle-aged officer at the desk recognized me. "Hi, Rascal. How's the new job?"

I liked this guy. He'd known my dad. Unlike most of the other cops around, he didn't believe the lies that buried Dad's good reputation. He still respected Ted Garden's memory. I smiled. "Job's great, Joe. Frank McCoy available?"

Joe threw me a curious look. No wonder. All the years I'd come here with Dad, I'd never asked to see a police detective.

"Sure. Upstairs. Either in the second office on the right or in the briefing room." He winked. "You two got something going?"

"Business."

Joe propped up a skeptical brow and grinned, then buzzed the lock on the high metal door.

I pushed through the heavy door. "Thanks."

I found Frank in the second-floor office, frowning down at a paper encased in plastic on his scuffed desk.

When I entered, he glanced up. "Look at this." He kicked a metal chair close to where I stood then used both hands to flatten the sheet on the desktop.

I bent over his shoulder. "Hi to you, too."

He didn't respond.

I leaned closer and peered at cheap typing paper covered with large and small letters clipped from magazines. My heart stopped like it'd been hit by a stun-gun.

I frowned. "A ransom note…without a demand for ransom." My stomach kicked hard enough to make me look for a wastebasket. This wasn't just my first case. This wasn't a stranger I was rescuing. This was my friend Matt in deep trouble! Otherwise I had no business searching for a kidnap victim. That was a job for the police. And maybe the FBI.

"What do you think?" Hard muscles worked in Frank's jaw.

Still trying to get a grip on my emotions, I quit looking for a place to heave, compressed my scared feelings for Matt into a tiny ball, stowed the lump under my sternum, and then digested the note.

No other cops or your player loses the game.
Your PI won't play ball. Bad boy, now you'll pay.
If you don't, your PI strikes out.

My heart jumped to my throat.

The gravity in Frank's piercing gray eyes launched a death march of chills over my body. "Where did you get this? Along with bad poetry, it looks amateurish."

"Anonymous mail-in. Found the envelope on my desk."

"Obviously the kidnappers sent you this because sometimes you're Matt's partner."

"So it would seem." His puzzled expression thwacked a new hit to my stomach.

"And your Thunderbird being smashed at Dolly's was no accident."

He nodded.

"And the shots?"

His hand jabbed the air. "I'd say a warning." His brows pinched together. "To both of us." He frowned. "The bullets came way too close."

Legs weak and knees knocking, I dropped into the metal chair facing Frank's desk. Gazing around the Spartan office, I noted the hidden surveillance camera and hugged my arms, partly to hide the goosebumps and partly to keep from shuddering.

"What now?"

Frank jackknifed to his feet. "You're off the case." His hand smacked the desk. "Whoever mailed the note knows I can't raise that kind of money. The kidnapper's not interested in ransom."

My eyeballs chilled. If they didn't want cash, what did they want? I swallowed and had to clear my throat. "The kidnapper has to be someone who knows you. Any idea who?"

Frank strode around the desk, loomed over me, and poked a finger at my nose. His short, clipped words made my hair stand on end. "If I did, I wouldn't tell you. Go home. I can't work with you. It's too dangerous."

I straightened. "And if I stay on?"

"I'll lock you up." Frank pulled a blank warrant out of his top drawer.

Superman-turned-Clark Kent ordering Wonder Woman to give up her golden lasso.

"Ha! You're joking."

"Not even." He flopped into his chair.

"What happened to you owing me?"

"Consider yourself paid up."

I'm not one to shy from a challenge. Besides, I couldn't stop thinking of Matt. I needed answers. With or without Frank, I had a plan. Thanks to the gunman/demolition demon, I knew where one of the wrestlers worked.

"If I give you a name, are we back to you owing?"

"You got a name?" Frank jolted up. His chair swiveled back and crashed into the rear wall.

I swallowed bad coffee as I gave my statement to Hal Jaconavich, the police detective. I told the sharp-nosed, slightly-built man everything I knew of Matt's disappearance and spilled my guts about the kidnapper's note. I talked as honestly and openly as I could about my relationship with Matt. During the half-hour interview at the police station, my insides skated from crushed ice cubes to quivering globs of jelly. I was talking about my BFF, Matt. Withholding background information could hinder the investigation. I didn't want anything to foil finding Matt.

"So McCoy has the note." Jaconavich settled back in his chair and rubbed his chin.

"Yes. But please, please, *please* be subtle in your investigation. The note specifically said not to notify the police." The jelly stomach threatened to upchuck. Had I done the wrong thing?

"We have a special Kidnapping Unit that will handle the case." Jaconavich put a hard hand on my shoulder. "Trust us. We'll take care of everything."

"Thank you. Please keep me up to date." I smiled my prettiest.

"I'm sorry. Are you related?"

"No. But—"

"I see." Jaconavich gave me that superior look that spoke volumes. I wouldn't be hearing from the detective.

"If I discover anything new, I'll notify you immediately." He didn't want my help, but I wanted all the help I could drag in.

I spent another forty-five minutes describing the wrestlers to a sketch artist. Then I was done.

On my way home, as my mind zipped and crackled, my driving might have been a little fast. I felt plenty hot under the turtleneck. Frank was running Chuck's shop and his license through the police files. I'd given Temple's guy my information, but he'd not promised to owe me anything he came up with except whatever my information brought to light.

I was pretty much on my own.

The traffic light at the bottom of the long hill flashed red. I touched the brake. Nothing happened.

I hit the brake again. Then pumped like a mad woman. The big Caddie sped way too fast. I pulled the emergency brake. Nothing.

Picking up speed, the car careened down the hill. Up ahead, an eighteen-wheeler gas tanker stopped at the red light blocked my lane. A school bus loaded with children waited in the adjoining lane.

I had nowhere to go. My heart ping-ponged between panic and dread. If the tanker exploded, it would take the children as well as me. The old Caddie had turned into a taxi to heaven.

Heart jack-hammering inside my chest, time slowed like a Matrix Moment.

Hands shaking, I laid on the horn and braced for impact.

CHAPTER SEVEN

Again I jerked the emergency brake. The car didn't even slow.

A picture flashed on the screen of my mind of a fiery crash enveloping the busload of school children.

Dear God, please, no!

Driven by either a white knight or a madman, a paneled ice cream truck sliced into my lane between the tanker and me. The driver hit the brakes and fishtailed.

My heart lit with hope.

Frantically I pumped the mushy brake, but the black Caddie didn't slow. The white- paneled side of the ice cream truck offered a softer landing than the tanker. If I hit the truck, I'd miss the school bus and maybe the tanker too. And we wouldn't explode and spew blood all over the road.

But the hero driving the truck would become an ice cream sandwich. In the flash it took for me to think these things, I switched off the ignition. My Titanic bucked and slowed.

I braced against the steering wheel. It would be—

Wham! The air bag exploded, and my body snapped back into the seat. Before I could take a breath, the bag deflated, leaving powdery dust on my forearms, face, and hands. A rubbery, singed smell clogged my nose. Groggy from the impact, I sneezed and coughed. Blinking repeatedly, I rubbed my lashes until my eyesight cleared. The stuff tasted toxic.

I had targeted the Caddie toward the ice cream bars painted on the truck's side. Bulls-eye. Now the vehicle resembled an open-air concession stand with the Caddie's front end nestled inside the refrigerated compartment. Twenty-gallon metal ice cream containers rolled in slow motion from the side to cascade over my car. Above a layer of jagged metal, squashed, frozen Snickers bars glued themselves to the Caddie's hood. Rainbows of ice cream globbed my front window so I couldn't see the full extent of the wreck. I lowered the glass on my side and craned my head out. Refrigerated air from the truck cooled my cheeks. The smell of chocolate and vanilla permeated the air.

My Titanic had shoved the damaged vehicle to within inches of the tanker. Horns blared. Brakes screeched. My radiator hissed. With a strange whooshing sound, the ice cream truck settled onto the pavement. But somehow the driver had managed to keep both our vehicles from hitting the tanker. God sent a guardian angel.

The light had turned green, and both the untouched tanker and the school bus had chugged down the street, leaving the crash site. I was sure they'd seen nothing and were completely unaware of the accident.

Leaning against the steering wheel, I let my breath hiss out like a hot-air balloon with a leak.

Thank you, Lord. But how's the other driver?

I brushed my trembling hand over my face. My teeth were all in place. No damage to my nose. Both arms worked. Fingers flexed. Except for slight burns from the air bag, no damage. My torso ached from the seatbelt gouging my chest. I was shaken but not broken.

Resting my forehead on the steering wheel, I again breathed a thankful prayer. Mark one up for me. Two accidents in one day. My guardian angel worked a double-shift.

A sinister thought sent a chill tiptoeing down my spine. Had Chuck deliberately issued me a car with faulty brakes? An image of him opening the Caddie's hood and tinkering sparked neurons in my gray cells. The accident could have been deadly. My whole body erupted into a delayed sweat. Not just for me; I was ready to meet my heavenly Father. But if I'd hit those children on the bus, they could suddenly have found themselves in eternity. I started shaking. And that brave ice cream man. How was he?

Aiming for the side of the ice cream truck, I'd missed the cab. It looked intact.

Motorists all around the intersection pulled over to the curbs. A crowd gathered around our two vehicles. Someone opened my car door. "You okay?"

"Yeah. Help me out, would you please? My knees are shaky."

"Here. Grab hold."

My hands felt like ice inside his warm ones. The stranger pulled, and I scooted out, stood on legs that trembled beneath my weight, and hoped I wouldn't be sick in front of the crowd. "Thanks."

"Should I call an ambulance?" Dressed in a well-fitted business suit, bald head shining in the sun, the man smiled. His face looked kind.

"Not for me, thanks. I'll be okay. Would you check on the person driving the truck?"

I stood, wobbly as a toddler learning to take her first steps, gazing wide-eyed at the Titanic. A few more dents marred the black fenders, but the front grill resembled an accordion. I forced myself to look at the demolished panel truck and clutched my roiling stomach. That pathetic vehicle would never refrigerate ice cream again.

75

A siren screamed, howling closer. Several men, also in business suits, worked on prying open the truck's driver-side door. I clasped my cold hands together.

Oh, God, don't let your angel be hurt.

A black boot slapped onto the glass-cluttered, ice cream-smeared pavement, followed by a black-clad leg then the other boot. Two men reached inside and hauled the driver out.

Thank you, God. The man can stand!

Wrappers, chocolate, sprinkles, and melting ice cream splattered his dark hair, dripped off his neck, and ran down the back of his shirt. He turned around. Blood oozed down the side of his face. He looked as white as his T-shirt. Then…I recognized him. How—?

Hanging an arm across the colossal fender, I bent over and retched. Keeping my head lowered, I realized I probably wouldn't faint. My hands shook as I pushed hair out of my eyes and wiped my mouth with the back of my hand. Leaning against the Caddie's fender where the metal impaled the panel truck's side, I sucked in the escaping refrigerated air. My head slowly cleared.

Those black boots, sticky with melted ice cream, slid into view and stopped, both rounded toes facing me. The jeans looked ragged, with new rips and raw, scraped skin peeking through globs of ice cream.

Forcing my gaze higher, I smelled chocolate and toffee.

The dripping white T-shirt clung to a familiar, trim, muscled body.

"Stryker?" How did he get here?

This was the man guaranteed to quake my knees at fifty paces… and they already shook.

"The same. You all right, princess?"

I nodded and tried to unhinge my jaw. "I'm so grateful you figured out my brakes were gone. Thanks for saving my life."

"My pleasure."

"I owe you big-time. How can I repay you?" I clamped my lips to avoid making the mistake of telling him, "I'll do anything."

He smiled as if he'd read my thoughts. "I'll think of something." Blood oozed from a nasty gash above his left eye, the same eye blackened last night. He swiped at the blood with his forearm and smeared melted ice cream over his face. His other arm cradled his ribs.

I took a couple fortifying breaths. "You don't look so good." Reaching through the Goliath's window, I fumbled for my red shoulder bag. "I always carry Baby Wipes because I'm inclined to create messes." Feeling sick but somehow all maternal as well, I had an overwhelming desire to dab the blood from his face. Instead I took the safe road and handed him several wipes.

"I've been worse." He pressed a towelette against the seeping wound and used the rest to swab ice cream. "Sure you don't carry a hospital in that red suitcase?" His grin seemed a smidgen forced. Minus the blood, his complexion emerged slightly gray.

"Are you sure you—?"

A siren hurt my ears and drowned out my voice until an ambulance screeched to a halt within a yard of where we stood. Immediately after, a black-and-white squealed up to block the intersection. Two EMS guys reached us first. They glanced at me then grouped around Stryker. Soon they shuffled him over to the ambulance, opened the back door, and began taking vitals. Sitting in the doorway, Stryker yelled over their heads, "Don't go away."

I scrutinized the medics. *Lord, please let those EMS guys be the real thing. I don't want any repeats of last night. Especially after this guy saved my life…and the lives of those kids on the school bus.*

The cops concentrated on me. While I kept my gaze on the ambulance and wondered how Stryker fared, I answered their questions. I told them everything, including my suspicions about

Chuck.

I didn't know these cops, but they shot an unbelieving look at one another and shrugged. No matter. I planned to interrogate Chuck myself.

I was bent over the glove compartment retrieving the loaner's insurance papers when the siren blared again. I hit the back of my head on the doorframe trying to back out in time to accompany Stryker. My effort gave me a glimpse of taillights rushing back up the same hill where my brakes had failed. I rubbed the back of my smarting head and sighed.

Yesterday medics whisked Matt away. Today they carried off Stryker. Coincidental? I didn't believe in twists of fate. Was God telling me I didn't have the right stuff to be a private investigator? Every time I worked the job, someone got kidnapped or hurt. I was a Sword of Damocles.

"Don't look so upset, miss." A trim officer patted my shoulder. "From what you've told me, this could have resulted in a fatality. Just relax in the squad car a few minutes." He steered me toward the black-and-white and opened the door. "You get a grip while I talk with these witnesses." He waved his hand at the staring crowd. "After that we'll call a tow for your car, and I'll give you a lift home." He turned his uniformed back to me and marched to the collection of people standing in the street.

I folded sideways into the seat and rested the side of my head on the back, my thoughts whirling between Stryker, Matt, and my second brush with death.

My stomach growled fiercely as the friendly cop, who told me his name was Sam Tucker, finally dropped me off at home. I didn't know Sam. He said he was new on the force. I was grateful for that since he probably didn't know about Dad, so he hadn't formed a bias against me.

I thanked Sam, who had to be about my age, grabbed the bag of detective tools rescued from the totaled Caddie, and waved goodbye. I headed up the veranda stairs, let myself in with my key, and hit the remote off button on my keychain to disarm the alarm.

Inside, the house was quiet. I guessed the maid had finished her work and left. Juanita, our cook, probably hadn't come on duty yet. I didn't know where Mom and Granny or the twins were, but the knots in the back of my neck eased some in the cool stillness. I walked through the hall, headed back toward the kitchen, plunked my tool bag beside a chair, dropped my shoulder bag on the table, and sucked in a deep breath. I had some thinking to do, and I wasn't feeling real perky.

I opened the fridge and snooped through neatly-packaged leftovers until I pulled out a low-fat King Ranch casserole. After piling several spoonsful on a plate and warming them in the micro, I settled at the glass table in the breakfast nook and downed a few bites.

I needed to go next door and talk with Matt's parents. Time was running out. It was too soon to hear from Frank about the information I needed, but I'd call him and ask for Stryker's cell number. Then I'd tell Frank what happened...or not.

He'd just order me off the case again. When I felt better, I'd call Stryker and check on him. But for now, I had to talk with Maddie and Ray Murdoch. I finished the rest of the reheated casserole, gathered my gear, and ducked out the back door.

I shimmied over the wrought-iron fence separating our yard from the Murdochs' and loped across the back lawn to escape the reporters staked out at their front veranda. I wasn't even out of breath when I rapped on Matt's back door.

Mrs. Murdoch's head popped out almost before I stopped knocking. Her subtly bleached blonde hair stood on end, revealing gray roots. Deep furrows lined her forehead, and she looked as though she'd slept in her mint-green pantsuit.

"Hi, Maddie." I kept my voice peppy to help cheer her up. "Along with the police, I'm searching for Matt. Can I ask you a few questions?"

"Oh, Holly. Have you heard anything?" She hugged me, grabbed my hand, and pulled me inside. Even during times of heavy grief, Dallas is Deep South in its welcome. As she ushered me into the kitchen, she held tight to my hand.

She pressed the intercom to the upstairs. "It's Holly, honey. She wants to ask us a few questions."

Her husband, Ray, had probably taken refuge in his study to escape the reporters.

When she turned back to me, Maddie's voice sounded unnaturally high. "The more people searching for Matt, the better." Her pale lips trembled. Usually subtle make-up allowed Matt's mom to look years younger, but today her skin appeared sallow, and dark circles lined the pouches beneath her red eyes. She looked two decades older.

"Sit and have a cup of coffee, dear. I've kept it warm. The police always appreciate coffee and cake when they drop in."

I had to swallow before I could answer. Maddie reminded me so much of Matt. "Coffee would be good."

"I'm glad you came in person, dear. The police are getting a court order to tap the phone."

"Yes, that's standard procedure." Matt inherited Maddie's warmth and concern for others, along with her twinkling sapphire eyes. They shared the same tall, lanky build and big bones. Though he leaned closer to nerd than athlete, he'd been popular with all the kids at North Dallas High. During the past four years, we both majored in criminal justice at different colleges, but we'd stayed in touch. Being three years my senior, he'd graduated and gone to work for my dad. After Dad died, Uncle Robert kept him on.

Maddie slid a cushioned chair out from the oak table and all but pushed me into it. "We've been up since Friday night without a wink of rest. Ray slept at police headquarters and wore a path to your uncle's office. You're lucky you caught him home." Her hand trembled as she poured coffee from the glass pot into a dainty china cup. Her red-rimmed eyes splashed over. "I just can't figure why someone would kidnap Matt. Did you see the note they left?" She shook her head as tears continued to trickle down her cheeks. "According to Detective McCoy, the kidnappers didn't ask for ransom because they probably know we couldn't pay much. I just don't know what we're going to do if—"

"Easy, Maddie, my girl." Matt's dad stepped through the doorway and slid his arm around her shoulder, hugging her close to his side. Still trim, with close-cropped silver hair, he stood two inches taller than his wife and wore a perpetual tan from spending hours on the golf course. "I'm sorry, Holly. Maddie's beside herself."

"Oh, Ray. Stop exaggerating." Her hands still trembling, Matt's mom wiped away her tears and cut a slice of coffee cake from a nearly-empty pan. She slid the goody onto a plate, and pushed the treat over to me. "Pastor Jenkins was here, and the choir and fellowship classes are praying for Matt. He started the prayer chain. He also said he'll lead the church in prayer for Matt during the service tomorrow." Maddie fluttered her hands and seemed to need to talk.

"I'm glad you're looking for Matt too. Jake Henderson's the name of the investigator Robert plans to assign. He said Jake was the best PI he had." Maddie gave a nervous laugh. "Other than Matt." Pink tinted her cheeks. "And you, of course."

My stomach flip-flopped. No one had any confidence in my investigative ability.

Ray steered his babbling wife to a chair and gently lowered her into it. He put a finger on his lips. "Sssh. Let Holly talk. Maybe she has news."

"I'm sorry, Ray." I shook my head. "I don't have anything to report. I've seen the kidnapper's note and talked with the police. I have some leads to follow, but I need to find out a few things first." I turned to Maddie who sat twisting her hands together on the polished oak surface.

"Do you know what case Matt was working?"

Ray raised his eyebrows and threw up his hands. "Goodness, no. Matt never discussed his cases with us. Said he had investigator/client privilege. We respected that."

"Of course." I knew Matt, as an only child, had a close relationship with both his parents, so I figured they could answer my next question. "I probably should know, but did Matt have a girlfriend?"

Maddie's mouth dropped open. She stopped twisting her hands.

Ray frowned. "What's that got to do with his kidnapping?"

I carefully measured my response. "He disappeared on Valentine's night. I thought perhaps a spurned love. Was he seeing anyone special?"

"Hmm..." Ray locked eyes with his wife. They silently communicated. When Dad was alive, he and Mom had often communicated that way in front of us girls. I felt sure Matt's parents asked each other how much they should reveal. My neck prickled. Why would Matt's dating be a sensitive topic?

Maddie sighed. Then she spoke much more slowly. "No. Ever

since you left to attend Baylor, Matt seemed a little lost in that department."

My heart somersaulted. I held my stomach, fearful I'd lose what little of Mom's King Ranch I'd choked down. Surely Matt wasn't hung up on me! He'd never shown any such feelings. My scalp burned, and heat painted my cheeks.

"Did he date much?" Matt and I had never dated each other. Where had his parents gotten their idea?

As if she feared she might be writing a signature to an anonymous Valentine, Maddie's voice hushed. "Oh, Matt saw a girl now and again. He said none of the females at church appealed to him since they all grew up together. But when you became engaged to Preston, he started visiting other churches. He met a few girls that way."

I was breaking into a house I feared I'd find haunted. Heat from my scalp and cheeks crawled down the back of my neck. I squirmed on the white-cushioned seat. To cover my feelings, I sipped the coffee, gazed out the bay window, and watched sunlight sparkle on the Murdochs' large kidney-shaped swimming pool. The coffee tasted bitter—like my life right now.

"Umm…maybe I will have a dash of cream." Pot had probably been on the burner for hours. Strong enough to make me choke on the secret Matt's parents tried hard to hide.

I'd never suspected. I realized I didn't know Matt nearly as well as I'd thought.

Maddie slid a blue-and-white creamer to me, and I poured a few teaspoons into the black coffee. "I checked Matt's timesheets at Uncle Robert's and found nothing. Could I take a look into Matt's timesheets for the clients from his moonlighting jobs? Those sheets will tell me where he's been working. I hope to find a lead in one of his cases."

Ray jumped to his feet and strode out of the kitchen. The man put thought into action more quickly than most people, a trait Matt shared with his father. Probably Ray's quickness made him a really good attorney.

I hoped Matt's kept him alive.

I listened to Ray's hurried footsteps on the stairs and thought about how strange it felt tracking down my friend. Matt was the type of guy who kept regular hours, did regular things, and people always knew where he was and why. Matt never had secrets.

The burn traveled all the way down to my toes. I *thought* Matt had nothing to hide. Sweat started to sprout from my pores. I was doing Niagara Falls in front of Matt's mom. Did he truly have a thing for me? What else about him had I missed?

Forcing my attention to the case, I looked for motivation. "Do you have any idea why anyone would kidnap Matt?"

"We have money, of course. But so does everyone in this part of town. Why pick on Matt?" Maddie's shoulders slumped. She looked like she needed a hug.

I got up, gave her a big one, and then resumed my seat at the table. "He's an only child. A kidnapper would realize you and Ray would pay fast and furious for his release." I scratched my pencil in lazy doodles on the pad I'd taken from my purse. "But the criminals didn't ask you for money. They asked a cop. Plus, it doesn't make sense to snatch Matt in such a public place."

"That's true. They could have kidnapped him on his evening run." Maddie rubbed her hand over her mouth. "Matt ran alone. Often late at night after he returned home from work."

"Right." I nodded. "The kidnap scheme was elaborate. Why go to all that trouble when someone could have snatched Matt on his run or even on his way home from work? Or late at night from his bedroom." I'd already thought of this, but to hide my new knowledge about

Matt's supposed love for me, I jotted these thoughts on my pad.

Maddie hung her head. "All the homes in this neighborhood have alarms, but we never bother to set ours. This neighborhood's safe."

Again I nodded. "I can count on two fingers how often neighbors called for police protection in the last eight months." I tapped my pencil eraser on the pad. "You don't have a guard dog. Even if you'd set your alarm, a kidnapper would find the job simpler to disable it and steal Matt from his bedroom on some dark and stormy night."

"True. Or even on a calm night. I'll let you in on a little secret. We've decided this morning to purchase a German shepherd as well as set the alarm. I know that's like locking the door after the horse is stolen, but we needed to do something."

I totally understood Maddie's desire for action. "To kidnap Matt on Valentine's Day, at a public party, smells like…revenge. A jilted love. Add the five wrestlers, who stood out like Halloween at the Meet-A-Thon, and you've got a revengeful publicity-seeker."

Maddie's eyes spilled over again. I handed her a tissue from the almost-empty box on the table. "But Matt never jilted any girl. He never even dated one girl more than three times. His heart was—" She glanced at me, then quickly away, and blew her nose on the tissue.

I gazed down at my untouched coffee cake. She did think Matt cared for me. I disliked butting in on Maddie's grief and pain and violating her privacy. Especially since Matt's parents were close friends and neighbors. People already important in my life, but I couldn't believe they were right about Matt's romantic feelings for me.

Ray strode in, a sheaf of papers in his hand. "This morning's newspaper followed your line of thinking. Look at these headlines." He thrust the folded paper toward me.

Private Investigator Snagged by Cupid's Arrow Missing from Valentine Date-A-Mate.

He shook his head. "I don't buy it. Sorry, Holly, you and the newspaper have the circumstances all wrong. Matt didn't have a girlfriend." His lips thinned, and he gazed narrow-eyed at me. "He never had one."

If only the floor would open up and swallow me. Even my ears burned.

But what if he did?

Vera Wang girl, Samantha Parker, shot to the top of my investigative list. What if Matt did know her before the party? I slopped coffee on my hand as I tried to take a sip. Obviously Matt knew how to keep secrets.

"Um…are those his timesheets?"

With his parents reading over my shoulder, I studied Matt's worksheets, timesheets, and notes on the various moonlighting cases he worked. Two recent cases stood out, one a blackmailing and the other a money-laundering scheme. Both perps had been arrested and immediately released on bail. Both men had cause for revenge.

From where they sat on either side of me, Maddie and Ray silently watched as I made notes.

Leafing further back through the papers, I checked the cases Matt worked since Dad had been murdered and the firm spiraled downward. Matt polished off more moonlighting cases than I'd have believed. Why did he still bother to work for Uncle Robert who had so few cases for him? I scribbled more notes.

"Matt worked with Uncle Robert three years while I finished up at Baylor. I already checked those cases and found nothing." I downed the bitter coffee in two gulps, gathered Matt's papers into a tidy pile, and thumped them on the table to align them. "There are two cases here that could motivate a man to kidnap. I'll look into them and let you know as soon as I discover something concrete. I'm sure we'll find Matt soon." I smiled, trying to remain professional and encourage them but not raise their hopes too high. With two good leads, I rose to leave.

"Oh, Holly, I'm so glad you're looking for Matt too. He'd want you to be the one to free him."

My stomach did a sick little flop.

"Thanks." I hugged Maddie. "Remember, God's in control, and He loves Matt."

Before I shut the back door behind me, I overheard Maddie speak to Ray in a grief-scratched voice. "When we get Matt back, I won't hear any more nonsense. He's going to law school and then straight into the firm with you. We've got to put an end to that dangerous investigative work."

I gave a dry, internal laugh. If she thought he'd fit in as a legal eagle, Maddie didn't know her son. Sure, Matt had the cool, analytical brain needed by lawyers, but like me, he loved adventure. Didn't she remember how, despite his skinny six-foot-three one-hundred-sixty-pound frame, he'd hung onto playing football even though he perennially warmed the bench? He'd made second-string on the varsity soccer team. Although mainly a brain, the man had speed and aggressiveness. Didn't Maddie remember Matt's outback adventures in Australia the summer after he graduated high school? And he'd hiked the Appalachian Trail and white-water rafted on the Colorado River. Nope, sitting behind a desk or arguing in a courtroom weren't Matt's calling. I sighed, refusing to give in to the tears pricking my eyes. Surely an adventurous, intelligent man like Matt could survive being kidnapped.

Please keep him safe, Lord.

My cheeks burned. *And please let Maddie be wrong about Matt's having chemistry for me.*

CHAPTER EIGHT

Just as I was leaving Matt's house, a police officer rang the front doorbell. I paused and turned back to see if I might learn something.

Maddie noticed my hesitancy to leave. "The policeman's just here in case we get a call from the kidnapper. He's going to stay with us until...until we get some sort of word about Matt." Again she twisted her hands.

"Yes. Standard procedure. And yes, God will bring Matt back safe and sound." *Oh, Father, please make my words true.* "I'll just let myself out the back door." I hugged them both and ran.

Once inside our house, I had to calm myself and dash back to work. I needed a cool head. Probably the police tapped Frank's phone as well.

I blew into the kitchen and plopped into a chair at the table.

For now, were there any new red flags I could follow up? Nothing sprang to mind, but though I didn't want to suspect him, Stryker seemed a unifying force. He'd been at the Valentine gala. He'd been at Dolly's Donuts just before the shooting and demolition derby. An hour and a half later he had used an ice cream truck to avert a tragedy. But why had he been there? And why the disguise? Why did this man pop up everywhere I went? I'd question him. Use my wiles to find answers. With a head wound, he might be dizzy enough to spill some worthwhile information.

But until then… I pushed up from the chair, opened my laptop, which I kept handy in the kitchen, and started a spreadsheet. I needed to piece this puzzle together. Computers crashed, so I liked to have hard-copy along with my spreadsheet. I pulled a package of colored index cards from a kitchen drawer.

I selected a red 4 x 5-lined card and wrote Stryker Black at the top. What did I know? Okay, Mom hadn't trusted me and hired extra security for the party. But why had an investigator of Stryker's caliber taken the job? I scratched my nose. Smelled fishy. Usually beginners like me, or older has-beens, manned such mundane jobs. Stryker fit neither profile. He had to have an ulterior motive for taking that job. Was he involved in Matt's kidnapping? Mentally I reviewed Stryker's movements and jotted each question they raised on his card. After I finished the index card, I typed in the information on my spreadsheet.

Stryker sent out Frank McCoy, Temple's current flame, as soon as Matt disappeared. I topped a blue index card with Frank McCoy's name. Had Frank really lost the kidnappers when he tailed the ambulance? Or had he been in league with the bad guys?

No way.

I trusted Frank. Reliance and integrity were engraved on the man's forehead. Was he an unwitting stooge for Stryker? Highly unlikely. Frank was too smart. Since I had such confidence in Frank, why did the cool, detached part of my brain distrust Stryker? Easy. He'd been outside the donut shop just seconds before someone shot at Frank and me. Was Stryker spying on us? Had he shot the bullets that demolished Dolly's front window? Since he seemed so tight with Frank, I doubted Stryker bulldozed Frank's prized car. Why did Stryker disappear? Had he eyeballed the shooter and chased him? That seemed the most likely scenario. I made a note to add that to the questions I planned to bombard Stryker with as soon as I could pin him down.

I had to be honest with myself. Did I really suspect Stryker, or did I distrust him on a different level entirely? Did I fear the hero who risked his life to save mine might creep into a tender, unguarded place in my heart and make himself at home? Whatever the reason, until I knew more about him, I dubbed Stryker as Dark Angel rather than Hero. Even Satan did wonderful things for people he wanted to entrap.

My chair scraped the floor as I pushed it back. I paced the kitchen. After Stryker sent out Frank, and Frank lost the kidnappers, had Frank turned up anything? Last night, when I first called the police detective, he'd claimed he chased a lead. Yet after Frank met me at Dolly's, he'd given me no information. I shrugged. Not like we'd had a lot of time to talk.

Another big question. How had Stryker known I drove the Cadillac rather than my Jeep? Was he in cahoots with Chuck? And how had Stryker miraculously arrived Johnny-on-the-spot with split-second timing to prevent my smashing into the tanker? Why would he risk his life for me? My head throbbed harder.

I jotted Chuck Eggleston's name at the top of a yellow index card and wrote out everything I knew about the Arena Repair mechanic. I'd grill the repairman about the defective brakes on the car he loaned me. Maybe that would loosen his tongue. Then after I talked with Frank again, I'd have more information to add to the full-time mechanic, part-time wrestler's card.

Soon a green card topped with the heading "Other Wrestlers" stared blankly up at me. Later I'd tack the cards to a bulletin board in my room and add answers as I discovered them. That way I could shuffle colors and cards any way I needed for chronology, clues, and answers. Then I'd work the computer spreadsheet. Using both methods, I could look at the clues from different angles and might see something I missed by gazing at the material from only the cards or only the spread sheet.

I did some deductive reasoning and dredged up tentative answers. Obviously Stryker had been tailing me, so he knew about Arena Repair. He knew I had the loaner. Or? I dropped my pen on the table and stared unseeing out the window. Had Stryker seen me stalled beside the highway and sent Chuck the muscle-man to pick up my Jeep? Had he arranged with Chuck to stab a hole small enough in the brake line to slowly drain the brake fluid from the loaner Cadillac? Would he then show up just in time to be the big hero?

I rocked my head from side to side to relieve the tension knotting my shoulders. If that were true, Stryker took a big chance. A very big chance. Of course, he couldn't have known the oil tanker and the school bus would be stopped at the light at the exact time my brakes went out. Or that I'd be on that hill above a busy intersection. He might not have expected such a bad accident. My heart flip-flopped. Still, he hadn't hesitated to insert himself in front of my run-away Caddie to keep me from igniting the whole intersection. Gratitude radiated over me, warming me from my scalp all the way down to the Tropical Blaze painted on my toenails.

I picked up the pen and rolled it between my palms. Had Stryker set up the whole accident thing to make me feel vulnerable? My heart fluttered. Yep. I was that. The puzzle piece didn't exactly fit, but it came close. The premise sounded completely ridiculous and totally plausible at the same time. Did he now expect me to blindly trust him? My thoughts wavered.

Did I? No, I did not fully trust him. But his action put him way ahead in the trust game.

I riffled through my cards. Then I wrote on a second red index card: Why is Stryker involved in every aspect of Matt's kidnapping? Why is he on the case at all? I brought the information on the computer up to date.

Today's accident swiped all my optimism. I needed refresher prayer time. I gathered the pitiful pile of index cards into a stack and tapped them on the table. I was smart. I'd figure out these answers.

In the meantime, Dark Angel remained on my list of suspects. I rubbed my chin. Wrestler Chuck ran neck and neck with Dark Angel and might be pulling ahead by a nose. With a leap and a quickened beat, my heart applauded.

Okay, time to view this puzzle from a different angle.

I hauled out a purple index card and titled it Matt Murdock. A mental image of Matt being carried out on a stretcher made me reach for a tissue to wipe salty tears from my face.

"Are you alive, Matt? Where are you? Is the kidnapper a rejected Valentine? Do you have a new girlfriend? Did she take revenge on you?"

My heart told me no.

But in the harsh light of my own disaster with Preston, this theory made sense. Though I'd prayed about forgiving my ex-fiancé, occasionally I still harbored fantasies of seeing the jerk suffer in the lowest depths of Dante's inferno, calling out for mercy with sweat dripping down his face.

Still, when Matt worked security last night, he'd been checking out the girl in the black strapless dress. And he'd never hinted to me about a girlfriend. I dropped my head in my hands and my shoulders shook. When I gained control, I placed Matt's purple card at the bottom of the stack and tapped my fingers on the glass tabletop.

Now what? I could check out the Vera Wang girl. I retrieved the spiral notebook containing Mom's guest list from my red shoulder bag.

The stunning blonde had been one of the few ladies to leave alone. And she left early, shortly after Matt's kidnapping.

Interesting…

My totally organized Mom had made notations regarding the various invitees during the party and planned to follow up later with more Sweetheart projects. I ran upstairs to her office and found the small notebook Mom carried to the party. The girl's name and brief description told me she was one Samantha Parker. She'd be easy to follow up. I took her card from the bottom of the stack, added her address, and placed the purple card she shared with Matt on top. I sighed. I didn't have much time. And I didn't have wheels.

Before visiting Samantha, I'd check with Frank. See if he knew anything new.

So what else did I know? I laid out the blank green wrestler's card and poised my pen above the first line. Wrestler Chuck confessed to crashing the Valentine party. On my laptop, I googled "Dallas, Texas, wrestlers." From my shoulder bag I retrieved my Android and typed in every wrestler listed. There weren't that many, and I suspected those who advertised were wanna-bes. Not much on-line information, but Google did list phone numbers.

I spent the next half-hour dialing and talking with men with raspy voices who spoke in short sentences. No red flags. All had alibis for other places they'd been last night. None sounded suspicious or worth following up. The other red cummerbunds must be part-time wrestlers like Chuck…*if* they were wrestlers at all. Maybe they were mechanics. Or hit men. I recalled each face but knew nothing about the men.

Since I really didn't expect anything to come from visiting Samantha but couldn't chance leaving any loose ends, and Frank hadn't called with his information yet, I'd reached a dead-end.

I phoned Uncle Robert. "Did the police lab come up with any

fingerprints on that stemmed glass I left with you?"

"Sorry, Holly. They've got a backlog. And we're not high on their list of people they lean over backwards to help. I should have dusted the stemware myself."

I sighed. As far as police labs went, we'd been blackballed and could expect little help until I cleared Dad's name.

Uncle Robert sounded tired. "How's the case working?"

"I've got some leads." I didn't dare tell Uncle Robert about my accident. He'd pull me off the case immediately.

Tires hummed on our long driveway. With the phone still pressed against my ear, I glanced out one of the floor-to-ceiling windows in the kitchen alcove. Mom…probably returning from one of her social engagements.

"I've gotta go."

"Keep me updated. Jake gets the file tonight."

"I know. I will, Uncle Robert. Bye."

Mom parked the Lexus in the front drive, so I knew she planned to go out again. She stepped out of the black sedan, decked out in swank. My heart squeezed. I hoped she hadn't been with Romeo. That silver-haired oilman seemed as slick as his product.

I gathered my cards, snapped a rubber band around them, grabbed my cell and both notebooks, and dropped everything inside my shoulder bag. Then I printed out my spreadsheet.

Thank you, Lord, that Mom wasn't home when Patrolman Tucker dropped me off.

I refused to upset her by relating the accident. On a routine day, she didn't want me pursuing my PI career. She thought the job too dangerous. Thought I had to work with scummy people. Thought I wasn't capable, and wanted me to get married. If I left out the scuffle with the ice cream truck, she'd feel easier about my job.

A crawly sensation crept over the back of my neck. What if Mom was right? What if God really didn't want me to risk my life? What if He did want me in a safer profession? What if I was going against His will? Still, finding Matt was a one-in-a-million job. Nine times out of ten I'd be investigating a suspect about insurance fraud or some mundane corporate crime. Private investigating really wasn't any more risky than say, teaching school.

Mom slammed through the door, worry wrinkles fading from her face when she saw me. She rushed across the Mediterranean-tiled kitchen floor to hug me. "Where have you been? Where's your Jeep? Why didn't you call? Any news about Matt? What—"

"Slow down, Mom. Take it easy." With Mom's nerves strung out like high-tension wires, I drowned in guilt. She didn't need the extra anxiety I caused.

"Calm down," I soothed. Mom's misgivings had gotten worse since drug lords murdered Dad and I spent the night in the slammer being grilled by the cops. She'd driven to downtown Dallas through a lashing thunderstorm at three in the morning to bail me out. She suspected I'd glimpsed some of Dad's killers and knew my penchant for landing in the wrong place at the right time. Ever since, she feared for my life.

After explaining about my Jeep but omitting the shooting and the loaner's demise, I twirled a strand of hair around my finger. "Mom, what do you know about those wrestlers who crashed the Meet-A-Thon?"

A pucker formed between her blonde brows. "Not a thing. Why would I be acquainted with such men?" She shook her highlighted head. "I have no idea who they were or where they went. Before I could order them to leave, they disappeared." She glanced at her Rolex. "That reminds me, I have to run. I just dashed in, hoping to find you." She stroked my hair. "Do try to stay out of trouble." She pointed a finger at me. "You'd make such a fine doctor. That's a safe, meaningful profession, don't you think?"

I nodded. At the moment, even eight additional years of school sounded more appealing than chasing intangible leads. My brush with death still had my stomach knotted. The few morsels of food I'd eaten hadn't stopped its trembling. I stiffened my back. Becoming Dr. Garden, Ob-Gyn, would never clear Dad's name nor keep his agency running. Or, for that matter, keep Mom from dating Romeo again.

I innocently widened my eyes. "Where are you off to?" I kissed her smooth cheek as she hugged me good-bye.

"Errands. Try to be home for dinner, please." She smiled and slipped out the back door.

I rustled up a glass of unsweetened iced tea and an apple to fill the sick places in my stomach, and resettled at the table. Leaning back in the cushioned chair, I draped one leg over the edge of the glass table and called Frank on our landline.

"Could you give me Stryker's cell phone number?"

"Sure."

After I added Stryker's number to my own cell, I started with my list of questions. "I figure if I feed you some information, you'll reward me with what you know."

"Give it your best shot."

"Okay. What—"

"Still shaky from your accident?"

"Why aren't I surprised you already know about the accident? Am I talking with Stryker's Siamese twin?"

"We're tight. What do you know that'll help me find Matt?"

"My questions first. Have you got anything from AFIS on the tow-truck's license plate number I gave you?"

"Yeah. Truck belongs to a Charles Eggleston. He just turned twenty-five."

"No surprise there. What about the Arena Repair address?"

Frank's end of the line went silent for a few beats. "Just opened for business this week. Seems you were one of the first customers. Everything's in Eggleston's name. Where would a kid that young get enough money to launch a business like that?"

"Yeah, that came to me too. And his truck's also next-generation." Disappointment quivered my voice. "That doesn't give us much to work on. Would you run a background check on Chuck for me, please?"

"Working on it."

"You're good. Now tell me what you know."

CHAPTER NINE

"Look, Holly, I gotta go."

Frank had toughed out a really bad day, but I wasn't done with him yet. "Did you tell Stryker we were meeting at the donut shop?"

"I really gotta go."

"No you don't, Frank. You owe me. Did someone hire Stryker to find Matt?"

"Ask him."

"Are you feeding all the information I give you straight to Stryker?"

Frank was silent for three beats then his cop-to-private-citizen voice rumbled. "Lay off the investigating."

I slapped the glass table-top. "This is me you're talking with, not some chump off the street. I'm a trained investigator."

"Someone tried to kill you today. Twice. Back off. Let the cops handle this."

Maybe I'd been thinking those thoughts earlier, but now the matador waved his red cape under my nose. I snorted and pawed the ground.

"I'm on this case, like it or not!"

"Then keep me posted on your whereabouts."

"So you can pass the info on to Stryker?"

"Give me your word."

Because I'd made a vow never to lie, I couldn't promise. "Stryker's working with you, isn't he?"

Silence on the other end. Then finally, "Don't make any moves without me. These people aren't playing around. This is no case for a rookie."

"I'm a fast learner. If you keep me updated, I'll do the same for you." Now why had I blurted that? Frank would run to Stryker with everything I told him. Did I *want* Dark Angel spreading his wings over me?

"I'd like you to carry a transponder. I need to know you're okay."

I didn't respond to that one. While circling the iced tea on the glass table with my free hand, I accidentally sloshed the liquid out into a puddle just as I posed the question burning in my cerebellum. "BTW, how is your boy? Is Stryker okay?"

"Sure. Man's got a hard head. A rib's cracked and a knee's injured, but good thing for you he played super-hero at the right place in the nick of time. What's that make him—Superman, Spiderman, or Batman?"

"Under-Suspicion Man. How'd that perfect timing happen?"

No answer.

I fired the next question like a lightning bolt, hoping it would jolt Frank into an unthinking answer. "You and I both know Stryker's tailing me. Why?"

Frank paused then answered, "Ask *him*. I'll talk with you after you make tracks right over here and put on that transponder."

"I'll think about it. If you answer one more question, your facts could help me find my way to your office."

"Shoot."

"Why did Stryker work security at the Valentine party?"

Frank's laugh rumbled over the line. "Maybe he hired on to catch a hot date."

The phone line clicked dead. I sighed. If Stryker hadn't followed me… I shuddered and bit into my apple. Juice squirted in my eye. Grabbing a tissue, I wiped away the sting.

Hard to suspect a guy after he saved my life.

While I fiddled with rinsing the dish and stacking it in the dishwasher, I tried to decide who to call next. An uproar in the front entry told me the twins were home. I wouldn't tell them about Matt just yet.

The star-studded blondes, Magnolia and Camilla, wearing flip-flops, identical sparkly pink off-the-shoulder tops, and hipster jeans laced with silver Concho belts, landed in the kitchen with their usual excitement and bubble. One wouldn't think a high-class mom like mine would stoop to naming all of us after flowers. Mom blamed that on Dad. *Dear Dad…*

Granny hobbled in behind them.

"Been to the Mall?" I dropped my Android into my purse. Of course they had. It was Saturday.

Cami puffed out her chest. "We had a double-date."

I grinned. Dating at their age was babysitting for Granny.

"You're the only early-riser in the family," Granny croaked. "Gone before we had breakfast."

My throat tightened. Dad had been up before the roosters all his life.

"Looks like you *should* have gotten more beauty sleep." Cami pushed hair back from my face and ran her warm finger across non-existent bags under my eyes.

"At least I don't have to lug a sister along on all my dates." I smirked at the twins as Maggie poured juice and Cami pulled bagels from the fridge. Granny cackled.

I come from a family of tall, slim women whose features resemble silent film stars. Mom looked melodramatic and pampered, Granny just dramatic. From watching the old classic movies with Granny, I'd decided the twins' delicate faces resembled double Greta Garbos. But I favored my tall, dark-haired father in looks and temperament.

As they scrounged up a snack, I parried the usual barrage of matchmaker questions from "The Flowers," as I dubbed my younger sisters. Each entertained Granny and me with different versions of their date. New boyfriends never lasted long with my vivacious sisters. To them, guys were a dime a dozen and as easily spent.

I took my last bite of apple and washed the sweet taste down with iced tea.

Granny put three teaspoons of sugar into her glass. "Eat your snack, girls, and let a body have some peace."

My grandmother and I share the same wavelength and curiosity. Unlike Mom and the twins, who keep both feet planted solidly on the ground, Granny's feet and mine detour toward trouble. Granny often finds herself up to her spiked silver hair in scalding water. We both endure embarrassing moments, but she never lets mortification bother her. Whereas I hit replay on the bad scenes until they warp.

Grandma Gardner is Pennsylvania Dutch from Ohio farm country. German with no Amish ties, she was stubborn, clung to superstitions, deliberately enjoyed shocking Mom, and aspired to be just like me.

"I like your hair the way it is." Granny smoothed her veined hand over my long hair then settled next to me.

I hugged her. Only Granny appreciated my tousled mess. "Yours looks good."

Granny patted her short hair. "Huh. Yeah. This is the latest."

HOLLY GARDEN PI, RED IS FOR ROOKIE

When Granny came to live here, my first-generation, southern, sweet-as-molasses mom took on what she considered her new burden with gusto, trying as hard to remold Granny as she did me. She failed just as completely.

"Peach Tree, did you snare a bird in your net at that Valentine matchmaking doo-dad? How about that hunk under the table? Tell me more."

The twins giggled and turned azure eyes in my direction.

"If he was cool…" Cami started.

"Holly didn't bag him." Maggie finished.

I winked at Granny. "Coolest man there. And…" I paused dramatically. "…he follows me wherever I go."

The twins blew out their cheeks and rolled their eyes in identical faces of disbelief.

Granny grinned. "Sounds like walkin' down Lovers' Lane to me."

I wrinkled my nose and snorted. "You know how I feel about weddings."

Granny sided with Mom on only one family issue. Both wanted to hear the patter of tiny feet more than air to breathe. Both insisted the teenage Flowers graduate from college first. That left me to bear all the baby-producing pressure.

Granny lived to meddle. "What's the dreamboat like? I ain't gettin' any younger."

I guess I came by prying honestly. "He's more like a stalker. And no, he isn't a Mafia kingpin." This was our private joke. Granny loved tall, dark Italians and thought I'd make a perfect mobster's moll. I had a sudden idea to get her off my case. "But Mom captured a man."

Granny sneered. "You mean that smooth-tongued Casanova who picked her up and hauled her off last night? Your ma's too smart for a Jasper like that. Money's all he's got. She'll dump him in no time.

What about you, Peach Tree? Tell all about that under-the-table hunk."

Granny just wouldn't let it alone. The twins sensed a new development and gazed at Granny and me with chatty lips sealed and blonde brows raised.

I sighed. "What makes you think he's worth discussing?"

"I still got two sharp eyes. I saw your expression when you mentioned Mr. Dreamy."

I made a show of looking at my watch. "I've got to run."

"She's not talking." Cami spoke with a mock-husky, seductive voice.

"She must be serious." Maggie jumped up and grabbed a banana to begin making a fruit smoothie.

I slid back my chair and headed for the door.

Granny walked me through the hall, one bony arm linked through mine. "Well, Peach Tree?" Granny squinted up through her rimless trifocals. "Find out anything about that nice young Matt who got himself kidnapped?"

"Not yet. I'll let you know when I do."

"Bet I come up with something for us to work on. I got my ear to the keyhole."

I nodded. "Thanks, Granny."

I wasn't too proud to follow any lead Granny picked up. Her grapevine originated at the Paradise Pet Spa where she volunteered three days a week. Her long list of friends traveled worldwide and wouldn't dream of leaving their beloved dog and cat babies anywhere else but the ultra-luxurious boarding and grooming establishment. Even the occasional movie star walked in and dropped off pets.

The palm-studded café overlooking the dog's splash pond provided Granny and her three friends a watering hole. If anything noteworthy happened in North Dallas, the elderly ladies— dressed in different colored velour sweat-suits, massive amounts of jewelry, and white sneakers—raised their antennas, gathered the news, then broadcast it. They discovered more secrets than "People Magazine."

Granny and the three other ladies who volunteered at Paradise Pet Spa formed the heart of the over-seventy North Dallas crowd. Very little information about the lives of the rich and famous living in the neighborhood escaped their attention. The rest of us didn't fare any better. All the women who belonged to Paradise had witnessed firsthand my humiliation at the altar.

Granny winked. "Think I could find one of those fancy short red dresses like you wore to the party?"

I was used to Granny's lightning thought-changes and nodded.

"I like red. If I had one, I could meet a hip man. Maybe an FBI agent." Granny's face wrinkled in a wide grin.

"Sure. You'd look great in a dress like mine." Granny usually liked her skirts sweeping her ankles, but you never could tell what she might do.

"Think I'll trot down to Willow Bend tomorrow and get one of those hot little numbers. I should have gone to that shindig myself." Grandma's grin brimmed mischief. "Bejiggers! Could have bagged myself a stag and kept an eagle eye on your mom."

I frowned. When my stay-at-home mom wasn't volunteering at church, she spent the bulk of her time with friends, frequenting plays at the local theater, doing charitable work, and shopping at the upscale mall. Mom was a giver...and she gave a lot. Showing up at the Valentine Meet-A-Thon with a date twisted her way out of character.

"I don't like it. Mom doesn't know the score. Lots of conmen lurk out there in the dark world of crooks. They live to target a well-heeled widow who hasn't dated for forty years."

My left eye twitched. *Lord, please keep Mom safe from money-*

hungry men. Please don't let her get involved with that silver-haired wolf she seems attracted to.

As if she were a Roman orator, Granny held up an arm. "It's okay, Peach Tree. Your mom's smarter than she looks. She'll be just fine. Leave her to me. That money-grabber ain't gonna get to first base. "

I hated to imagine what would happen to Mom when Granny took her on.

"Just give me a heads-up if I need to keep tabs on her myself."

Granny giggled, sounding younger than The Flowers. "Count on it." She smacked me lightly on the bottom then hobbled back toward the kitchen. I knew as the day wore on and her hip loosened, she'd walk easier.

I took the wide stairs up to my bedroom, pulled my gun from beneath the hollyhocks, stuck it in my red shoulder bag, and ran down to the porch, slamming the front door behind me.

The familiar ache settled in my heart. "How I miss you, Dad. We could search for Matt together."

But what if Dad really had been dirty? What if the police were right about him and I was wrong? I thumped my fist on the veranda railing to dislodge my disloyal thinking. Not knowing drove me loopy.

Obviously Mom had gotten over Dad's death. Did she realize what bad shape the business was in? A sudden thought froze my foot in mid-stride. Hmm. Maybe that answered her sudden dating. Maybe she thought she needed to sink an oil well herself.

"Get that worried look off your face," Granny called from the kitchen door where she'd waited to see me off. "Just leave your mom to me."

Nothing got past Granny. I grinned at her. "Tell Mom I'm borrowing Dad's Toyota."

As I ran down the long driveway toward the garage, my cellphone played "When the Saints Go Marching In." I dug the glittering red-coated smartphone out of my purse. "Holly here."

"I need to see you in my office. How soon can you be here?"

"Twenty minutes, Uncle Robert. I'm on my way."

In record time I slid into the front seat of Dad's dark green Toyota Highlander, the car he used when he wanted to be inconspicuous. Half the population of Dallas drove SUVs.

Breathless, I gasped into my cell, "Any news about Matt?"

"Just get here."

Twenty minutes later I rushed into Uncle Robert's plush office, my hair tangled about my face from the wind. I stopped short. Jake Henderson sat stiffly in the client chair.

As usual when I met him, my first thought was that in a group as small as two people, Jake would be overlooked. I figured Jake's ex-wife probably couldn't recall a single feature of his bland face. No man alive was more overlooked and underestimated by the criminal mind. Therein lay his great value.

Uncle greeted me with a scowl and scooted his swivel chair back from his desk until he hit his bookcase. "Should have dissolved my partnership with your father when he married. Marriage and investigative work don't make good partners." He stood to all his rugged, though slightly paunchy, six-foot-three-inches, flattened his hands on his cluttered desk, and glared at me. "Your mom ordered me to take you off the case."

More than half-expecting this disaster, I stuck out my chin. "You promised I had twenty-four hours." I slid into the other chair facing Uncle's desk.

"Now you don't. Jake's taking over. I should have let him work the case from the beginning." He pinched his forehead into his ferocious daddy-bear expression. "Fill Jake in on everything you have."

Knowing the futility of challenging Papa Bear, I glared back. But because Matt remained in danger, I shared everything I'd learned. And outlined every idea I had.

"Not much to go on." Uncle Robert took a monogrammed handkerchief out of his breast pocket, closed his eyes, and wiped them as though his eyeballs ached.

My own left eyelid spasmed. I'd seen Uncle use a handkerchief like that only two other times—when the police brought news of Dad's murder, and when the doctor told my uncle his wife had only a short time to live. Uncle's out-of-character tears meant he held little hope of finding Matt alive.

My stomach knotted. My throat ached. My chest hurt. I could do only one thing. I closed my eyes. "Oh, God, please protect Matt. In your Psalms You promised 'Because he loves me, I will rescue him. I will be with him in trouble. I will deliver him and honor him with long life.' So we're trusting You to keep Your promise, Lord. In Jesus' powerful name I pray."

When I opened my eyes, I noticed Jake gazed at the floor, his head lowered.

"Amen." Uncle Robert folded his hanky and kneaded the white square between his long fingers. "There are some reports on your desk I need typed. I'd like you to take care of them."

"But—"

"That's it."

I dragged my feet to my windowless office. Slumping into my desk chair, I rubbed the knots on the back of my neck. Uncle Robert thought Matt would be murdered before I could find him. He thought I'd botch this job like I had that stakeout with Dad. Like Mom, he had no faith in my ability.

But I'd ventured on that stakeout before I ever trained as an investigator. Things were different now. *I* was different now. But was I still a screw-up?

I folded my arms across the desk and dropped my head on them. Synapses flashed in my gray cells. Different or not, I had to find Matt.

Why would someone kidnap a man on Valentine's? Did the kidnapping have something to do with unreturned love? Revenge? Hate? Or was I barking up the wrong tree?

I jerked my head up and slammed a fist onto the desk. I knew about rejected love firsthand. Why else was I without someone warm and fuzzy on Valentine's day? Being dumped leaves emotions raw, maybe even gives a person strong enough motivation to kidnap. The pain might scorch enough to land Matt in deep danger. But who had he cast off? And did he really have feelings for me?

I jumped up to pace back and forth across my small office.

Uncle Robert couldn't bar me from what he didn't know. On my own, I'd visit Stryker, the Vera Wang chick, talk with Chuck, and check into Matt's personal life. Maybe he *did* have a romance.

I clenched my fists. The past few years while I'd been busy getting my Criminal Justice degree, Matt and I hadn't been as close. Before that, he'd been like the brother I never had. He'd seemed an uninvolved bachelor at the party, pursuing the girl in the black strapless dress. So a rejected girlfriend didn't seem plausible.

Frank needed to clue me in on the cases he worked with Matt.

This afternoon, regardless of family fall-out, I'd follow my ace-in-the-hole lead.

I finished typing the stack of reports for Uncle Robert and shut down the computer. Drumming my fingers in a perky beat against the mahogany desk, I watched the second hand of my Seiko slowly tick to five past five. From the bottom drawer I gathered my neuron spray, extra flashlight, camera with the telescopic lens, and added them to the

9mm Glock in my already-heavy shoulder bag. I reapplied lip gloss.

Even though I was officially off the case, Uncle Robert couldn't keep me from tackling Matt's disappearance. With Matt's life in danger, I had to admit I was eager for Jake's help. But first I'd find Matt. I pumped myself a shot of courage via Tommy Girl Perfume and jumped up. What I lacked in brawn and experience, I made up in brains.

I grabbed a bottle of water from the bottom drawer. Besides, I had Dark Angel flying near while I worked the case. Just the thought of Stryker kicked up my pulse. I was sure to run into him again. My heart did a flippity-flop.

I couldn't wait.

I hitched my bag over my shoulder, bolted out the door, and dialed Temple.

She answered.

"Girlfriend, I'll meet you at the station in half an hour. We're working a stake-out."

CHAPTER TEN

Private Investigator Rule #4: In a Dangerous Situation, Call for
Backup.

I turned the corner and switched off my headlights. I glided to the
curb, stopped the SUV, released my seatbelt, and rolled down the front
window.

On the opposite side of the street, about fifty yards away, Arena
Repair stood like a wrestler showing off his strength inside a ring of
light. The shop's new white stucco exterior contrasted starkly with the
neighborhood's rundown frame houses. A single streetlamp at the far
end lit the street. I hunched forward to peer out the front windshield.

Light illuminated the repair shop's office interior and the inside of
each closed bay. Through separate compartment windows, I saw empty
car lifts. The neon Arena Repair sign cast an eerie red glow over the
office area. Due to a row of live oaks shadowing the concrete drive
and the rear of the building, the surrounding concrete nestled in inky
invisibility.

About thirty yards away, a Beemer, headlights off, slid to the curb
on the same side as the long, low repair shop.

I spoke into my cell. "Building looks deserted." I pushed up my
sweater sleeve and glanced at the lighted dial on my Seiko. "Three

minutes past six. With rain threatening, it feels more like nine-thirty."

Temple, tonight's backup—who, I could bet, also wore black jeans topped with a black turtleneck—was a vague shadow inside the dark interior of the luxury sedan facing me. I'd taught her that with our cars positioned this way, if our suspect drove away in either direction, one of us could follow. Then the other could make a U-turn and keep in contact from farther behind the suspect. If Chuck identified one of us as a tail and tried to get away, the one following in the distance could leap-frog up to take her place.

"Our party-crashing wrestler doesn't seem to have drummed up much business yet. Do you think he's still inside, Holly?"

"We'll wait here for a while and watch." If Chuck had already called it a day, I planned to get into real close proximity to the office. "The building appears to be in lockdown. I don't see my Jeep anywhere."

"Are you sure we should be here?" Temple sounded worried.

"Think about Matt. He'd be here for you if our positions were reversed." I squared myself in the seat and stretched out my legs. "Not to worry. I worked a stake-out with Dad once. Besides, the police and Jake are on Matt's case now. We're just here to see what we can unearth." I hoped my use of the last unfortunate word didn't include finding a body. Shivers spiraled down my spine. I wanted to locate Matt…but I wanted him alive. Without Matt in my life, I'd be left with a huge chasm to fill.

"Wasn't it on a stake-out that your dad—?"

I cut in before she could finish. "Yeah. This one's different. No drug-bust-gone-sour here."

"No. Just a kidnapping."

Temple sounded seriously nervous.

Before I could think of a snappy comeback to relieve her anxiety, she asked, "And *this* is less dangerous?" Temple must have opened the lid on a cola because I heard the pop.

"Sure. We're snooping for something suspicious, not barging in to confront a drug lord." I pulled my knees up and cupped my hands around them. "Take it slow drinking. I don't see any public restrooms nearby. We might be here a while."

"Wish Frank were here. He told me he warned you off the case. Maybe we should leave."

I reached into the backseat and retrieved a thermos. "Frank wanted me to stick a GPS transponder on the car." I unscrewed the thermos and poured steaming Starbucks Coffee Latte into a travel cup. The gurgle of coffee and the heavenly scent brought comfort to the Toyota's dark interior.

"Good. I'm glad Frank can find us."

"Didn't have time."

"Oh, Holly, I should have known. Why are you so hardheaded?"

I gazed through the windshield at the peaceful building. "Frank would have been bored. Not much going on over there." I took a small sip of the latte. "Mmm. Hits the spot."

"Thought you weren't drinking."

I blew on my coffee. "Not drinking. Sipping." I gazed at the empty premises. "Why would Chuck vacate the shop so early?"

"Maybe he had a wrestling match."

"Or maybe he had to check on a kidnapped man." I took another delicious sip, licked my lips, and stared at the vacant-looking building.

"This is tedious." Temple tuned in the radio. The music sang over my cell.

"Sorry, but you have to turn that off. Someone might hear. Stakeouts are mind-numbing…until something happens. We can't let anyone know we're spying out here."

"Don't think there's a remote possibility of that. I bet every person within two miles of us is glued to their tube. No one's close enough to hear us." Temple began humming softly.

I fished around in my shoulder bag and brought out an apple. "Munch on the apple I put inside your ice chest."

"You could have brought a couple chocolate-nut donuts. Isn't that what cops eat on a stakeout?"

"We don't need trans-fat and calories. Besides, after the sugar-hit, those carbs make you sleepy." Temple never worried about health issues. "So how're things with you and Frank?"

"We've only known each other twenty-four hours. You're the preachy gal who says take it slow with a new guy. Friends before romance. Remember?"

"Glad you're using our system. Has he called?"

"Sure. Twice. I'll phone him tomorrow." Temple sighed. "That is, if we make it back alive."

"Are you scared?"

"You kidding? This is deadly dull."

"Frank's a good guy, but I can't get his mouth unhinged." I licked latte sweetness off my lips.

"I hope you mean as in answering questions and not as in kissing."

I laughed. "He's so taken with you, he only sees me as a nuisance."

"Or maybe Stryker ordered Frank to keep his mind—and hands—off you."

Hmm… The thought swirled in my brain and left a pleasure trail. "You think?"

"Sure. Stryker's got eyes, doesn't he?" Temple giggled. "You didn't give him your usual get-lost signals did you?"

"Actually, I did. As much as I could. Stryker's pretty persuasive."

"Got to you, did he?"

I didn't answer immediately. Finally I said, "I can't deny the sizzle, but I don't dare free my feelings."

Temple whistled. "Cupid hit a bull's-eye."

"Not on your life. And you're one to gloat."

She giggled.

Ten minutes passed while I slumped low in the seat, drumming my nails on the Toyota's steering wheel. Patience is not one of my few virtues.

To break the boredom, I started talking again. "Remember last week when I complained I had no challenge at work? I'd been on the job a month, and private investigating had been as exciting as watching the weather channel."

"Absolutely." Temple sang, "What a difference a day makes."

Ten silent minutes later she said, "This is *so* exciting."

"Get used to it."

Keeping both eyes glued to the corner shop, in an attempt to get my mind off Stryker and Temple's mind off the monotony, I cleared my throat then blurted, "I've always wanted to be like you."

Temple's laugh pealed out through my earphone. "Unbelievable!"

"Shush. Of course I can never have your tawny skin tone."

"Not unless you're a quarter Afro-American, half-Vietnamese, and a quarter Caucasian."

I ignored the laughter in her tone. "You have that ability to be totally yourself with all kinds of people." I made my next sentence sound like a joke. "They're drawn to you like starving artists to a beautiful landscape."

"Did you just make that up?" Temple grew serious. "Thanks for telling me. If people do like me, that began when I became a Christian. God showed me that since He loves a blended-racial female, He can love anyone. So rich, poor, or in-between, beautiful, plain, or average, intellectually-gifted or slow-to-learn, I know God loves every person. And if He loves them, why can't I?"

"Yeah. Makes sense." We'd been friends a long time, so speaking of spiritual things was easy with Temple. "You never gave the impression you thought of yourself as different. You have so much—"

"I don't think that anymore," she cut in. "I'm a daughter of the King…and so are you."

"Mostly I think of myself as Dad's daughter. A crusader with a soiled name."

"Take your pick." Temple's tone indicated there was no contest between the choices.

"That's another point in your favor. You don't press your line of reasoning and become annoying."

"I take that as a hint."

"Take it as a compliment."

I bagged my apple core, screwed the lid on the thermos, and wiped out my cup with a moist towelette. I might be accident-prone, but I'm obsessive about cleaning my messes.

"Boredom's getting to me. I've less patience with stakeouts now than I had with Dad." I retrieved my gun from my shoulder bag and tucked the Glock into its special-made holster under my sweater at the small of my back. I dug for the flashlight, stuck it into my belt, pulled the keys from the ignition, and slipped them into my jeans pocket. "You head left around the building, and I'll go to the right. We'll meet in the back. If you see anyone, hide." I took a deep breath. "Okay, let's go. Out the window."

"What? Go?" Temple's voice sounded breathless over her cell. "Out the window?"

"Yeah. Through the window. If you open the car door, the interior light comes on and stays on for a few minutes. It's a sure tip-off that we're here."

"You didn't say we'd leave the car."

I wriggled up on the seat and thrust one leg through the open window and over the door. When I tried to follow with the other, my Glock snagged. There I was halfway out the window, hung-up on the door. My Blue Tooth caught and tangled. I pulled it off and tossed it on the seat.

I squirmed and twisted until I wiggled free and landed off-balance on the pavement. Kneeling by the car, I watched Temple's shadowy form slide out the Beemer window and land lightly on the street. She exited far easier than I had. I should reconsider my aversion to starting an exercise program. I rose and started for the shop.

I was so concerned about Temple staying out of sight that my gaze was on her when I tripped. The bush scraped both my ankles. My Sketchers slipped on some loose pebbles. The small noise sounded loud, filling the street's silence. From her position at the left corner of the repair shop, Temple turned my direction, her shoulders shaking in silent laughter.

"Are you okay?" she called softly.

"Fine." My quiet answer sounded defensive.

After scrambling to my feet, I cat-walked through the shadows past the lighted shop front then rounded the corner into pitch-blackness. Back sliding against the rough stucco wall, I tiptoed the length of the building. I made it to the rear without tripping again and peeked around the corner.

Really dark back here.

As far as I could see and sense, the shop's backside was as empty as the front. The pavement narrowed. An alley and a high wooden fence separated the shop's concrete from a series of dimly lit, dilapidated homes.

A deeper darkness loomed near Temple's end. I stopped dead. Then forced myself to edge closer. An area in front grew blacker with each step.

Where was Temple? I tiptoed on toward the black bulk. The thing didn't move. When I reached the hulking mass, I extended tentative fingers and touched something smooth, metallic…and strangely familiar. I ran my palm over the dark form, bumped into an oversize truck tire, felt rough canvas, and my heart soared with endorphins as if I'd reached a runner's high.

Bunny!

Feeling around the front bumper, I discovered the metal still crumpled and rubbing the wheel. Why hadn't Muscleman repaired her? He certainly wasn't too busy.

Then a shiver struck down all my good endorphins, making my hands icy.

Chuck thought I'd never return to claim my Jeep. He expected me to die when the Cadillac's brakes failed. I took a few deep, calming breaths.

After my heart stopped jerking, I turned the Jeep's door handle.

A cough spurted from inside.

I jumped back two feet, hit the building behind me with my back, and clamped my lips to smother a scream. My knees turned to rubber bands. I stiffened the traitors. Only fancy balance work kept me from falling on my rear again. I stepped forward. Reaching behind my back, I fumbled around until my hand closed around my Glock. *Where's my backup?*

"Who's there?" My words came out strangled.

"Who's there yourself?" The voice sounded sharp, rough, and street-smart. I couldn't tell if the timber was male or female.

I stood in semi-paralysis until my brain clanked on. Street-savvy or not, that's a young voice.

"Come out. We need to talk."

"No way. You don't belong here. I'll call the cops."

I jerked on the door, but it was locked. "Come on out." I wanted to tell the voice inside I *was* the cops, but I couldn't lie. Instead I put all the authority I could force into my voice. "I'm a private investigator, and you're trespassing." I stuck my Glock back into the holster and flicked on my flashlight, shining the beam into the backseat where I thought the voice originated.

A small girl, stringy blonde hair hanging about her face, stared into the light like a frightened armadillo caught in a vegetable garden. Both hands grasped a faded sweater way too big for her and held the garment over her face so only her big eyes peeped out. She was either cold or had used the old sweater to disguise her voice. My guess was both.

I softened my words. "I won't hurt you."

"Like cats don't hurt mice. Big fat chance." She lowered her sweater to her chin and poked out her lower lip.

I changed tactics. "Out…or I'll call CPS."

She screwed her face and looked about to cry, but jerked her chin up and narrowed her eyes. Obviously she knew the initials stood for Child Protective Service. She'd probably had a run-in with them in her short past. Or she was a run-away.

"Don't." She uncoiled from Bunny's worn upholstery, reached up, and undid the lock.

I jerked open the door before she could change her mind. She shrank back on the seat like she expected me to backhand her. Her movement sent a whiff of unwashed body odor my direction.

"It's okay. I won't hurt you."

"Don't call CPS."

"I won't. Yet. I've got hot coffee and apples in my car. You want some?"

"You some kind of freak? Bribing me to get me into your car?" She twisted her mouth. "No way, Jay."

"Actually, you're sitting in my car. This is my Jeep."

She cursed.

Shock tightened my shoulder blades at the words she used, but I didn't let the jolt show. Instead I lowered the flash from her face.

"This your pile of junk?" Tugging the sweater tight around her neck, she inched toward me. "This old thing's a wreck. I thought Chuck was sending this old junker to the car cemetery."

Chuck! "Come on out. I won't hurt you. Let's talk." I held out my hand. When she flinched away, I almost dropped the flashlight in my other hand. She scooted through the opening and slid out. I shut the door behind her.

"Where's this coffee?"

When she stood, she came to within four inches of my height, which made her older than I'd first thought. I turned the flash on her. The ancient sweater bagged over faded jeans and ragged holes-in-the-toes sneakers. No socks.

"I'm parked in front. Refreshments are in my car." I started to put my arm around her shoulders.

She back-stepped. "You said this was your car."

"It's a long story."

"You said apples. Like in more than one?"

"Yep. At least two." She followed me around the other end of the building where I expected to meet Temple.

No Temple.

When we reached the BMW, Temple called from the driver's seat, "Finally! Who's that?" She lowered the window.

"What's this? A party?" The girl turned away.

I grabbed the back of her sweater and whispered to Temple. "I'll call you from the Toyota."

I hurried the girl over to Dad's Toyota, opened the passenger door for her, finally coaxed her inside, then ran around to the driver's side and slid in.

Under the glare of the interior light, I got a good look at the girl's thin white face and one big aquamarine eye.

I clamped my lips and grabbed the steering wheel.

One baby blue was black, swollen, and closed. Someone had belted her really hard. My hands trembled when I opened the ice chest and handed the battered girl the remaining apples, then poured the rest of the hot latte into my cup and handed it over.

"I can make an ice pouch for your eye." My strangled throat made my voice hoarse.

"Naw. Won't do no good now. It's been too long." She tore into the apple like she hadn't eaten for a month. From what I'd seen of her thin frame, maybe she hadn't. Her knowledge of how soon to apply ice to a wound made my skin crawl. This wasn't the first black eye she'd received.

"What's your name?"

She looked away and spoke through a mouthful of apple. "Joy."

By her furtive expression, I knew she lied. "Did you run away? Was someone abusing you?"

"You could say that."

"Chuck?"

She laughed, a hard cynical sound that should never have come from a child who looked about eleven. "Naw. Chuck's sweet. He just looks scary. He's a teddy bear."

Teddy bear was not what I would name Chuck. Kidnapper rang

truer. "Then who?"

"What's it to ya? You some kind of Mother Teresa?" She spit an apple seed onto the floor.

"Do you live around here? You want me to take you home?"

She stiffened. "Never! I ain't *never* goin' back to that trailer. Not with him there." She sniffed and her shoulders trembled.

"Your father hits you?"

"He ain't my dad." She lowered her head. "Just shacks up with Mom." She threw the apple core on to the carpet and gulped the last of the coffee.

"You're mom doesn't protect you?"

"Listen, lady. What *you* doin' out here in the middle of the night? I'm gettin' out of here." She reached for the door handle.

I'd locked the door as soon as the child and I got inside, so I made no attempt to stop her. "Look, Joy, it's—"

A siren wailed in the distance and squalled nearer. I locked eyes with Joy.

My cell rang my melody. The lighted read-out told me it was Temple.

"Um, Holly. I called Frank when you were gone so long. I was afraid…" Her voice trailed off as a black-and-white squealed to a halt, neatly blocking the Toyota. In seconds, two policemen stormed the car. The shorter one arrived at my window first. The second officer hunkered at the passenger side, a vast dark shadow.

Something about the first officer struck me as familiar, but I had no time to mentally run down my list of suspects because an unmarked sedan screeched to a stop behind the Toyota, blocking any chance of exit. The driver raced up and peered in my back window.

The first cop shone a light inside. I blinked and shaded my eyes.

"Everything all right in there?"

Recognizing that deep voice, I leaned back against the leather cushion and relaxed.

"Fine."

I still held my cell, and Temple's voice come across loud and clear. "I recognize that bass voice." Her own changed timber and she fairly sang, "Hi, Frank."

"Temple?" He flashed his light on my cell, my Blue Tooth lying nearby, then shifted the glare to my face, blinding me before he turned the beam on the trembling girl huddled against the passenger window.

The driver of the unmarked car moved from the rear window to lean into mine.

A shiver skittered up my back. "Stryker?"

"The same." He spoke into Frank's ear. "Dim the spotlight." Resting both elbows on the sill, he poked his head inside. His voice took on a chiding tone. "I heard-tell your uncle took you off Murdoch's case."

"Word sure gets around. Is there *anyone* who doesn't know?"

"Apparently you don't."

The Toyota's door barely separated us. He had a serious personal space violation going here. I inhaled his woodsy aftershave and tried to sound annoyed. *"You got a twenty-four hour tail on me?"*

"What gave you that idea?"

Why else would you be here? "You tell me."

I saw his jaw clench. "You're paranoid."

He wasn't going to admit anything. "Last time you showed up, the EMS had to cart you off. I heard your head's okay. How's your leg? You limped when those Good Samaritans extracted you from that ice cream sandwich."

"I'll live."

"Do you have any other injuries?" Though I didn't want it to, my voice reflected genuine concern.

"Just a cracked rib and the bum knee. Could have been worse."

I didn't want to dwell on the intriguing thought of his rib cage, doubtless encased inside a muscular chest above a six-pack abdomen. "Any headaches?"

"A man's got to have a hard head in this business. A few stitches, and I'm good as new."

In the dark I couldn't see any stitches, but I wanted to reach out and feel for them. "I never got a chance to thank you."

"Yeah. Well…I'll think of a way."

The frightened girl had her hand clamped on my arm or I would have slid out the door and kissed him. The man could duck under all my defenses and cause my heart to dance faster than lightning could strike a utility pole. I prayed for a cool head to act as a grounding wire.

And, um, yes. I thought of fifty ways to thank him too. A candlelit dinner. A walk in the park. I ignored the urge to nibble on the muscular neck so close to my lips.

Frank cleared his throat.

And brought me back to my senses. Angel possessed a dark side I couldn't afford to forget.

Frank's partner flashed a light from the passenger side of the car, illuminating all of us. "Let's take a look at your license, registration, and insurance."

Joy shrank further back into the upholstery and slid lower in the seat. The hand that had been clamped on my arm now grabbed mine and held tight. Her body language yelled, "Don't tell them about me. Please!"

I didn't want to turn her over to CPS. I sensed Joy needed a lot more care than an overworked CPS caseworker could offer. I wanted to take Joy home and show her how much God loved her.

So I said to Stryker, "Tell Frank that Temple was afraid I'd run into trouble so she called the cops."

I fumbled in the glove box for Dad's papers, hoping somehow Mom had brought them up to date.

As I rooted in the glove box, I whispered to the trembling girl, "If I don't snitch on you, will you tell me the truth?"

Stryker had his eyes on me. He didn't miss a thing.

The girl nodded.

From where he was crossing the street, Frank spoke over his shoulder. "I'll check on Temple." He sprinted toward the Beemer.

I handed the papers out the passenger window to Frank's partner. "Turns out this is a false alarm. I'm so sorry, Officer."

"You know this lady, Black?" The officer ruffled through my papers and handed them back.

"Yep. Meet Holly Garden."

The officer winked. "Ah, the rookie you been gabbing about."

Light from the officer's flash lit up the color darkening Stryker's face. "Shut up, Hugh. She's a PI with Garden Investigations. That's Temple Taylor in the BMW across the street. The two ladies are just leaving a stake-out."

"Garden." The unknown officer frowned and thinned his lips.

Obviously the big officer remembered Dad. He thought dad had gone bad. Had been the guilty party in the high school drug bust. Had shot three high school seniors in an execution-style slaying before getting shot himself.

I stuck my torso out the window and lifted my chin. "And you are?" I needed to know all the Dallas area officers. I had Dad's good name to clear up with them.

Stryker's PI voice disguised any emotion. "This is Hugh Oliver, Frank's sometime partner."

"Oft-time partner," Oliver snapped.

I stretched out my hand.

After a too-long hesitation, Hugh shook it and mumbled, "Huh. The famous Garden girl."

Their squad radio squawked. Hugh Oliver back-stepped all the way to his black-and-white, his gaze fixed on me as if I'd just smuggled in a load of illegal aliens.

I plopped back down inside the Toyota, bristling like a defensive porcupine.

Stryker leaned in and swiped his thumb slowly across my lower lip. "Take it easy, Bloodhound."

Warmth filled my whole body.

He stepped away from the Toyota. "Nothing happening here."

"Flash," Hugh yelled to Frank from the black-and-white. "It's a 9-1-1."

Stryker leaned in the window, his face close to mine. "With the storm coming in, I'd head for home if I were you. And that kid should be in bed." The way Stryker spoke made me feel certain he'd picked up on Joy's problem and decided she'd be better off with me, at least for tonight.

Dark Angel climbed a step up the ladder of what I liked in a guy. Try as I would, I couldn't keep him colored dark. He'd softened to gray. Actually, a very light gray tinged with gold. Like a dark halo.

"I'll call you." Stryker's voice seeped promise.

"Do that." I kept my tone professional. I desperately feared being snared into an entanglement with a man who could easily break my heart even worse than the poor thing had already been shredded. "But this relationship is strictly business."

Except the touch of his thumb still burned my lips.

Oh, he was bad news.

CHAPTER ELEVEN

I sat on the tropical-patterned upholstered chair in our guest room. The child who called herself Joy lay propped on the pillows of the nearby king-sized bed. She was stuffing baked chicken, mashed potatoes, and salad into her thin frame, the glass of milk on the tray already emptied.

Watching her, I tried to figure how to pry answers from the street-smart barrier she'd raised against revealing herself. A hot bath, shampoo, and conditioning of her natural blonde hair transformed Joy from a scared urchin into a pretty girl. She looked older than I'd first thought.

"You're thirteen, aren't you?"

"Almost fourteen."

She had a pert little nose, one big sapphire eye, one swollen, black-circled eye, and a generous mouth. Her delicate bone structure caused me to grind my teeth. What beast could smash a fist into that innocent face?

"So you think Chuck's a teddy bear?"

"Yep."

Huh. I'd seen the results of Chuck's fist on Stryker's face. The muscleman could inflict serious damage.

"And Chuck's not the man who hit you?"

"That's what I said, ain't it?"

"You run to Chuck when your mom's boyfriend throws his weight around?"

"Yeah. Chuck's safe. He's a good guy."

I pictured her unknown abuser as a raging weasel who relieved his frustration on a defenseless girl.

Though angry to the bone, I unclenched my hands from the upholstered chair arms and adopted a relaxed posture. Each time I spoke I made my voice as soothing as I could.

"We have apple pie or cheesecake. Which do you prefer?"

Her heart-shaped face lit up like a Christmas angel. "Can I have both?"

I had to lock my jaw to keep my mouth from gaping. The slender girl perched on the edge of womanhood, with her curves just beginning to blossom, had already eaten as much as my ever-so-much-taller-and-bulkier Uncle Robert.

"Sure." Did her mother even feed her?

I called through the open bedroom door, "Juanita, could you bring a piece of pie with ice cream and a slice of cheesecake?"

"Si, Señorita."

Soon the heavy sound of our cook's steps echoed on the stairway. She entered the room, her quilted yellow robe a bright splash of color.

"Thees niña es hungry." She set the desserts on the end table.

"Thanks, Juanita."

"No problema, Señorita."

As she left, Juanita's signature scent of cinnamon and mixed spices wafted after her.

Joy grabbed the tray and started in on the apple pie ala mode.

It took all my willpower not to lean forward and brush wispy hair back from Joy's rounded forehead. "I know it's late, Joy, but…"

The girl looked up from her munching. "I haven't been straight with you. My name's really Allison."

"I knew Joy wasn't your name. And I promise I won't make you go home until you're ready. Please tell me your last name."

Allison blinked rapidly and gazed across the room, focusing on the picture Mom painted of the Grand Canal in Venice, spotlighting a man and woman laughing together inside a gondola.

"My last name's…Gold."

Again, I knew she lied. Too obviously she'd taken the cue from the golden haze Mom painted over the Venetian scene. Besides, Allison's rapid eye-blinking gave her away. She was not a good liar.

"Okay, Allison…*Gold.*" I emphasized the name to show her I knew she wasn't giving me her real one.

She grinned, showing small, straight teeth.

"You must go to school somewhere."

She fidgeted and toyed with the ice cream dripping from the warm apple pie. "I do, but the rat will go over there lookin' for me. He'd grab me before I got very far from school. I don't want to go back."

"I see." I didn't want Allison to return to that school any more than she did. How could I legally keep this girl safe and in school? A man who hit a child would be capable of doing even worse to her—if he hadn't already.

"Okay. I'll have to figure out how to get you back into your studies without dropping you into that man's clutches." I hated to work this already prickly conversation around to Chuck, but I had to find Matt.

I tried to sound casual. "Do you live near Arena Repair?"

She spooned ice cream into her mouth like she feared I'd take it away from her. "Not too far."

"Allison, I don't want you to go back to that abusive situation.

129

I'll find out how I can protect you. I do want to help, and so does God. That's why He brought us together. Will you trust me?"

One skeptical blue eye gazed at me long and hard. Then she concentrated on her dessert. "I'll do anything you want. Just don't send me home."

"Won't your mom worry?"

"I'll get word to her that I'm all right."

I leaned forward. "Through Chuck?"

"Right." She set the empty pie plate aside and pulled the turtle cheesecake toward her. "Chuck'll tell her. Mom knows Chuck takes care of me when things get too bad at home."

Ice rippled down my spine. I gripped the chair arms. "How often has this happened?" Some care Chuck gave. Didn't the man know to contact CPS?

"Lots of times. But that big bully usually doesn't hit me in the face. He hits me where the bruises don't show."

I jumped to my feet. "Your mom could get a restraining order."

"Chill. Mom's had those before. They don't last long. Pretty soon she opens the door and lets the jerk-wad slink back home." Allison released a sigh that moved her whole body. She wrinkled her lightly freckled nose. "Mom thinks she can't pay the bills unless Jerk-face's sitting in front of the TV getting drunk. When he dozes off, she sneaks money out of his wallet." Allison licked her lips, pushed aside the empty cheesecake plate, and lay back against the pillows.

I had to hug my stomach to stop my insides from trembling. "How does Chuck help? Is he your brother?"

She giggled. "Nope. Now that the shop's built, he said I could sleep in any car that's parked behind the garage. Yours was the first. And he buys me Big Macs and lets me hang out on the property."

"That's it? That's all he does?"

"He got Mom to help me get the first two restraining orders." Her eyelids began to droop.

Since he's male and probably lives alone, he can't take her into his house. "Where does Chuck live?"

"He used to live in a little trailer on the property until he got his new shop built. They sure got it up fast. Now he lives at the garage. He's got a cot inside the office. But he wasn't there tonight, so I helped myself to the Jeep."

Allison looked sweet and cuddly as she lay against the pink pillowcases. I swallowed and hoped she didn't really know what my next question meant.

"Does Chuck ever try to touch you?"

"Naw. He ain't like that. I told ya, he's my teddy. He's a good guy."

Of course she knew. Kids had to know a lot these days. Hate for her mom's boyfriend almost made me choke. I couldn't bear to ask her how far the man had gone with her.

"Do other men ever come around your mom's house?"

"Naw. Just Jerko."

"How about when you're with Chuck? Do the other wrestlers hang with him?"

"Sure. They come over a lot. And they come every Friday night to play poker. 'Cept when they have a gig wrestling."

She giggled again. "Don't look at me like that. Chuck don't let 'em touch me. He's got three sisters in Ft. Worth. He don't let any man lay a finger on me. He's big enough the other guys leave me alone."

"Does he face down your mom's boyfriend?"

A look of fear flashed across her face. "Even Chuck's afraid of Max when he gets mad. Max's got a gun." She hugged the extra pillow to her chest. "Anyway, Max catches me when no one else is around."

"Oh, Allison, we have to keep that man away from you." I plopped back down into the chair and thought for a few minutes. "Does he hit your mom too?"

"When he can't find me."

Just talking about the boyfriend with the gun had Allison's slender chest heaving. I didn't want to upset her with more questions.

"Well, sweetie, let's not think about Max right now. Let's think of nicer things."

"Mom used to call me sweetie." She looked content for the first time since I met her.

"Used to?"

"Un huh. Before she got too busy."

I wanted to clutch this neglected child to my chest, but she was too skittish. I had to change the subject before I burst into tears.

"You said Chuck has sisters living in Ft. Worth."

Allison closed her eyes. "Yep. Three younger ones. He's got brothers too."

"Do you know the Eggleston brothers' names?"

"Not Eggleston—Chambers." Allison's breathing deepened.

So, either Eggleston or Chambers was an alias. He probably used Chambers in the ring.

I stood and watched Allison's small relaxed form, face peaceful but cupid lips still turned slightly down at the corners. She barely made a dent in the middle of the king-sized bed.

Tears dripped from my cheeks onto the sleeve of her pink and white jammies. I swiped at the wet glaze I couldn't hold back.

Oh, dear God, please show me how I can help this little one. I'm not at all sure what to do with her. She needs a safe place.

Next morning The Flowers proved useful, and I felt proud of them. Maggie and Cami took Allison under their wings. They rummaged their closets and put together a cool outfit for the smaller girl to wear to church.

The swelling had receded from Allison's eye. The twins cosmetically turned the injured eye into another beauty. The three entered their teen fellowship class as tight friends. A twinge needled my heart. I hadn't been chummy with my sisters since I returned from school. As a college grad with a new job, I shared few common interests with high school sophomores.

At the classroom door, I waved what I hoped was a cool good-bye. With this age group, you never knew if you were cool, from the nerd-geek pool, or invisible. Breathing a prayer for Allison, I jogged upstairs to teach my fourth-grade class.

"'If you remain in me and my words remain in you, ask whatever you wish, and it will be given you.' John 15:7." As I spoke, I wrote the promise on the white board in front of the five round tables occupied by about thirty children.

"Miss Holly, what does the Bible mean when it says to *remain in*?"

I smiled down at the freckled nine-year-old face. "Taylor, remain in means to live in, like you live in your house. So if we remain in Jesus, we stay with Him. And His words stay with us. How do His words remain with us? Anyone know?"

Red-haired Elizabeth waved a hand, almost jumping up and down in her seat. "First we read the words in our Bible. Then we think about them."

Sweet Elizabeth. Her parents are doing an excellent job of raising their daughter in the Lord. If I ever have a daughter, I pray I do as well. "Right, Elizabeth. What is another way we can remain in Jesus' words?"

Puzzled expressions gazed up at me. Suddenly the boy from India raised his hand.

"Yes, Josuf?"

"We can memorize Bible verses." His dark face and large, intelligent eyes beamed excitement.

I clapped. "Absolutely!" If only every child could experience His love. Their innocence made knowing evil, such as Max committed, even more horrible. "And Jesus wants to live *in* you and love *through* you each day."

When I was a third-grader, I trusted Jesus as my Savior. I walked hand in hand with Him right up until I faced my first real test of faith, my first encounter with the underbelly of society. And I learned firsthand how easy it was to end up on the wrong side of the law. Now my faith wobbled at times.

"Let's all form a circle," I invited.

Girls grabbed hands, but no boy would hold a girl's hand. Instead the boys made faces and pretended to gag, making the girls roll their eyes.

I looked around the treasury of upturned faces. "Who has something for us to pray about?"

Hands shot up all around. Darcy asked prayer for her brother, a professional hockey player with the Dallas Stars, who'd broken an ankle. Paige wanted prayer for a safe delivery for her new baby brother.

"I have a request today," I said. "I have a new teenage friend. She doesn't have a safe home like you do. The man who lives in her house hits her."

Innocent eyes widened. A murmur of questions hummed.

"*Ssh*. She needs a safe place to live so she can go to school. Please pray for her."

Taylor called out, "What's her name?"

"God knows her name. Help me pray for the sweet girl who's been hurt." I bowed my head.

All around the circle, children scrunched their eyes closed. One after another, a sweet voice prayed. As I peeked at them, sunshine filtered through the tall windows, painting each lowered head with light.

I believed John 15:7 with all my heart. And didn't I remain in Jesus? Without any doubt, He remained in me. Why then did my faith seem weak? Was I looking at my two big problems instead of the God Who created the universe? The God Who said He is the great I Am. The God Who is enough. The God Who said if I abide, He will do it. God promised.

Give me the faith to believe.

When the children finished praying, I said, "When God answers, I'll tell y'all how He answered the hurting-girl prayer."

Um. I hadn't thought about giving the children a week-by-week news report about Allison. The words just sprang to my lips.

Okay, God, these kids are expecting answers for Allison.

I wanted to add, *Don't let any of us down*, but figured He was way ahead of me there.

By now I felt hung out to dry. I still didn't know what I could legally do for Allison. I had faith in God, but I'd heard too many bad stories about our legal system and children being returned to intolerable home situations.

A mother stuck her head in through the open door. "I'm here to pick up my daughter."

I handed out take-home papers, and although I knew the parents' faces, dutifully matched the children's badges with parents' badges before letting them leave together. I wanted no children kidnapped on my watch.

As the children herded out, I wondered why I hadn't prayed for Matt. Deep down, I knew the answer but didn't want to confront it. I wasn't sure my faith stretched that far. If Matt was dead…

I heaved a huge sigh. Did I think God wasn't big enough to keep Matt safe and help me free him? A verse nagged me.

And He did not do many miracles there because of their unbelief. I sighed. *Lord, help my lack of faith.*

With the room empty, I gathered leftover take-home papers, craft material, and empty snack wrappers. Then I sank on one of the small chairs at a round table and propped my chin in my cupped hands. With the smell of crayons and clay tormenting me with everyday normality, I gazed out the window at departing families heading home.

Lord, I've got these two lives I'm responsible for. And I'm not sure I can handle the job.

Thoughts of the reports I typed all last week—surveillance of an unfaithful husband, tracking a missing heir, and interviewing people for a security clearance—flashed through my memory. Those were jobs a PI did. Tracking kidnappers wasn't part of the job description. Nor was clearing Dad's name.

A hot flush spread over me. I'd only worked with Dad before I earned my license, so I'd never had a chance to make him proud. I had to face facts that up until now, I'd been a bungler.

Take the time Dad asked me to photograph that couple in the

restaurant. I could have snapped a pretty good picture from where I hid at another table behind the artificial palm tree. But no, I had to move closer. I kept the couple in my lens-finder as I crouched, creeping toward them. Just when I clicked the frame, a waiter ran smack into my rear, which I guess in my stooped position stuck out too far. We both slammed into the floor, showered with hot soup and garlic-cheese bread. The couple fled. And the errant husband never met the other woman in a public place again. Topping that, my shot was blurred beyond identification. So the wife never got the proof she needed.

And then there was the time—

No. I couldn't continue listing my mistakes. I jumped up and headed for the door.

Matt's case has to turn out differently. And what am I going to do about Allison? And is Dad really innocent? God, help me believe!

CHAPTER TWELVE

I was stiff from the accident, but the ache didn't slow me down any.

Lunch at Juan Hernando's was great. Delicious fragrances swirled through the air, and waiters rushed by with sizzling fajitas, juicing-up my appetite. Mom and The Flowers kept Allison all but rolling on the restaurant floor with their stories of my past embarrassments. I tried for the cool, yes-they-were-funny-but-now-I'm-more-mature tone but itched to escape. They planned to catch a movie, and I needed to get to work.

I usually don't work on Sundays, but time flew by, and I was no closer to finding Matt. I couldn't wait to check the Ft. Worth address Allison leaked to me. I'd called Chuck, and since he wasn't at Arena Repair, I hoped he spent the weekend with his family in Ft. Worth. In my optimism, I dreamed I'd find Chuck holed up in the Eggleston family garage, guarding a bound, gagged, but alive-and-kicking Matt.

The drive to Ft. Worth on Sundays would only be a thirty-minute jaunt rather than the usual hour or longer trip during weekday traffic.

Mom dropped me off at home and left again in the Lexus, taking The Flowers and Allison with her. By 1:30 I'd changed into jeans and a lightweight sweater, both black. I didn't know if I might need to stake out the Ft. Worth address, so I wanted to be prepared. I hated to spy on Chuck's sisters during the day, since there's nothing more conspicuous than someone sitting alone in a parked car in a residential neighborhood. But the crucial first forty-eight hours since Matt's kidnapping fast approached. So I loaded my Glock, pepper-spray, handcuffs, flashlight, and several apples into my red shoulder bag and left a note for Mom.

Since Jose had weekends off, I backed Dad's Toyota from the garage, drove around our circle drive, and out onto our boulevard. We didn't really need Jose, but the legal Mexican needed a job while he attended college, so Mom hired him to maintain our fleet of cars. We all liked Jose and were glad to have a male on the premises. Mom let him use the two rooms over the garage, paid him a small salary, plus gave him all the food he could eat. And she adjusted his hours so he could finish his degree. While working for us, he'd completed his Associates Degree and planned to go on to earn a Physician's Assistant certification. Today he was probably up in his room, studying.

After turning onto the state highway to Ft. Worth, I dialed Stryker on my cell.

No answer. I left a message telling him where I was headed. What did he do on Sunday afternoons? Probably had a hot date. Probably took his dates skydiving or bungee-jumping. Both sounded like fun to me. But not with Stryker. No time spent with the dangerous heartbreaker sounded good to me.

I forced my thoughts away from Gray Angel and wished I could invite Temple along. But she worked with underprivileged kids in South Dallas every other Sunday afternoon, and this was her day. She'd started a club with three girls and now had about twenty-five. I visited once in a while, but I'm no good at music, painting, drawing, designing clothes, or the other creative things Temple shared with the girls.

My talks weren't nearly as popular either. I spoke to them about obeying laws and staying out of pregnancies. Most of the time my speech came too late, but I hoped to steer the girls away from future unwed motherhood. With little money to spend on dates, boys in the South Dallas projects lured girls into the sack with no thought to the little lives they might create.

I dialed Frank and gave him the lowdown on my whereabouts and what I was doing. He didn't sound happy.

He used that authoritative cop voice that allowed no disobedience. "You're off the case."

"Just think of this as my visiting girlfriends. What could possibly happen in broad daylight on a Sunday afternoon?"

Frank snorted. "I'm over my head with work now. Give me the address and I'll take a look-see later."

I huffed but gave him the address. I'd do anything to find Matt.

"You stay in touch," Frank ordered.

"Will do." I didn't need to tell Frank I wasn't leaving Matt's kidnapping alone. From our short acquaintance, he knew me well enough to realize I'd hang in this investigation like a junkyard dog fighting for a bone.

"Watch your back."

"Sure. You'll let me know when you learn something about Matt?"

"Roger."

I knew he wouldn't.

Investigator Rule #5: Tell a Cop Where You're Going in Case You Don't Come Back.

Frank didn't know he was my only backup at the Ft. Worth address.

CHAPTER THIRTEEN

I encountered more traffic than I expected. A Monet exhibit premiered at the Ft. Worth Art Museum, but I had no idea what caused the other jams. A good forty-five minutes later, I found the house.

Chuck's small home was tucked inside a confusing maze of narrow, winding streets. Pick-ups, motorcycles, SUVs, and aged cars lined the pavement. People clustered in tiny yards and in front of open one-car garages. Children spilled over into the road. Most residents looked up, smiled, and waved as my Toyota crawled past.

The Eggleston garage door stood wide-open to the world and revealed the usual clutter—but no Matt.

The contrast between Matt's house and this one couldn't be greater. The evidence seemed pretty obvious as to where a man as young as Chuck got the money for his expensive new garage. Whoever hired him to stage that fight and kidnap Matt must have paid Chuck well.

I feared my late-model Toyota SUV would stand out but raised my eyebrows at the many costly vehicles parked in the same drive as dented, vintage jalopies. After slowly weaving through the line of parked cars, I finally pulled into the one empty space on the block, just two houses down from the address Allison gave me. I lowered the windows and cut off the engine. Warm air, muted chatter, and the odor of spicy food and dog poop slammed my senses. Intermittent roars from lawn mowers and motorcycles drowned out most opportunities to eavesdrop.

This wasn't a tree-lined, spacious neighborhood like mine. Small houses, dribbling out large families, revealed an ethnically-diverse population. Groups of dark and light-skinned men in muscle shirts and tattoos prowled the sidewalks. Girls wearing skimpy tops and short-shorts ambled, arm-in-arm, laughing and chatting. I could bet more girls in this neighborhood had babies than high school diplomas. Would Temple like to start a club here? I'd help her.

Movement at the Eggleston house caught my attention.

Chuck—and by the family resemblance, two older brothers— sauntered out the front door. I slid down in my seat until I could just peep above the dashboard. Leaning close to the open window, I couldn't make out what the trio discussed.

The porch was too small to hold all three wide-shouldered men. Chuck stepped down to the narrow walk that zigzagged to the uneven front sidewalk. Face toward my car, he propped a foot on the tiny porch.

Three girls, hips swaying, cruised by. All the brothers ogled them. After the girls passed, the men resumed their talk. Chuck's face turned red. His hand slashed the air, punctuating his comments. He looked hard-put to keep his temper in check. Six muscular arms flailed the air. If the curb hadn't been lined with cars, I'd have driven closer to hear since the three were so intent they'd never have noticed me.

I shivered. Chuck, the red-faced muscleman, didn't look anything like a teddy bear.

Both older brothers raised their fists and seemed about to smash Chuck. He held his ground. Seconds later the two pushed past him, leaped from the porch, strode to a late-model black Corvette parked between two pick-up trucks, piled in, and screeched off, leaving behind the odor of burnt rubber.

Chuck gazed after his brothers then headed around the yellow house toward the backyard. I pondered what to do. Was he exiting via the alley? A minute later he answered my question when he swung down the driveway peddling a silver multi-speed mountain bike.

My jaw dropped.

He shifted gears and cycled into the vehicles trolling the street. He wore no helmet, so his hair shone gold under the bright sun. I flipped on the ignition, waited until he reached a curve in the long street, then eased out into the traffic.

This was novel.

I tailed a suspect riding a bike. I'd have laughed if the situation hadn't been serious. How could I stay far enough behind and yet keep him in sight without his spotting me? I prided myself that I knew how to tail as well as the best investigator, but a guy on a bike?

At the end of the block, I took a chance and pulled into the alley behind Chuck's house to look for signs of Matt. I parked Dad's Toyota behind some tall garbage cans, slid out, and ran up to the rear door. A dog barked, but I stayed long enough to peek into one of the un-curtained windows. Two older ladies worked in the kitchen washing dishes. The other window revealed three girls primping in front of a vanity inside a tiny bedroom.

Just then a gang of boys sprinted in my direction, yelling in Spanish. I ran to my Jeep, bolted inside, and cranked Bunny up.

Back on the street, I held my speed to fifteen, slowed to ten, and steered around a curve. Cars snarling behind me, I spotted Chuck a half-block ahead. He hunkered down, calf muscles defined below his khaki shorts, pumping madly.

In my rearview mirror, I glimpsed the black Corvette one of his brothers drove. The car rounded a block and inched closer. My pulse sped up much faster than the traffic.

Were the two big Tom cats chasing the spying mouse?

Legs thrusting like pistons, Chuck turned into a wider boulevard where the two lanes *Y'd* into separate directions. Should I follow or, with the brothers tailing me, lead them in a different direction? With only two cars separating us, I skimmed in behind the speeding bike.

When the black Corvette pulled alongside, my pulse went wild. The brothers gazed up at me, suggestive grins cracking their rugged faces. I ignored them.

Okay. Just don't try to stop me.

They motioned for me to lower my window.

Guys, just keep going and leave me alone.

The Toyota barely moved at a snail's pace. Horns blasted behind me. The two men resembled older copies of Chuck, minus his dimples and good looks. Nice, if you liked the murder-mystery-man type clad in identical black sleeveless tees.

Me, I like a man with brains…and enough brawn to show his muscles on a crowded beach.

The brothers revved their engine. Were they wrestlers too? Had they been at the party? Both sported buzz-cuts, so I wasn't sure.

I ignored them.

Finally they turned a corner and took off.

My breathing slowed, and I seized a deep lungful of air.

Whoa! Chuck had disappeared.

My neck felt stiff, and my head throbbed before I spotted him again. He cycled three blocks ahead and had his right arm extended, indicating a turn. A spasm twisted my stomach. With my Directional Dyslexia, I could so easily get lost in this unfamiliar neighborhood of winding, intersecting streets. I needed a GPS. I'd buy one first thing tomorrow.

But for now, I was hopelessly lost. Did Chuck know I tailed him? Would he lead me to a lonely destination where he could—?

Remember, Allison said he's a teddy bear.

Legs flashing, body pumping, Chuck peddled as if he had to be somewhere and was late. I figured he stayed in that tip-top shape by riding his bike instead of driving. I'd do well to follow his lead. I did run three miles every chance I got. Who knew when I'd need to chase a bad guy? But on a bike, I'd never keep up with Chuck. He probably took weekend trips to the hill country.

He arrived at an intersection and barely stopped. He merged into the dense traffic and moved to the far right lane where his bicycling slowed the fewest cars. I finally got a break in the traffic and made the turn. With me trailing as far behind as I could, we headed toward Ft. Worth.

That's when I noticed I'd picked up my own tail.

The nondescript gray Taurus carried only one man. He hung so far back he was little more than a dark image. Well, nothing I could do about him in this slow chase. I'd stick to Chuck until he arrived at his destination, then I'd lose the tail and double back to confront Chuck. If the sometime-mechanic didn't lead me to Matt, I'd get him alone and force him to talk.

My watch read four o'clock. As we slowly progressed through the Ft. Worth neighborhood, traffic turned sparse. I stayed as far behind Chuck as I dared. I doubted he'd look back, but I didn't want to chance it.

Off the labyrinth of narrow residential streets in Chuck's neighborhood, I breathed easier. I knew where I was. Most Saturday nights tourists crowded this area of downtown Ft. Worth close to the historic Stockyards. The old west architecture, wooden sidewalks, covered walkways, and hitching posts lent an air of authentic Wild

West. I loved coming here myself. The restaurants offered huge western-style steaks served by men and women in tight jeans, western shirts, fancy cowboy boots, and bandanas. On weekends, mock shootouts livened the streets, and ranchers ran longhorn cattle down Main Street to the pens in the Stockyards. It didn't take much imagination to believe you'd fallen through a crack of time and landed in the old west.

During the stock show, cattlemen bought and sold lowing, long-horn cattle penned inside the well-maintained corrals. Cowpunchers climbed up and walked on wooden platforms above the pens to select stock amid the pungent odors of manure and hay. I opened the car window. Mouth-watering odors wafted in. I could almost taste a thick, juicy Ft. Worth steak. Somewhere onion rings fried.

But today, Main Street looked all but deserted. Only a few cars parallel-parked adjacent to the wooden sidewalk. To keep from overtaking Chuck, I scooted into an opening behind a pick-up truck. A shotgun hung across the rear truck window, a common sight in Texas.

The nape of my neck prickled when the gray Taurus parked almost a block behind me. I figured the driver guessed I knew he tailed me and wanted to throw me off his track because he jumped out and hurried into a pipe-and-tobacco store. The man wore a black Stetson, tight jeans, Roper boots, a plaid western-style shirt, and a black bandanna. He could have been one of the performers in the shootout, except I was certain he tailed me. And he didn't have a six-gun strapped to his side.

My neck eased its prickling, so I turned my attention back to Chuck. Idling my engine, I watched him peddle down the authentic brick street. A breeze gusted in the sweet odor of tobacco from the swinging doors of the pipe shop.

When Chuck peddled almost out of sight, I eased out of my

parking place and crept down Main Street, pretending to be a gawking tourist. If Chuck noticed me, he paid no attention. He rode past a dance hall with a mechanical bucking bull out front.

Then Chuck slammed on his brakes so fast I grazed a fire hydrant when I tried to slip into an open spot along the wooden sidewalk. He hopped off, lifted the bike under one arm, and stepped up onto the sidewalk. A look in my rearview told me the tail in the gray Taurus still lingered in the tobacco shop. Maybe I imagined his following me.

Chuck whipped out a lock and chain and secured his bike to a hitching rail. Without a glance in my direction, he pushed open a wide wooden door and entered the Lone Star bar/restaurant.

I crouched where I was and watched. In about ten minutes I grew antsy. Because Chuck had seemed in such a hurry, I figured he was meeting someone. I wanted to know who. Five more minutes ticked slowly by, and the cowboy driving the Taurus didn't swagger back out of the pipe shop. How long could a man shop for tobacco?

I sweated out a few more minutes, but I was getting nowhere. I'd have to go inside.

After pulling my key from the ignition, I grabbed the red shoulder bag, slid out, and locked the doors with the remote. I jumped the giant step to the wooden sidewalk and peeked through the brown tinted window. Too dark. I couldn't see anything inside. Sidling up to the door, I cracked the heavy wood ajar and peeked in. A tall, rustic wood panel separated the restaurant from the entry. I slipped inside, let my eyes adjust to the dimness, and stuck my head around the panel.

A number of round tables surrounded by captain's chairs circled a dance floor. An older man and woman sat at one. The rest were vacant. A long, old-fashioned mahogany bar ran along the right side of the room. Behind the bar, a mirror reflected the entire place to anyone seated on a bar stool. Country-western music blared. My foot wanted to tap in time to the fast Texas Two-Step.

Then I saw Chuck. He sat alone at the far end of the bar. No one occupied the other stools.

His forehead puckered in a frown, Chuck glanced at his watch as if he'd checked it a number of times since he'd sat down. He nursed a beer and tapped a sneaker on the brass foot rail in time to the music. His left hand lay inside a half-empty basket of bar nuts.

What now? I had no other option. I walked boldly in.

When he heard my sneakers squeak on the wooden floor, Chuck jerked his head up, a wide grin making his even features very appealing. Silhouetted against the light, I knew he couldn't recognize me. He probably saw a girl's outline. Apparently that's who he'd been waiting for because his welcome grin lasted until I slid a leg over the stool next to him.

"You?" His mouth pulled down like a little boy who'd just seen his dog run over.

"I'm glad to see you too." I lost the sarcasm. "Is my Jeep ready?"

"You're not my date?" A scowl took over his face. "You didn't come here to ask me about your wheels. How'd you find me?"

I took a stab in the dark. "Blind date?"

"Yeah. Blind on my side. For a one-two count, I thought you were her."

"Was that disappointment or relief on your face?"

His expression shifted to hurt.

I almost wished I hadn't asked. Who'd stand-up a cool, athletic type like Chuck? I figured women formed a line to date him.

"Afraid your date's not coming." I tempered my words with a smile. "So how'd you find me?"

"Little bird named Allison. Ring a bell?"

"Allison Taylor?"

I almost laughed at his raised brows and open mouth. For a man, he wore his feelings on his sleeve.

"How—?"

"Never mind how. I'm a private investigator, remember?"

"Doesn't take a detective to figure I've been dissed." His expressive face looked like he'd squatted with his spurs on.

"Not detective—investigator." I flipped out my license and slapped the leather container on the counter for him to see.

His long blond lashes lowered as he studied my license. I hadn't had that many chances to toss it out for people, and I enjoyed seeing the tinge of respect tighten his face. Then his whole demeanor changed. He jumped off the stool, huffed out his noteworthy chest, and growled like a lioness protecting her cubs. "Is Allison okay?" He slammed a balled fist on the bar, making the basket of beer nuts shiver. "That step-dad of hers hasn't—"

"Yes, he did. But she's okay. For now." I smiled. "She thinks you're a teddy bear."

Red flooded Chuck's cheeks. "Naw. The kid's just—" He broke off and slapped my license still lying on the polished counter. "What do ya want? Why'd ya follow me here?"

I slid off the stool and pushed my face right up to his. Not as effective as I'd hoped since my 5'8" was a head shorter than his 6' something. He wore some kind of nice aftershave, no doubt for his missing date. "Who paid you to kidnap Matt? I want answers, and I want them now."

Sweat broke out on his upper lip. I hadn't shoved him into a corner hard enough to make him back down, but he turned away, gulped his beer, pulled at his ear, and swiped his nose as if the situation stunk.

Good. He didn't like having the spotlight glare on him. "Someone paid you so much money to kidnap Matt that you were able to finance your garage. Was it enough money to pay for a good man being murdered?"

He slammed his empty beer glass on the bar. "We didn't know nothin' about no kidnapping. The gig was supposed to be a joke. We'd get the mark into a fight, the paramedics would barrel in and haul him out, and he'd end up at his girlfriend's house." He leaned both elbows on the bar and took a deep breath. "That's the honest truth. The lady said the mark liked…" He gazed around the almost empty room then lowered his voice. "…his dates rough."

I hadn't known what to expect from Chuck, but certainly not this. The kid had been a patsy. If I didn't find the kidnapper, Chuck could spend a chunk of time in jail for aiding and abetting. Pleading innocence was meaningless. I couldn't believe he'd been so dumb. On the other hand, the pretty boy hadn't seemed extra bright all along.

But something didn't set right. What was I missing? Maybe I was the dumb one. I couldn't let myself be taken in by Chuck's looks and young age or by the fact he'd been stood up. Or even that he'd helped Allison. I had to develop a hard core if I expected to work with the dark underbelly of society. I jutted my jaw.

"What's the woman's name?"

Chuck lowered his head and stared down at his empty glass. "She didn't tell me."

"You stuck your neck out for a woman who wouldn't give you her name? How stupid are you?"

Chuck hung his head like a ten-year-old caught stealing jelly beans in a candy store. "I met her in that backroom of Billy Bob's."

I didn't know the backroom of the famous dance palace, but I believed the cavernous place had any number of backrooms.

"Did she pay you with a check?" I had him rattled and wanted to find out all I could before he recovered.

"Naw. Cash. Threw a hundred-thousand on the table. Twenty-five for each of us. That's what I needed to finish getting my loan."

Mentally I whistled. "What does she look like?"

Chuck glanced toward the door, tightened his lips, and frowned.

"If I don't find her, you're going to jail." Probably will anyway. "If she kills Matt, you'll get the lethal injection for his murder. I promise." I'd never used that hard tone before. I'd unleashed the iron. Matt was in danger.

"She was real nice. I don't think she wants to kill him. I think she likes him."

"Don't be an idiot. Describe her."

"Well, she's real tall and has lots of red hair that goes all the way down to her waist." He turned, slipped his hand around me, and patted my lower back.

I slapped his arm away.

"She's probably about five years older'n you." His blue gaze swept over my face. "That'd be about thirty, I reckon. She's got more curves than you." He used both hands to cut the air into a top-heavy hourglass shape. "She's a real looker." He smirked. "Had me pantin' like a hound dog on a scent." His dimple showed. "Had me believing the gig was a gag. Any man would."

"But you're not so sure now. And rightly so. Who helped you?"

"I ain't rattin' on my pals." His brows drew together, and once again I realized this man was no teddy bear. His muscles bunched beneath his t-shirt in a way I found threatening. As the older couple shoved back their chairs and left, he glanced after them. Only the bald bartender at the far end of the bar and Chuck and I occupied the room. And the bartender had his back to us.

A chill swept my spine.

Chuck didn't look like a pretty-boy now.

"I'll get a warrant—"

"Don't try it. We can get rough if we need to. We made a mistake, but we ain't paying for it. All we did was start a fight. Can't send us to the slammer for that."

I wasn't getting any more information with my tough-girl bit, so I changed tactics. I hopped up on the barstool and leaned close to Chuck. "Help me find Matt, and I'll see the police know about your input. I'll say a good word for you." As if the daughter of Ted Garden could get a good word for herself from the police, let alone for a criminal. Still, I'd do my best. "What can it hurt? Tell me everything you know."

His manner softened. "You tell the cops I spilled my guts and told you everything." He nodded, and his blue eyes cleared, looking open and honest. "I met this Barbie Doll in Billy Bob's backroom. She paid cash and didn't give no name. I don't know where the ambulance took the mark. End of story."

His body language told me he wasn't lying. Except for discovering one of the kidnappers was a woman, I'd run into another dead-end. Outside, the setting sun darkened the room, and fake gas lights twinkled on, giving the bar an old-timey atmosphere. I started grasping for straws. "Can you draw a picture of her?"

"You kiddin'! A stick picture maybe. She's got a real pretty face though—big green eyes and a mouth a man wants to—" He broke off and coughed. "She has this look of being real innocent, but something in your gut tells ya she's been around the block a time or two. Know what I mean?" He slid a long leg over the barstool next to me and straddled it.

I nodded. "Sort of a Marilyn-Monroe type."

"Who?"

When Chuck looked puzzled, he really didn't seem too bright. And unlike me, he didn't watch reruns of old movies. "What else can you tell me?"

"I followed her out into the alley to her car and watched her leave. She got into a big black stretch-limo. You know, one with dark windows. She had plenty of the green stuff because she packed big rocks on her fingers and in her ears. I was bowled over that she went into Billy Bob's alone. Some of them cowboys get rough when they're drinking. She needed a bodyguard." He grinned like a sheepish little boy. "I woulda done that."

I nodded and kept my mouth shut. Now he was talking, and I wasn't about to interrupt.

"She seemed right at home there, not scared at all in that backroom alone with me, standing as close to her as I dared to get. She had this confidence like…like she knew I'd never have guts enough to touch her." He shook his head. "She's way out of my league."

"Did you get the license plate?"

A sly look glazed Chuck's face. "I didn't just fall off the turnip truck."

"You thought you might get other jobs from her, so you wrote it down." His expression told me I was right. I kept my face bland.

"Sure. I ain't no dummy."

I pulled my small notebook from my shoulder bag. "What is it?"

Chuck smiled like an experienced safecracker who just broke the combination. "What's it worth to ya?"

"It could keep you out of jail."

"Yeah. Well, that ain't enough. I don't think what we done will land us in the clink." He put his big hand over mine, covering pen, pad, and all, and pressed hard. "One date's as good as another. You're a looker yourself." His gaze raked my body.

Left-handed, I reached for my shoulder bag, which I'd deposited on top of the bar. I needed my pepper spray.

He grabbed my left hand before I could touch my purse.

Crushing both my hands hard against the bar he hissed, "Lady, this ain't no one-way street. Ya got what ya wanted. Now it's my turn."

"Allison Taylor said…"

"Aw." At Allison's name, Chuck eased the pressure on my hands. But he was too late.

A tornado wearing a western shirt and Stetson roared in between us. The tall cowboy grabbed the collar of Chuck's white polo and jerked him off the barstool.

Chuck's face turned ashen then red as he struggled to breathe.

The cowboy growled, "Not a good move, tough guy. Don't touch the lady. Keep your hands to yourself."

Under the black ten-gallon, I glimpsed the man's profile. "Stryker!"

Still gripping Chuck's shirt, Stryker winked. "The same."

I huffed, pulled my hands off the bar, and massaged the needles of pain. "I don't need your help. I was doing just fine."

"Sure you were." He shook Chuck.

"Let him go."

Here was Gray Angel, flying in to rescue me again. But Stryker's jaw bulged where he clenched his teeth. It took me a second before I realized he still had to hurt from the ice cream truck wreck. His limp hadn't slowed him down, and the black hat covered the stitches I had yet to see in his forehead. But his tight expression didn't hide how much his ribs hurt while he man-handled Chuck.

Just as I once again grabbed for my bag to reach inside for the pepper spray, Chuck executed a wrestling move, knotted Stryker's legs with his own, and they both crashed to the floor.

CHAPTER FOURTEEN

If I wanted to succeed at this detective business, I had to learn to react faster.

Grunting like stallions fighting for mares, the two men wrestled each other on the slick floor. I grasped my pepper spray like a life raft on the Titanic and waited for the chance to use the weapon on Chuck. My heart did a tom-tom beat that I felt all the way to my throat. Stryker was already injured and should be home recuperating in his bed. His wounds were my fault, and I sure didn't want him hurt again—especially on my behalf. I told myself his disabilities didn't panic me. I just needed to do a couple deep-knee bends, and I'd be okay. But I wasn't. I hyper-ventilated.

Bent over the fighters, I hopped around the professional mat-pounder punching the broken-ribbed private investigator, my finger primed to spray. The younger face grimaced with his efforts to throttle the dark-haired man who'd saved my life. Both grunted and swung wildly.

Oh, God, please don't let Chuck hurt Stryker.

Stryker smashed a fist into Chuck's face. The classic nose spurted blood. My stomach heaved like a cowboy's bronc.

Okay, I'm not one of those women who enjoy having gladiators fight over me. In my angst, I hesitated too long to spray the bloodied face. Muscular arms locked Stryker's neck in a wrestling hold. As Stryker's face grew red, I tucked in close to Chuck, used my body as well as I could to protect Stryker from the spray, and pressed my finger hard on the trigger. *Psst! Psst!*

Chuck let out a yell and dropped his hold. Both hands flew to his bloody face and he kicked free of Stryker. The wrestler huddled on the floor, hands frantically wiping his streaming eyes. He cursed.

After Stryker's face lost its mottled crimson color, he heaved himself up from the floor to lean against the bar, stuck his chest out, and tried to look manly. But I didn't need to hear his raspy breathing to see through his charade. He cradled his injured ribs and panted. Chuck crouched on the floor, eyes, mouth, and nose streaming like he'd gone over Niagara in a barrel. I'd never used pepper spray before, hadn't known what to expect, and now had no idea how to help Chuck.

One hand limply dangling the pepper spray, I gazed at Stryker. "You didn't have to do the macho-man thing."

He touched the stitches on his forehead, which now seeped blood. "Princess, he had you pinned to the bar."

"Yeah, well…" To divert attention from how much I really had needed Stryker's help, I called to the bartender, "Hey. Could you bring some water?"

The big man lumbered over, a sweating glass pitcher in hand. He stood over Chuck and splashed the whole jug over him, dousing him from blond hair to khaki shorts. Chuck lolled, hunched over, coughing and gasping.

"Water won't help. Don't touch your eyes." Stryker panted. "Rubbing makes the pain worse." Satisfaction radiated from his expression.

But Chuck looked so pitiful that I wished I hadn't sprayed him.

Both eyes swollen closed, he moaned between coughs and gasps.

I stood by, wringing my hands. "What will help him?"

Stryker raised an eyebrow. "Soap and ice."

I dashed for the ladies room and double-timed back, carrying wet, soapy paper towels and several sections of dry ones. The bartender brought ice. I knelt by Chuck, who sprawled bent double and gasped like a derailed locomotive. Sweat slicked his face, and every orifice dripped. Dabbing gently, I washed his face and swollen eyelids with the soapy towel.

"Remember, *he's* the bad guy." Stryker's voice sounded strained

Glancing over my shoulder, I caught a flash of something that looked suspiciously like jealousy in his expression before his detective-face locked into place.

He leaned against the bar. "Leave the soap on a few minutes before you rinse it. He'll be good as new in about forty-five minutes." He hooked both thumbs into his western belt, making the huge, silver bull-riding-champ buckle gleam in the flickering gaslight.

My heart did a new flip-flop. Did he win that trophy or buy that huge buckle at a souvenir shop? Something about this virile cowboy-type tied my tongue.

I used a clean, wet paper towel to rinse Chuck's hot, swollen face and clenched eyes, then shook my head. "I'll have to be in a really tight spot before I use pepper spray again."

Investigator Rule #6: Develop a Hard-Core Stomach When Taking Down a Criminal.

I fashioned an icepack from the paper towels, pushed Chuck to a lying position on the water-spotted floor, and laid the ice pack over his face. His erratic breathing slowed, and he appearing to be recovering.

I stood and faced Stryker. "Your stitches are bleeding." I grabbed one of those small paper napkins that bars seem to think are adequate and inched closer to him with the intention of dabbing at his pulled stitches.

He backed away. "I'm fine."

"You're bleeding."

"Don't worry about it."

Again I moved toward him. "Just let me…" Unbidden, my thoughts flashed from cool investigative mode to a personal analysis of Stryker's appearance. That mistake shot a bullet straight through the body armor around my heart. My protection momentarily penetrated, the intrepid Stryker appeared dangerously lovable. *Whoa. Slam on the brakes!* At this crucial time in my life, I had no time for a new man. No time even for casual dating. Especially no time for a charmer like Stryker. Nope. Out of the question. Just thinking about this man was overkill.

I ran for the ladies' room, calling over my shoulder, "I'll bring a damp paper towel." Once safe inside, I leaned over the sink and rested my forehead on the cool tiled wall. Preston's tire treads had left deep grooves in my heart. I wasn't about to venture on another disastrous road-trip of love. Not caring about germs, I rubbed my forehead on the clean, horse-decorated white tile. Surely I simply felt gratitude to the investigator for saving my life. I glanced up and caught the fletchings from Cupid's arrow vibrating between my eyebrows. I gripped the edges of the sink. Oh, I was in deep trouble.

Okay, so I couldn't deny the sizzling attraction between us. But pheromones were quicksand, not solid grounds for a relationship. I doused my face with cold water but felt like I needed a dip in the Arctic Ocean next to an ice flow.

Sure, Stryker was the best-looking man I'd run across in my twenty-four years of life, but looks faded, men grew big stomachs, and skin sagged during life's long years. I'd never counted appearance as a criterion for a long-term association. Straightening, I drilled wet fingers through my tousled locks. Despite the man's undeniable good looks and physique-to-die-for, I wouldn't start counting physical charms now.

My stomach quivered like vanilla pudding. Not if I could help myself.

But Stryker showed incredible bravery when he sandwiched himself between the run-away Caddie and the gas-tanker. Each time I thought of his action, my knees turned to chocolate syrup. And now, fighting for me when he was hurting. Delighted goosebumps shivered through me.

Grabbing the sides of the sink with both hands, I spoke to the pale, dripping face gazing back at me from the lavatory mirror, pupils dilated so wide that most of the hazel showed black.

"Far, far away. Keep the man far, far away. Admire him from a distance, but don't let him snare your heart. You don't dare risk the poor shredded thing again."

I stood there talking to myself until my heartbeat slowed and some color returned to my cheeks. Then I patted my face dry, straightened my shoulders, and would have applied lip gloss, but in my mad rush, I'd left my purse on the bar's long mahogany counter.

"Holly, get a grip. The heartbreaker's probably not a Christian." I watched the mirrored face set her jaw and silently vow *not* to find out his spiritual state.

I turned from the mirror and spoke sternly over my shoulder to my reflection. "Stryker's the competition—nothing more. You remember that."

I wet a paper towel and marched out of my hiding place back to the two men, one of whom was fast screwing up my emotional life.

"Here." I shoved the wet towel toward Stryker and knelt beside

Chuck. "Let's get you over to one of the chairs so we can talk."

Chuck groaned and remained lying flat, icepack covering his face. So I sat down cross-legged beside him.

"Mind if I join the party? I hate being baffled without you." Stryker grunted and held his ribs as he scrunched down to sit beside me. He braced his back against the mahogany bar.

Oh, how could a man smell so good when he'd just been fighting? I kept my attention away from the hazardous-to-my-health aura surrounding him and stared at the icepack on Chuck's face. His respiration looked normal, and I suspected he'd almost recovered from the pepper spray. I'd have to be quick with my questions.

"Okay, Eggleston, who ordered you to poke a hole in the Caddie's brake-fluid housing?"

Chuck's body jerked. He sat up, and the icebag slid into his lap, spilling cubes across his nicely-blond-haired bare shins. "What?"

"Don't go all innocent on me. I saw you mess around under the hood before you tossed me the keys to the Caddie."

His blood-shot-eyed expression looked too stunned to be feigned. "Something happened to my Caddie?"

"As if you didn't know." I took advantage of his dropped mouth and pressed on. "The police impounded your car after the wreck."

"Wreck? You wrecked my Caddie?"

I could tell by the raised-eyebrow look Stryker threw me that he believed Chuck's innocence too. "*Your* Caddie? Wasn't it a vehicle to use as a loaner?"

Chuck swallowed, the sound loud in the quiet room. "Um…no. I just opened the shop and hadn't gotten a loaner yet. The Caddie's mine." As if he thought we didn't believe him he crossed his heart. "Why else would I ride a bike to a blind date?"

He had me there. Used to cleaning up my own messes, I gathered the melting ice cubes, rewrapped them in the used paper towels, and laid them beside the empty pitcher.

"When did you last drive the vehicle?" Stryker's voice sounded unobtrusive, as if he were a best friend commiserating about the wreck.

"I never drove it. She had the car delivered."

Like a crawling spider, a shiver crept vertebrae by vertebrae down my back. "She who?"

"The lady who paid me."

"Did any of the other wrestlers see her?"

"Nope. Just me. She only wanted contact with one of us. I had no job, so the other guys tapped me." Chuck shrugged. "She insisted I take the Caddie as part of the payoff." He glanced from my face to Stryker's, his skin graying in front of my eyes. His face melted to mush. "I, uh, thought it was kinda funny she had the car hauled to the garage instead of having somebody drive it by."

I could see he understood the implication of the wreck. So he wasn't as slow upstairs as I'd previously thought.

I saw the confirmation in the frightened way his gaze darted around the room, in the pulse that started beating at the base of his throat, then in the straightening of his back, the shaking of his blond head, and the red that stained his lean cheeks.

Flash to self. Chuck wasn't dumb. He'd taken a big chance to make an impossible dream come true. He'd taken the fight-at-the-party-job as the only way to ease his way out of poverty. He'd seen the money as a magical flying carpet to a new life.

I sighed, hurting deep inside for him. The young man had never glimpsed his own potential. I'd talk with him about that. Soon. But first I had to find Matt.

He grimaced. "Then the S.O.S. came in about your stranded Jeep, and I took off to tow you."

"What did you do under the Caddie's hood before you threw me the keys?"

He blinked. "Just gave her a quick oil check. Some of those old cars burn oil worse than they guzzle gas. And I made sure the battery cables weren't corroded."

"So you were the intended target, not me." The knowledge should have made me feel better. Instead the creepy-crawler spiraled my back again. My shoulders slumped. If the kidnapper wanted Chuck dead, he obviously didn't want any witnesses who could finger him.

I slapped a hand over my mouth and fought against being sick. If Matt saw the woman's face, even if she was just a gopher, he was a dead man.

Oh, God, let him be blindfolded!

CHAPTER FIFTEEN

I pulled my galloping emotions back together and scooted closer to Chuck. The floor already dented my rear.

"The kidnapper tried to murder you, Chuck. You're not safe. Tell me what you know. Give me that limo license."

Chuck's pale face and mushy expression showed he fought against spilling his cookies too. "You'll tell the cops I cooperated? You'll keep my brothers out of this mess?"

So his brothers were involved. That's why the new haircuts. They didn't want to be remembered as being part of the kidnapping. Why hadn't Chuck cut his? I glanced at Stryker. He barely nodded.

"I'll do everything I can for you," I patted his arm. Poor Chuck. He didn't know his life would definitely be ruined if I spoke up for him. Stryker'd have to put in a good word for the wrestler.

Stryker used one long arm to grab my purse from the bar top and shoved my big red bag toward me. I slid my small notebook out, flipped to a clean page, and poised my pen. "What's the license number?"

Chuck hemmed and hawed but finally blurted the Texas plate.

"Now tell me about the EMS pretenders." I doubted Chuck knew anything, but maybe he could identify more than he gave himself credit for.

"We're all wrestlers. Wannabes, I guess. We get a gig now and then."

"Give me names."

Surprisingly, he did. His hands shook, and he looked too young to be a wrestler or even a mechanic. He should be back in high school. And like Allison said, way down deep Chuck Eggleston was a teddy bear.

"Where did the ambulance take Matt?" I held my breath.

"I dunno. Haven't laid eyes on those clowns since the brawl. It's not like we're chicks and text all day." He brushed long, dripping hair back from his face. "Just so you know, I had to drop off that monkey-suit I wore at the cleaners." He scowled at Stryker. "You bled all over the shirt and cummerbund."

Stryker's lips tilted a fraction at the corners.

I had to give credit to the PI. Most men would have raised their fists, ready to up the score. Not Stryker. He kept a cool head and stuck to business. Still, I noticed a vein in his temple throb.

I turned my full attention back to Chuck. Almost recovered from the pepper spray, the would-be wrestler's face hardened into a determined look. I doubted he'd answer any more questions, but I kept digging. "Did the woman mention who she works for?"

"Must be a real rich dude to have a dame like her for a gopher."

"Did she mention any names?"

"Nope."

"Do you have any idea why someone would kidnap Matt?"

"Like I said, we all thought the gig was a gag."

"You knew when you started the fight that Matt was security. Why kidnap him?"

"Like I told you, the lady said her friend liked his romance rough." Chuck's demeanor turned sullen. He shrugged and struggled to stand. "Correction. What she actually said was, 'My friend likes to surprise her boyfriend.' Guess I was the one thought her friend's approach seemed downright rough." He held up both hands in an I've-told-you-everything-I-know gesture. "That's it. That's the way it was. She paid me, and I vamoosed out of there."

I shut my notebook and slipped it back into my purse.

"Oh, yeah. Come to think of it, I did do a double-take when I saw the mark. He sure wasn't in her league. But who am I to question love?"

"No, Matt definitely doesn't look like a millionaire. But neither does Ross Perot."

"Who?"

"Never mind. Just one more question. Why didn't you repair my Jeep?"

The red tinge on his cheeks deepened. "Aww…" He hung his head.

I tapped my foot on the floor. "I'm waiting."

He continued to gaze at his high-tops.

"Answer the lady." Stryker stood to his full six-foot-three, impersonating an angry gorilla.

Chuck mumbled incoherently.

"Speak up." The gorilla flexed his muscles.

"There wasn't much wrong with that old Jeep. Something knocked the gas tank around and caused a leak. She was out of gas. I fixed the tank. It'll only take a little elbow grease to straighten the fender and bang out the dent. An hour's work."

"So why didn't you call and tell me my Jeep was ready?"

Chuck glanced at Stryker. "You want the truth?"

Stryker glared. "You'd better spill it."

Chuck kept his gaze on Stryker. "You can see this chick's a looker. I wanted her to check in a couple of times…so's we could like…get to know each other. If I told her the Jeep was ready, she'd pick it up, drive off, and I'd never lay eyes on her again."

Stryker raised a skeptical brow. "But you knew she was investigating you."

"Yeah. That spooked me yesterday. But I chewed it over and knew I didn't have nothin' to hide. I didn't do nothin' wrong." He finally glanced at me. "I thought with me owning my own place, you might want to hang out together."

I made a show of gathering my purse and the blood-tinged paper towel Stryker had used then headed for the ladies room. "I'll be right back."

For now, Stryker could handle Chuck. I shook my head. For a first-time offense, I figured Chuck would get off with probation. And rather than encourage his crush while I talked with him about his spiritual life, I'd ask Pastor Jerry to speak with him. If Chuck didn't go to jail, maybe the pastor could invite the guy to the singles group.

Someone needed to clue the teddy bear in, for now…and for eternity.

"Of course you'll stay for dinner, young man." Granny clamped a fist around Stryker's arm.

Stryker had given me a ride home because I'd parked in a no-parking zone in front of a fire hydrant near the Lone Star. While I was inside, the Fort Worth Police towed Dad's Toyota. With it being Sunday, I couldn't pick the SUV up from police impound until tomorrow.

"Oh, Granny, he's in a hur—"

"I'd like that, ma'am." Stryker tipped his Stetson.

Granny gave me her most conniving smile. "See, Peach Tree? The hunky cowpoke wants to stay."

I bit my lip. Okay, maybe the western get-up wasn't fake. It would've helped if Frank had filled me in on Stryker's background.

He'd probably grown up in the Mesquite area of the Metroplex and was a real cowboy. The bull-riding trophy buckle looked genuine. The high-heeled boots peeking from beneath the frayed hems of his tight, well-worn Levi's looked as if they'd seen real service too.

The long-sleeved plaid shirt with the western yoke didn't look new either. I easily pictured chaps and Stryker straddling a huge, frightening bull doing frantic whirls and jumps to unseat the fool with guts enough to climb aboard and hang on for the eight magic seconds.

The man holding the Stetson loosely at his side definitely courted danger.

"Okay, Granny. But he has to leave immediately after. He has things to do and places to go."

Granny gave a little hop. "Yeah. Like taming those bulls."

"Oh, I'm pretty free tonight."

Granny didn't need that charming smile to set her heart skipping like a girl's. Her face lit up like a film star at the first sight of a camera. No doubt about it, Stryker had Granny hooked.

"Free tonight. Fancy that," I said dryly. "No doubt this is an anomaly." Okay, so some women were swept away by Stryker. I shrugged and muttered aloud, "Probably only the ones who are breathing." And right now my own breath came pretty fast.

"What?" As we walked through the front door, he put his hand in the small of my back.

"Nothing." The man was hot as a jalapeño pepper. In the entry hall, I moved away from him. "So where do you conceal your weapon?"

"Ho. That's a leading question." He grinned.

"Your gun. You *know* I'm talking about your gun. Do you wear an underarm holster?"

"*That* gun." He grinned wider, eyes twinkling. "Yep. It's right here." He patted his right side.

"I need a side-holster. Sometimes I can't get to my shoulder bag."

"I noticed that."

He kept on grinning and, as usual, charmed everyone around him, especially Granny.

She nestled close to his side, the top of her white head barely reaching his armpit, her shining brown eyes on me. "Peach Tree, you'd never get one of those holsters under that black sweater." She gazed up at Stryker, hero worship popping from her eyes. "Right, handsome?"

"I'm afraid you're right, ma'am."

"Yes. Your back-holster gives you more panache." Granny patted the hollow of her own back. "I think I'll get one, too."

Mom chose that moment to glide from the dining room and wave us inside. "Hello, Mr. Black. This is an unexpected *pleasure.*" Her tone betrayed exactly the opposite emotion.

I squirmed. Why was Mom so upset with Stryker staying for dinner? Even Jose ate with us on occasion. Mom wasn't a snob.

She turned her back to Stryker and spoke to Granny. "What are you planning to buy, Naomi?"

"I need a back-paddle holster for my thirty-eight. Wish I could shoot a nine-millimeter like Holly does." Granny held up her veined hand and wriggled the crooked fingers. "But my arthritis doesn't like that stiffer action."

"Do you have a concealed handgun license, ma'am?" Stryker slid his hand in the small of my back again. I tried not to enjoy his warm touch. He seemed unperturbed by Mom's rude reception.

"Sure do. You don't think I can help Holly catch her crooks if I don't carry, do you?" Granny stuck her arm through Stryker's and headed him through the front hall toward the dining room. "Let's go eat, and you can tell me all about how you landed under the table and won Holly's broken heart."

"Granny!"

My red face and watering eyes almost made me miss Stryker's I'm-standing-on-the-winner's-podium, I-hear-the national-anthem, and I-won-the-gold-medal expression.

"Did I mention that Granny's in the last stages of Alzheimer's?" I only half-joked, my head down.

"Now, Peach Tree, is that a nice thing to say?"

Mom turned and glared at Granny. "Of course, Hollyhock would never pursue an interest in a..." She tipped her head up and iced Stryker with a glance. "...a man who chases a dangerous profession." She turned and led the way to the dining room. "Holly's attracted to doctors or investors or... businessmen. A private investigator is simply out of the question." She glanced back. "As are rodeo professionals."

Stryker had his cop-face on, so I couldn't tell if Mom's words affected him.

I searched for a hole in the wide-planked polished floor to fall through. None being available, I decided to intervene before either Granny or Mom brought more of my real romantic status to light and put my failures under the microscope for Stryker to dissect. I gave the heartbreaker a thin smile.

"Poor Mom. She wanted a debutante daughter and instead got an adventuress more interested in sniffing out a cheating husband than in marrying a plastic surgeon." I waved a hand. "Though Dallas is jammed with both—plastic surgeons and wandering husbands, that is."

We entered the dining room where The Flowers and Allison already sat at the long table. All three gazed up, expressions painted with curiosity. Mom glided to the head of the table and took her seat. She tilted her head up and glared at Stryker. "Holly has many suitors."

Maggie's eyes widened. "Is Preston back?"

Cami's mouth dropped. "Did he call, Holly?"

"No and no." I glared at the twins.

Stryker pulled out the closest of the four chairs on the opposite side from my sisters. "Preston, huh?"

I plopped into the upholstered chair. Most dysfunctional families refuse to acknowledge what they don't want to deal with. Mine delighted in spreading our problems under a spotlight for anyone who happened by to marvel at—especially my problems.

I had to stop further conversation about my romantic status and clue my family into the fact that I merely worked with this man. There was no intention to date. So in a brisk, businesslike tone, I asked, "Stryker, did you call the DMV to check that limo license number with the title department?"

Stryker gave me a look as if he thought I was fairly dense. He sat down next to me. "You know I did. After they pull up the info, they'll call." Then he winked. "You've been dating a plastic surgeon?"

My face heated.

Granny raised a fist. "Not if I catch sight of that forehead-lifter first. I'll shoot him between the eyes. Nobody gets away with leaving my Peach Tree dumped at the altar."

Allison's wide eyes darted from Stryker to me. "Your fiancé dumped you on your wedding day?"

I squeezed my napkin into a wad, jerked it open again, and then dropped the wrinkled linen in my lap. "Ancient history. Water under the bridge. Much ado about nothing."

Like a frying pan whacking the back of my head, my conscience hit me. Lies. I promised God I wouldn't lie, not even tell a small white lie to spare someone's feelings. In this case, the feelings were mine.

I swallowed and fiddled with my knife and fork. "Well, mostly water under the bridge." Afraid to look at Stryker's reaction, I honed in on Allison's sympathy-dripping blue eyes. Her pity closed my throat.

Tears prickled the back of my eyelids. I grabbed my glass and forced water down my throat. Didn't work. I coughed and sputtered, water filling my nose.

Granny jumped up, flashed to my side of the table, and handed me a napkin. She opened her mouth.

Before she could say a word, Stryker's baritone purred, "Missed his chance, I'd say. Left the treasure under the rainbow for a better, wiser man."

With my face buried in the napkin, I heard Granny say, "You got that right, young man. This here girl's a peach."

I never expected the soothing warmth Stryker's words spread over my battered heart. Lifting my face from the napkin, I turned toward him, hoping my voice worked. "Stryker, the twins are my sisters, Cami and Maggie, and the younger girl is a friend, Allison Taylor."

Stryker nodded. "I met Allison last night." He smiled at her. "Nice to see you again."

Even in my agitated state, I detected some swift, unnamable message pass between the two of them. I almost missed it. But the communication generated so much electricity that if I raised a hand between them, I'd have been zapped. On some level they connected. My intuition buzzed. What secret did they share? Did Stryker know Allison from some other time or place?

Mom's radar pinged as she honed in on a different signal. She glared at Stryker. "You were *with* my daughter last night?"

"Yes, ma'am. On the job."

"Does your job necessitate you being *in* my daughter's company?" Now it was Mom's turn to send an unspoken message to Stryker, but hers blasted cannonballs.

Granny cocked her head, looking as quizzical as I felt. "More secrets flying around here than at Los Alamos during World War Two."

I was about to agree with her when Mom shot another broadside salvo.

"Is there some minimum IQ test you took to become a PI?" She stared at Stryker. Frost dripped from her face and posture.

I dropped my mouth. You can relocate a Southern Lady into the African Serengeti, but if you were born in Texas and raised in North Dallas, you're a lady for life—all magnolia smiles and sugary hospitality. This was so unlike Mom. She was Scarlett O'Hara, pistol in hand, facing the Yankees. Poor Stryker. If Mom's lack of hospitality took him by surprise, his face didn't betray any tension.

"Holly, we got a situation here." From across the table, Granny wiggled her eyebrows.

I fussed, smoothing the puckered napkin in my lap while I worked to put on my detective face. I knew Mom was deeply hurt by Dad's death and didn't want me to wind up facing the same kind of situation in the highly unlikely scenario I ended up falling for an investigator. That was clear enough. But what did Allison and Mom know about Stryker that I didn't?

"Yes, ma'am. I *was* on the job. And no, ma'am, I was not *with* your daughter."

"I see." The pulse beating at Mom's temple slowed. The slight pink left her cheeks. She turned to me. "So, Holly, have you discovered anything new about Matt?"

I put my curiosity in my to-be-examined-later compartment, let her change the subject, and brought her up-to-date.

My briefing finished, Cami, the more apt to strike-out-into-unchartered-territory twin, tinkled a spoon against her water glass for attention. "Mr. Black, I never even had my picture taken in my junior bridesmaid dress last June. And pink's my favorite color."

My throat tightened with an almost anaphylactic reaction.

"Yeah, Mr. Black." Maggie wiggled up and down on her chair.

"And Holly's eight bridesmaids didn't get their pictures taken either. They had awesome dresses." She chimed her glass in imitation of Cami. "And all us girls spent the whole day at the spa getting our faces, hair, and nails done."

"The church was filled with Stargazers." Cami closed her eyes and sniffed deeply. "I know I'm weird, but I love their scent. And those flowers looked heavenly."

Allison's eyes grew wide. "Were the invited people inside the church?"

"Yep." Maggie bobbed her head, making her ponytail bounce. "We *ladies…*" She tossed a superior look at her twin. "…were standing inside the Bride's Room just off the sanctuary, and we heard the special wedding music being played over and over."

Cami held up a slender purple-nail-polished finger. "I wanted to run out into the church and find out what was going on, but nobody would let me. We *ladies* waited and waited." She frowned. "Finally, Matt, who was best man, poked his head into the room and called Holly over. He whispered in her ear that Preston never showed up. So Matt had gone to Preston's house. The maid said the runaway-groom left that morning for Tahiti."

I took a deep breath and opened my mouth, but not even a squeak came out.

Granny spoke up from where she sat on Stryker's other side. "I don't know how the media got the news, but those reporters made a three-ring circus of Preston jilting Holly."

Mom sat stiffly at Granny's right. She darted icicles at Stryker. "You probably read the tabloids. The newshounds brought up Ted's death again and said our wealthy family had drug-cartel connections. They said that once he found out, Dr. Preston Porter wanted no part of us."

"The man's an idiot."

I'd never seen Stryker angry, or if I had, he knew how to conceal his emotions. But that single sentence held murderous intent. He gazed out the dining-room window at the fountain with its Greek woman eternally emptying her pitcher of flowing water. His jaw clenched and unclenched. His skin darkened.

Granny spoke up. "Guess the twins think any *friend* of Holly's should know what happened."

I didn't like how Granny said friend. But when Stryker turned back to Mom, I forgot to reprimand Granny.

"Um, in answer to your question, ma'am, no, I didn't read about an undeserving fool deserting an incredible woman on her wedding day."

He didn't look at me, but his profile appeared rocky. "I moved to Dallas in August. Moved from Montana to work for Ace Investigations."

"I see. And now you're here." Her tone implied he should crawl back under the rock he came from.

I lost track of the conversation after that. I found I could breathe, sip water, and smile. Eight months had eased the ripping pain in my heart and the absolute embarrassment that came from Preston's public rejection. I no longer fled to my room at the mention of my humiliation. But my determination to clear Dad's name exploded into a vow. I was ninety percent certain Dad hadn't been on the take from that drug cartel. And absolutely sure he hadn't murdered those three teenagers. Somehow I'd prove his innocence.

And Stryker's pain-quenching words soothed my amazingly not-quite-so-shredded heart.

But dinner had more firecrackers in store. Sunday nights we usually ate in the kitchen, and as Maria brought in the soup, I asked, "Why have we gone formal this evening?"

I tasted the spiced acorn soup and my question got its answer.

The doorbell chimed, and Maria rushed to answer. Mom's face

turned moist, and her hand trembled when she set her soup spoon on the platter beneath the bowl.

Maria appeared at the doorway. "It's—"

"So sorry I'm late, Vi." As if he were a frequent diner, the silver-haired man strutted to the empty chair at the head of the table at Mom's right, pulled it out, and nested. "I had an international call I couldn't cut short." He bowed over Mom's hand and kissed her fingers.

I spilled the water in the glass I set down. As the liquid spread over the damask, I lost the little appetite I'd regained.

Mom beamed around the table. "Y'all have met J.C. Hogg."

Granny, Allison, The Flowers, and Stryker all nodded. Since I hadn't seen J.C. in church, that meant the silver-haired Romeo visited Mom earlier today. None of the others seemed any happier than I at the oil shipper's sudden appearance. But Mom glowed.

During the salad course, conversation picked up again. The usual differences of opinions ping-ponged around the table.

Maria served the main course. I cut my grilled steak into tiny pieces and feigned eating.

Granny broke into the jousting around the table. "I forgot to tell you about this woman who sailed into Paradise Pets yesterday." She gazed at each face to make certain she had everyone's attention. She didn't. Romeo and Mom gazed dreamily at each other as if they starred in a romantic commercial. Granny spoke louder. "This woman created quite a stir. Mrs. McNary was there picking up her big tabby cat. You know, the one with the ragged ear."

Granny's voice reached a decibel that could shatter glass. "That tabby caught sight of this woman, froze, arched her back, and bristled her whiskers. No way would she let Mrs. McNary shove her into her cat carrier. That big cat hissed and stared with her unblinking yellow eyes at that woman as if she were scared to death." Granny leaned forward and waved her knife toward me. "Doesn't that beat all?"

Not interested in the cat, I forked a tiny piece of steak and pushed it around my plate. But Granny's dark eyes sparkled like a kid with a lollipop, so I asked, "Who is this cat-scaring lady?"

"I don't know her name. But she's really tall."

Granny only comes to my shoulder, so to her, "really tall" could be my height.

"Why was she there?" I asked out of habit, my mind swirling over the revelation that I might actually be getting over Preston.

"She brought in her two standard-size poodles. Beautiful dogs—one apricot and one white, named Cinnamon and Vanilla. That cat spooked those two beauties too. Mazie and I had to run out from behind the counter and chase them down before we could walk them back to their kennel suites."

Allison wasn't used to Granny and didn't know Granny would continue telling her story even if no one showed a spark of interest. She asked, "How tall is the woman, Granny?"

"Taller than Danny. He's the boy that grooms the dogs."

I knew Danny, and the forty-five-year-old was a good four inches taller than I. My interest spiked. "Are you sure? If she's taller than Danny, she'd have to be almost six-feet tall."

"'Course I'm sure. I might be old, but I'm not blind."

For the first time since my dismal past spilled out, I looked at Stryker. We locked glances.

"Can you describe her, Granny?"

"Well, the first thing I noticed was that big rock on her right hand. Biggest diamond I've ever seen. And she has long red hair."

"Anything else?"

"Yeah. Funny thing. The woman's only a little older than you, but she's got a real bad limp." Granny scratched her white head. "It was chilly yesterday, but she wore little gold sandals with those fake gemstones on the straps." She shook her head. "Those sandals weren't much more than sparkles running across her toes. And her feet looked strange."

I leaned forward. "Strange in what way?"

"Well, I don't know. She's a slender lady, but her feet looked thicker, like they were swollen, and her toes were crooked. And the little pinkie crossed over the toe next to it."

"On both feet?"

"Yep. She wore her pants so long I didn't notice at first. But when she limped, I edged over and gave her slacks a little tug so I could get a gander at her feet."

I gave Granny a thumbs-up.

"She didn't like me doing that one little bit. I'd sure hate to get on that gal's bad side."

"Was she attractive?"

Of course Stryker would ask that. Granny didn't seem to like his question either.

"Some of the other girls who help out thought so." Granny's answer sounded grumpy. "Not me. She's too gaudy for my taste, what with that big ring and that low-cut blouse showing enough cleavage to make a priest blush."

When Maria entered, instead of spinning her story out until our eyes crossed like they usually did, Granny asked, "What's for dessert?"

I figured she still didn't like Stryker's question about the pet shop woman's beauty.

When dinner was finally over, I walked Stryker to the front door.

"I like your crazy family." He leaned against the doorframe and eyed the crystal chandelier in our hallway. "None of you five females agree on anything. This is a 'madcap mansion.'" He smiled, showing those heartbreaking dimples. "Your house has a nutty aura all its own. But I like the wacky element."

I had my mouth open to answer when he leaned down and brushed a light kiss over my lips.

"You take care."

When I could breathe again, I whispered, "I'm so not good at being careful."

CHAPTER SIXTEEN

After Stryker left, I started going and blowing with my hair on fire. I borrowed Mom's Lexus and pranced out to pay a Sunday night visit to the Vera Wang dress-owner, Samantha Parker.

Somewhere between Preston Road and The Shops At Legacy, I picked up a tail. Because it was dark, I couldn't identify the make of car but assumed Stryker followed me again. He was getting careless.

I did my dodge-car thing to lose him.

My watch said the time approached nine when I knocked at the door to apartment 234 at the Preston Hollow Apartments in Plano. No surprise here. This was a Vera Wong dress-type-up-scale apartment complete with surrounding parks and lakes.

I heard locks open then Samantha spoke through the crack above her door's burglar chain. "Yes?"

I shoved my badge close to her eyes. "I'm investigating the Matt Murdock kidnapping. Let me in, please. I have a few questions to ask you."

Her blue eyes widened. She glanced up and down the hall as far as she could see through the two-inch slit before she slipped off the safety latch and opened the door. She wore no make-up, and her blonde hair flowed straight to her shoulders.

"Who's kidnapping?" Her ringless left hand clutched a blue sweatshirt to her neck.

"Matt Murdock was kidnapped two days ago at the Valentine-Meet-A-Thon. Let me in and I'll explain."

"Oh." She repeated the scared-rabbit glances up and down the hall. "May I see your badge again?"

I held the official square up. She examined it and checked the picture with my face.

"You can come in, but I don't know how I can help."

Her feet were bare, and the exercise video playing softly in the background agreed with the loose sweatpants she wore. She locked the door behind me, switched off the TV, and gave me a quizzical look. "One of the other guests told me the man went to the hospital after the fight."

So she knew exactly who I was asking questions about. "No. The whole brawl turned out to be an elaborate kidnapping."

"Really?" She padded to the white overstuffed couch, plopped down, and waved a hand for me to join her.

"Thanks." I sank into the cushions. My info hadn't surprised her, so I settled back to find out why.

Before talking with Mrs. Murdock, I'd thought Matt had a romantic interest in this striking blonde. But now, according to Matt's mom, Matt carried a secret torch for me. So I felt pretty awkward. Still, I'd proceed on the premise that Maddie Murdock wasn't up-to-date on her facts—or she was dead wrong.

I plucked my little notebook out and poised my pencil. "Did you and Matt meet before the Valentine party?"

"Was that his name?"

A shiver shook me, and the lead in my pencil broke. I'd not allowed myself to think of Matt as being a *was.* I grabbed my red shoulder bag and rummaged through the interior until I fished out a ballpoint pen. The beautiful Miss Parker's question seemed as fake as her smile.

"Yes. His name *is* Matt Murdock. I take it you didn't know him?"

"I noticed him looking at me from time to time during the party, but no, I didn't know him."

Well, I'd seen that much. "Did he approach you? Introduce himself?"

"No. He seemed to be kind of looking at everyone. Almost like he was working." Even the petite blonde's shrug looked attractive. "I found the men at the International Banking table interesting, so once I made contact, I didn't think about the cool guy again."

Cool? Matt? "But you had observed him."

"Sure. He was tall, nice-looking, and younger than most of the other men there. He had a great build and wasn't pushy. I would have been interested enough to take his card, but since he wasn't sitting at one of the tables, I didn't."

I worked for a hard-shell detective face. This number-ten blonde thinks Matt's attractive enough to date? Have I been overlooking something? Taking him way too much for granted?

"You left early?"

Becoming pink blushed her cheeks. "Well, yes. Jason Jetter asked me to meet him at his private club." She glanced at the door as if she wanted me to leave, then down at her polished toenails. "I mean, that's what the whole thing was for, wasn't it? To meet someone."

I sighed. Yeah, a girl that looks as good as you would definitely score. Samantha's mom probably wanted grandbabies too.

"Yes. So you and…" I looked down at my notes. "…you and Jason left together?"

"No. I met him at his club." She rose. "I'm sorry, but I have to leave now for an appointment."

"And the name of the club?"

"The Dallas Country Club, of course."

I stood up to face her. "Well, thanks for your time." I didn't buy her story. Miss Samantha Parker wasn't telling me everything she knew. And someone frightened her so much she wanted me out of her apartment.

As she hurried me out the door, I stopped and looked back over my shoulder. "So you made no contact with Matt at all?"

She shook her head.

"Then how did you know which man I asked about?"

Her creamy skin pinked again, and she all but pushed me out the door. "I'm late."

The door slammed, and the locks clicked.

Back in Mom's Lexus, the time headed on toward ten, and the night was dark as a bat cave. As soon as I pulled away from the apartments onto Preston Road, headlights behind me flicked on.

I shivered. Not Stryker. He tailed too well to be so easily detected. Who, then? This guy wanted me to know he stalked me. The guy I'd thought I lost earlier? Maybe I needed a renewal course in ditching surveillance. Or maybe the tail was a professional.

Probably due to nerves, I pressed the gas pretty hard.

A siren shrilled, and the red light flashed until the cop car all but hit Mom's bumper. I sighed and pulled over to the curb.

The black-and-white slid into the angled cop-car-stop position, blocking my rear bumper. A loud speaker blared "Out of the vehicle. Hands up. Now."

Wild. I grabbed my shoulder bag, raised my hands so the cop with the spotlight beamed on me could see, and stepped out of the Lexus.

"Drop the pocketbook on the street…slowly."

My hand shook as I plunked my heavy bag down.

I couldn't see well because of the blinding spotlight, but about a half-block away where the street lay in darkness, my tail switched off his lights. Now the cop's spotlight blinded me.

Cars slowed and crawled by as drivers' got an eye full. I counted at least ten just on my side of the six-lane street before the cop horn blared again.

"Hands on the hood, and spread your legs."

In a moment of déjà vu, I was back with Dad at the take-down just before shots punctuated the night, and Dad crumpled at my feet.

The heat on my hands from the Lexus hood brought me back. The cop let me stand that way for a full two-minutes before he opened his door and climbed out.

When I recognized him, my stomach did a flop and I was glad I hadn't eaten much dinner. "P.J., it's me. Holly Garden."

The grossly over-muscled former parajumper-turned-cop grunted. He pushed one heavy leg in front of the other, shifted his gun-belt around his size-fifty waist, and thudded toward me. His big, meaty hands did a too-invasive search of my body to see if I wore a hidden weapon.

"Stop groping me. My gun's in my flower pot at home."

He ignored me and continued running his hot hands over my torso and legs. "Can't be too careful."

"Watch your hands!"

"Just keep facing the car."

I tried to pull away, but he pressed in closer.

"I know I was probably going five miles over the speed limit."

"I clocked you at forty-five in a forty-mile zone."

I turned to face him.

"Hold it." He grasped my arms and turned me back toward the

Lexus. "Keep your hands on the hood and your legs spread."

I looked over my shoulder and watched him loosen the baton at his back.

"This is ridiculous."

"Before I caught you speeding, I saw you park in a VIP spot at the Preston Hollow Apartments. You don't live there. I think you planned a B and E."

"Come on!" What could I expect from P.J.? Every time he saw me, he bullied me. Now, in the dark of night, we were alone. Why didn't Stryker show? Surely he, as well as everyone traveling Preston Road, could see P.J. hassling me. Where was Gray Angel when I needed him?

"What's the matter? You got a slow night? Nothing better to do than harass a helpless girl?"

"Shut your trap. I could get rough."

I didn't doubt he wanted to. "I could get a lawyer."

"You were stalking. I got a call." He took his cuffs out, jerked my arms behind my back, and snapped them tight around my wrists.

"What—?"

"Shut up." He grasped both my arms and pushed me toward the squad car.

"You can't—"

"No? Watch me." He opened the rear door of the black-and-white, shoved his beefy hand down on the top of my head, and forced me to sit in the caged backseat.

I didn't believe for a moment Samantha called him. She hadn't had enough time.

"Move over."

"And if I don't?"

"You think I can't make you?"

He could, of course. He had at least a hundred-fifty pounds on me, the law on his side, and muscles the size of the Hulk's. I scooted.

He opened the front door and switched his spotlight off. The red light on top of the car and his radar screen followed. Except for headlights from passing cars, we sat in blackness.

"What are you doing?" Despite the chill air, sweat beaded my upper lip.

He grunted, put the black-and-white into gear, and pulled away from the curb.

I hoped to see the headlights from my tail flick on and his car follow us, but that didn't happen.

P.J. veered into a U-turn, sped down a side street, drove about ten minutes, and slid into a spot under a viaduct where I figured he must lurk to eat donuts. He switched off the headlights.

The place was dark. Our car was dark. We were totally isolated.

I could see nothing. After he twisted off the ignition, I heard the gurgle of water from someplace nearby and the occasional croak of a frog.

"This isn't the police station." I tried to keep my voice from quivering.

He rustled around in the front seat, did something to the light, and opened the front door. No light when he opened the front door and no light when he opened the rear door.

I couldn't see a thing, but I heard him fold over, grunt a few times, and felt the seat mash down like a beached whale landed next to me. Then a massive leg stuffed into a too-tight uniform pushed against mine. He smelled like an overdose of after-shave trying to mask body odor.

Fear left a metallic taste in my mouth. My wrists hurt from too-tight cuffs. And my eyes, after being spotlighted so long, burned and refused to adjust to the dark. "So are you arresting me?"

"You could say that."

"For parking in a reserved spot and going five miles over the limit? What else do you have on your mind?"

I wished I hadn't asked. Pictures of this massive man having his way with me, whether in rape, torture, or murder, flooded my imagination.

He chuckled long and low, like his thoughts echoed mine. "Well, Miss Troublemaker, out alone on such a dark and dangerous night… you're asking for trouble."

My insides quaked like jelly on an unsteady spoon. I didn't want to know what trouble he meant. "I'm not alone. Didn't you notice my friendly tail?"

"That's no friend of yours." His low rumbling laugh shook his huge body.

CHAPTER SEVENTEEN

P.J.'s hand burned heavy on my thigh. His acrid odor cut into my senses. Arms cuffed behind me, I shifted away until the door handle bit into my side. "This is police harassment."

"You'll never tell anyone." He pressed against me, one hot hand on my thigh, the other caressing the back of my neck, making the hair stand on end. His bad breath so close to my face, I could breathe nothing but beer, garlic, and sweating male.

Cold chills dried the sweat between my shoulder blades.

I kicked him hard on the shin. My toes screamed as if I'd slammed them into a steel bank vault.

A mistake.

He slapped a beefy leg over both my thighs and tightened his grip on my nape.

He pushed his face close to mine. Our noses bumped. "You make any waves over your father's death, and you…will…hurt." He squeezed my neck hard. "One word, and you're very sad."

"Ow!" I believed him. Like I hadn't already lost all feeling in my fingers and my neck wasn't already bruised and smarting like a hot pepper. A chill that made me shudder iced that heat. I knew he could hurt me a lot more. He knew it too.

"Your old man was a dirty PI. Leave the case there."

At that point, I knew P.J. wasn't going to kill me. But the trembling that shook my body came from wondering how far he'd go to make me obey.

"Understand?"

I tried to nod, but he held my neck in such a vise, I couldn't.

"You tell anyone about tonight, and those cute little sisters of yours won't make it home from school. You'll never see them again."

"You better not touch—"

"Shut up." He squeezed the back of my neck so hard I couldn't breathe. Shockwaves of pain shot up and down my arms.

"Don't dig into things you've no business shoving your nose into." He released my neck, and I gulped air. "You think anyone's going to take your word over mine?"

He had a point. Without proof positive, no policeman would believe me. P.J. was a long-time officer. And as far as I knew, a respected one.

When I could speak, I said, "I've been working on Matt Murdock's kidnapping."

His eyebrows vaulted to his receding hairline. His two-hundred-ninety-plus pounds jerked back against the cushion, bouncing me against the door. He recovered quickly and seized both my arms in a vise. Helpless as a target on the pistol range, my teeth rattled while he shook me.

He bellowed, "I know exactly what's going on in this town. I better never hear you're trying to fabricate evidence against the brotherhood to whitewash your old man's name. I know you're in cahoots with Frank McCoy and Stryker Black. You stick your pretty little snout back into domestic disputes and adulterous couples, and leave police work up to the experts."

He shook me until my breath came in big gasping pants then released my arms. Though I could barely see his face, I felt the heat of his glare. "It's real easy to arrest your little sisters, make them disappear, and no one is ever the wiser." His growl came from somewhere deep inside his chest, like the snarl of a pit bull. "When I say you'll hurt, you'll wish you were dead."

I'd heard of teens in Dallas being kidnapped and ending up as sex slaves in China. Austin and San Antonio had tracked missing girls to the Mexican border and then lost them. I didn't want that nightmare for my sisters. I didn't want this monster anywhere near them.

I recovered my breath enough to say, "If anything ever happens to the twins, I know exactly where to look f—"

"You won't be able to look for anybody. You'll be inside a body bag."

Okay, so I believed him.

"Now, then, do we have to go through this whole thing again?" He grabbed the back of my neck where bruises already made my skin tender and squeezed tight enough to make my head throb. "Or you got the message?"

I was feeling pretty wrung out by then. "I hear you."

He sat beside me, breathing heavily for a full five minutes while I prayed for escape. Neither of us spoke.

Finally, the cushions groaned and the stench of his body lessened as P.J. moved across the seat toward the other door. A wave of clean, breathable air hit me then the door clicked shut. He leaped into the front seat faster than I thought a beefy man could move, locked the crime-proof locks, screeched the black-and-white into reverse, and sped back to where he'd shoved me into his squad car.

He pulled up behind Mom's Lexus, and I started to breathe easier. Except for an occasional late-night driver, traffic had pretty much emptied from Preston Road. Finally he opened his door and climbed into the backseat close to me.

"Make me feel sure you got the message."

Again he dropped his hot hand onto my thigh. A shudder shook me. *Oh, God, not again!*

Something in his tone and body language made me wonder if I'd ever get out of that squad car. The windows were tinted so dark even someone walking by couldn't see inside. "Look, you made your point."

"You gonna keep your trap shut?"

Now I'd made that pesky vow. I wouldn't lie under any circumstances. So what could I do?

"You ain't saying nothin'. Remember, the law has a long arm. I can get to you and your sisters anywhere…anytime…anyplace."

My voice only trembled a little. "You made that quite clear."

"Swear to me you'll leave your old man's death right where it lies."

My head pounded, my wrists ached, my hands were numb, my neck pulsed, my arms hurt. And let's admit it, the big man scared me. I tried side-stepping.

"You want me to never investigate the case that painted my father a criminal."

"You got it, toots."

"Because you're involved."

I thought he'd hit me. In the dim light from the distant streetlamp, I saw the reflexive jerk of his arm and hand.

"I ain't involved. What affects one man in the department affects us all. I don't want any dirt thrown on the brotherhood." He tightened that painful hold on my thigh until I squealed. "Understand?"

"Not guilty? But you'd murder me and kidnap my sisters?"

He cursed. "Look, lady, you got more guts than brains. Just leave it that something real bad will happen to all of you if you mess with that dead case."

"I understand."

He heaved a deep sigh. Then he fumbled in the dark for the keys hanging on his utility belt. He jerked my arms around, unlocked the cuffs, opened my door, and head-butted me out into the empty street.

"Get lost before I change my mind and make you wish you'd never thought of sticking your beak where it don't belong."

"Um—my purse."

He threw my shoulder bag into the street. It thudded heavily at my feet.

Late that night, lying in bed between my own clean, vanilla-scented sheets, I still shook.

But I had learned a few things. Number one: There was a dirty police officer in the Dallas department. Maybe more than one. And they didn't want me to clear my dad's name.

Number two: Samantha Parker knew something about Matt's kidnapping, but she was scared and wasn't talking.

Number three: I had to move out of Mom's house. I didn't want any bad guys I encountered in my work coming after my family. If I didn't live with my loved ones, I'd have at least one degree of separation.

Number four: Always carry my weapon. Although tonight using my gun wouldn't have been a good idea. Shooting a police officer never goes over with the cops. Being the daughter of a PI who'd supposedly gone over to the dark side, I already stood on shaky ground.

Number five: Did P.J. connect Dad's murder with Matt's

kidnapping? Were the two related? If so, how?

I overslept Monday morning and almost missed seeing The Flowers and Allison off to school.

Sunlight glinted through the window, highlighting Allison's golden hair and puckered brow. As she pushed crisp bacon around her scrambled eggs, she didn't seem hungry

"Holly, I tried to call Chuck to ask him to tell Mom where I am, but he didn't answer his phone. I called right after supper last night, and before I went to bed, and again this morning."

"He's probably just away from his phone." I sipped my strong, fragrant coffee, feeling my stomach tighten as I lost my own appetite.

She laid her fork carefully on the glass table and looked at me with her blue eyes wide. "He keeps his phone hooked to his jeans."

A knife of fear slipped into my tired brain. "Maybe it's not charged."

"He never forgets to charge his phone. He doesn't want to miss a wrestling gig or a garage customer…or me. I only call him when I need him bad."

I glanced at Mom, hoping she had a solution. I'd not had time to check with Allison's mother about keeping the child at our house for a while to separate her from the live-in boyfriend. So we'd agreed last night to drive Allison to her school, contact her mom, and ask if we could keep the girl until the live-in cooled off, and go from there. We had to find out what CPS would let us do, or if they'd put Allison into a foster home. We didn't have a license.

When Mom raised her brows and shook her head, I said, "I'm driving over to visit your mother first thing this morning, Allison.

We'll talk, decide some issues, and then Mom will pick you up early from your school this afternoon before your mother's live-in has a chance to find you. How's that?'

"Awesome." Her lips curved into a smile, but her hands fluttered like butterflies unable to find a place to land. "Only…I'm worried about Chuck."

I pushed my untouched eggs away. So was I.

"Okay. Just to ease your heart, after I talk with your mom, I'll drive over to Arena Repair and check up on him."

I had some questions for Chuck. Then I'd visit Jason Jetter.

CHAPTER EIGHTEEN

On the way to the trailer park, I held down the pedal pretty hard when my cell started playing "When the Saints Go Marching In."

I clicked on my Blue Tooth. "Holly here."

"It's Stryker."

The usually smooth baritone sounded rough, and the silence began to drag.

"Yes?" My heart quickened inside my tightened chest. Had the tough PI found Matt?

"Can you meet me at Arena Repair ASAP?"

"Did you find Matt?"

"No. Take it easy. It's not Matt."

My pulse and breathing slowed until they were nearly normal.

"Are you okay?" Matt's voice sounded like he soothed a child…or a hysterical woman.

I guess my response hadn't been as calm as I'd wanted. So he hadn't found Matt's body. My brain cells ignited. Then a chill washed over me. Somewhere deep down inside, I knew why he'd called. *Oh, dear Father God, no! Please…* "It's bad news, isn't it?" I gripped the steering wheel hard.

"Where are you?"

"Driving on 75 toward Allison's home."

"Okay. I want you to slow down, pull into the right lane, and take the next exit."

My hands started to shake. For once in my life, I obeyed. My intuition told me I didn't want to hear his news. "Shoot. I'm turning on Renner Road."

"Okay. Now pull into the first residential area and park."

Like a robot, I obeyed, numb from head to toes. Had P.J. kidnapped the twins?

As soon as the wheels brushed the curb in front of some brick ranch homes, I said, "I'm parked."

"Engine turned off?"

"Yes. For heaven's sake, what's the news?"

"It's bad. It's Chuck Eggleston. He's dead."

Blood rushed from my head. The tree-lined street outside my window began to spin. I rested my forehead on the steering wheel. I hated when my gut was right. "When? How?" My voice sounded small.

"I know this is hitting you hard. I've seen your sympathy for the guy. When you're feeling better, meet me at Arena Repair. You can see for yourself."

A good ten minutes later, when the landscape returned to normal and so had my stomach, I felt well enough to turn on the engine and head south to Chuck's place. Since I had a hard time maintaining concentration, I exited 75, drove slowly, and made a couple wrong turns before I managed to pull up behind the lines of police cars stacked around the new automotive shop.

Yellow crime-scene tape surrounded the entire end of the block. The white van with "Forensic" painted on the side and the Medical Examiner's van each parked near the front of the shop.

I slid to the curb across the street, turned off the engine, stagnated and stared.

Cops and official-looking people in suits swarmed from one end of Arena Repair to the other. Some held cameras, some paper evidence bags, and some barked into radios or cellphones. An ambulance slowly pulled out of the drive, no lights or siren blaring.

While I tried to put my emotions back where they belonged, Stryker walked over. I pushed the button, and the window rolled down.

"Mind if I sit with you?"

I clicked open the lock on the passenger side, and he slid in.

He didn't ask if I was okay. It was pretty obvious I wasn't. Actually, he didn't look so great himself. Bags puffed under his dark eyes.

"Sorry I had to tell you over the phone."

"Yeah."

"It was murder."

"How?"

"You don't want to know."

"I have to."

Stryker sucked in a deep breath and narrowed his eyes as if he had a personal score to settle. "Someone tied him up then crushed him beneath a Hummer. Officers found four jack-stands nearby. The killer jacked the truck up on the stands, shoved Chuck under the Hummer, and kicked away the stands."

I dropped my head in my hands. If Stryker had knocked me out with a gut punch, I couldn't have felt it more. When I could speak, I asked, "Was he conscious when they murdered him?"

"Looked like he was."

I lost it then. Right there on the console between us. Some vomit flecked over onto Stryker's neat black suit. He didn't even jump away.

Just held out both hands to steady me, took out a clean handkerchief and wiped my mouth. Then he sopped up what he could from the leather seat, reached into my red bag, pulled out some wipes, and cleaned up the rest.

We languished in silence. As I tried to erase the picture of Chuck's last moments from my mind, deep anger hardened my heart. I would settle this score too. After a while, I quit trembling. "What exactly are jack-stands? Are they the same as jacks?"

"No. Not jacks. Jack-stands look like eighteen-inch-high oil derricks. They operate with a jack-handle and have a saucer-type top. You put the jack-stand under the car frame and use the handle to pump it to the right height to set under the frame and hold up a car. Use a jack-stand in each corner of the car to get it high enough to work beneath it."

I swallowed hard, the picture in my mind making me even more determined to find Chuck's killer. "So the murderer didn't even try to make Chuck's death look like an accident. Did the police find anything? Fingerprints? I see they have a full forensics crew working."

"They're not talking."

"Can we get hold of the report?"

"Frank'll get it for me."

"I'm going over. I can't see anything from here except officials swarming the place."

I had my hand on the door handle when Stryker reached over the console and parked his hand on my arm, his shoulder brushing me. "I don't think you should."

"Walk over with me. Help me gain entrance through the police barricade." His face was so close, I saw indents where his dimples showed during the infrequent times he smiled.

He blew out a breath, drew his hand away, and slid back into his seat. "If you promise not to look at Chuck." He frowned. "You'll never see anything worse, no matter how long your detective career." He opened his car door. "I should have my head examined."

I hopped out. He lifted the yellow plastic, and we walked together toward the front of the shop. The killers hadn't even tried to hide the death scene. I sidled just close enough to see Chuck's legs, his feet splayed to the side.

A photographer was shooting multiple views of his body. A videographer circled the scene and recorded everything in the vicinity. A man and a woman held a measuring tape from the body to the exact location of all the objects in the area near and around the front of the shop. Nearer to the body, a man stood in front of a computer positioned on one of the new tool carts. He had the laptop opened and sketched the crime scene, aided by his CAD software program.

A man I recognized as the new Medical Examiner knelt by the body, taking temperature and doing other things to ascertain when Chuck had been murdered. He put some instruments back into his bag and took out several paper bags. Though I couldn't see him, I knew he slipped the bags over Chuck's hands. I remembered those young hands knuckling desperately at his eyes after I pepper-sprayed him. I gagged.

A man standing by, holding a large tarp, stepped toward me. I waved him off.

Even from where I stood, I saw and smelled huge quantities of blood. A woman wearing a dark pantsuit used markers and placards to show the blood splatter. I turned away. I hoped Stryker was right. I never wanted to witness such a brutal crime scene again.

"When you get the report, will you share it with me?"

Stryker cleared his throat and loosened his tie. "You should let the police handle this case from here on in."

Tears were bursting through the dam, and I couldn't hold them off much longer. My throat clogged. "Chuck was so proud of his shop." Then I jerked up my head. "You think Matt's dead too?"

"The only thing I know for sure is that he's in danger…and so are you. Be reasonable. Holly, please let the police handle this."

"You don't think Matt's dead?"

Stryker put his arm around me and steered me back to my car. "The kidnappers don't have whatever it is they want yet. Matt's no good to them dead." He opened the passenger door for me.

"How do you know that?" As I crawled into the seat, my mind reeled.

"Trust me. I know." He stood by my open door.

Before I could question him, my thoughts flashed back to Chuck. I took a stab at being professional and calm. "So Chuck did his job, provoked the fight, and got Matt kidnapped. After that he was no more use to them, and they didn't want any loose ends."

"You got it."

Then slobbery, choking, hiccuping tears erupted. Stryker knelt beside me, half inside the car. He took me in his arms. Hardly knowing what I was doing, I wet down the front of his shirt, his suit, his tie, and probably his nerves. My eyes scrunched shut, my lips pressed against the slightly rough texture of his suit, and I babbled.

"I never told Chuck about how much Jesus loves him. How Jesus could forgive him for his part in the kidnapping. How he could become a child of God. I never told him!" My voice rose all on its own. "Oh, Stryker, I never told Chuck how to gain eternal life. Now he's entered eternity, and it's too late for him!"

Stryker massaged his hand through my hair, his strong, warm fingers easing the tension in my scalp. His heart pounded under my cheek, and I realized he was taking Chuck's death hard too. Finally my tears ran dry, but my heart felt like one of Chuck's heavy wrenches had worked it over. I straightened.

"I'm sorry." My eyes burned, my nose was running, and my face was wet.

Stryker rummaged in my purse and came up with some tissues. He handed them to me, and I cleaned up my face as best I could. So much for being professional.

"You've nothing to be sorry for. Chuck was a good kid. Dumb. He did something he shouldn't have and paid dearly for his mistake."

I choked down another bout of tears. "He wanted to better himself. He wanted to own that repair shop."

"But just to set the record straight, church isn't for everybody." A muscle in his lean cheek bulged. All the sympathy inside him had turned hard. Buried deep. "Don't go there with *me*."

The rigid tone of his voice told me that conversation was over.

I swallowed. "Okay." I looked out the window.

His smooth, warm baritone was back. "Police are packing up."

If Stryker didn't want to talk about eternity now, there was nothing more I could say. For now. "What will happen to the shop?"

"Dunno. Go back to the bank, or maybe his brothers will take the business over."

"You know about his brothers?"

Stryker gave me a sad, crooked smile. "Sure, Bloodhound. I know everything you know about this case. Probably more. So lay off it, will you?"

I hurt too much to answer.

I sat in silence until he scrambled off his knees, zipped around to the driver's side, and slid behind the wheel.

The squad cars pulled away, leaving the repair shop looking empty and forlorn, bound inside yellow tape.

"You okay now?"

I sniffed and blew my nose on one of the tissues. "Yeah."

"I gotta get to work." He put a big hand on the door latch. "You want to go for a cup of coffee before I leave?"

"I'll be fine."

"Sure?" He smiled that enticing way that weakened my knees even after this tragedy.

"Yeah."

He reached over and gently rubbed a thumb across my lips. "Go home, take a shower, get a massage. Do whatever you do to relax. Chuck's not your problem now."

I forced a smile and thought, *Yes he is. He'll always be. I'll never, never again put off telling someone who needs to hear about God's gift of eternal life.*

I drove home. The clock read fifteen after three before I felt recovered enough to go on with my life. I showered and changed my stinky clothes. *Thank you, God, that Jose took the train to Ft. Worth and retrieved Dad's Toyota from the police impound. Looks like I'll be driving it until I get my Jeep.* Before climbing into the SUV, I opened my ice chest to grab a Sprite to control the sickness still churning in my stomach. Grief would have to wait. I needed to talk with Mrs. Taylor before Allison spent another night at our home. I took a second gulp of Sprite. Sometime I had to go back to the Arena Repair and pick up my Jeep. Or would the police impound my wheels for forensics? I gulped.

Tonight I'd have to break the tragic news to Allison.

I set the Toyota in a straight line to her house.

She lived in a mobile home parked inside a trailer court on US

75. Except for being adjacent to one of the busiest freeways in Dallas, the park wasn't bad. It had trees, a Laundromat, and a gas station/ convenience store. Medium-sized trailers permanently anchored inside picket-fenced yards that wandered up a hill.

I rang the bell of one of the more attractive units. A tiny woman with Allison's big blue eyes, wearing a pink waitress uniform, opened the door.

"Hi. I'm Holly Garden. My mom called."

"Oh, yeah. You're the lady who found my baby." She waved an arm. "Come on in. Any friend of Alley-oop's a friend of mine. It sure was nice of you to take her in." She plunked down on a newish-looking overstuffed couch and patted the cushion beside her. "Here, sit down. Tell me what all the kid's into now. She don't say much when she puts in an appearance here." The woman's blonde curls, with white roots showing, shook from side to side as she moved her head. "Ain't you the pretty one? I always did say Alley could weasel out good friends for herself."

She picked up the TV remote and muted the blare, but her eyes kept straying from my face to the cop show she'd been watching. "Alley and Ben don't get along too well, you know. Ben don't like her backtalk." She smiled, showing either perfect teeth or a nice set of false ones. "Course, Ben's a real good step-dad, regardless of what my little fibber mighta told you." She lifted a graying eyebrow. "Why, he still likes her to sit on his lap, big girl that she is." As a cop chase began, her eyes fastened onto the TV. She clicked on the sound for a minute then muted the raucous noise again. "Yep, he even tucks her into bed some nights until she starts in on him."

Shivers sent me to the edge of the cushioned seat. "She starts in on him?"

"Yeah, the little monkey. She starts hollering for me. Like I don't have a carload of work to do when I get home at night. Like I don't have dishes and cleaning and washing and what-not to get done before I go to bed." She glanced at me, most of her attention on the muted TV. "I got to get my uniform washed and pressed for work the next day." She pushed herself back against the cushions and sighed. "I'm on my feet for ten hours at the restaurant. When I get home, I like to kick off the shoes and put my legs up." She put on a pitiful face. "Ben says no woman my age should work so hard. He says as soon as he gets on his feet, he'll bring in enough money so I can quit my job." She smiled. "Ben's a good man. He'll take care of me."

My stomach was in knots. "And you get home from work what time?"

"Oh, around ten-ish. If I don't have to work late. Then I don't get home 'til around eleven."

"So, Allison's home alone with Ben when he returns from work?"

"Oh, Ben don't have no job at the present time. He's been out looking and collecting unemployment and food stamps. I just don't know what we'd do without his unemployment and those food stamps. Lifesavers they are. You ever been unemployed?" She took a closer look at me. "You even work? You old enough?"

I wasn't about to be sidetracked by this poor woman whose mind flitted from one thing to another like a moth from one street light to the next. "So you're saying Ben is here in the trailer when Allison gets home from school."

"Sure. Wouldn't be good for her to come home to an empty house, now would it?"

"Does Ben drink?"

A sly look flashed across her face. "Oh, he'll take a tiny glass once in a while. It's hard on the man not finding work all these months. Not good for his self-es-es…not good for him, you know. So he kind of takes over the job of being daddy to Alley." She frowned. "Except Alley don't like him to boss her around."

Afraid I might get sick right in front of this misguided woman, I glanced around the small trailer for a bathroom. "What does Ben do when Allison...back-talks him?"

"Oh, locks her in her bedroom and one thing or another. He don't say much about it."

Suddenly Allison's mom seemed immersed in the TV show, though nothing much was happening. Her shoulders slumped.

"Mrs. Taylor..."

"Oh, my name's Lil. Lil Switzer." She was all smiles again. "Jill Taylor was my niece. She was Alley's mom. She disappeared when Alley was a year old. I've had the little fibber ever since. And a handful she's turned out to be." She leaned in close and whispered, "Just between you and me, sometimes I think about disappearing myself. You know how trying these teen-age girls can be. Always coming up with one weird story or another. Drama Queens, I think you call them."

"Did you ever think Allison's stories might not be just to gain attention? She might be telling the truth."

"Like I said..." Lil's once pretty mouth drew down at the corners, and her eyes narrowed. "...Alley fibs. She don't like Ben, even though he's been really good to her."

"How do you know her stories aren't true?" I kept the rage flooding every brain cell out of my tone.

"Cause." Lil sat up straight and patted her blonde curls. "Ben's not the first man that's found me attractive enough to move in. Before Gil left, Alley fibbed about him too."

Oh, dear God!

"And Gil was also a good stepfather?"

"Nope. Not him. He didn't want to go, but he packed up and left after Alley called the cops on him. She made up this story about him touching her, and Gil didn't want no part of that. So he up and left even before the cops got here. And because of that little fibber, me and her had to eat peanut-butter and jelly for weeks. Then I met Ben, and everything was all right again."

"You mean financially?"

"Yep. Ben's unemployment check gets us over the hump." Her eyes strayed back to the TV, and she turned the sound back on. "Ben's a good man. Don't know what Alley and me'd do without him."

"Does Allison know you're not her mother?"

"Nope. And don't you tell her neither. Wouldn't do her any good to know her own mother run out on her." She stood up. "Hey, you want a drink? I got beer, wine, spritzes." When I shook my head she added, "And I might have a root beer."

"Do you know Allison spends some of her time with a mechanic named Chuck Eggleston?"

"Oh, you mean Chuck the Tux. He's a professional wrestler, not a mechanic. And yeah, I know Chuck. Chuck lets Alley have a slumber party at his place whenever Alley gets an itch to run off. Alley's got itchy feet just like her mom. Don't surprise me none she's that way. Apples don't fall very far from their tree."

"Allison said she goes to Chuck when Ben gets drunk and hits her."

Lil sighed. "Alley fibs. I told you. I told them children's workers when they came snooping around. I told Chuck. I'll stand on my rooftop and yell to the whole world: 'Alley fibs.' Her ma did. She does." Lil stood and jammed her hands on her hips. Her voice rose with each word. "Drama Queens, the both of them. If Alley keeps it up, I'll wash my hands of her. She run off one good man, and I won't let her run off Ben."

I rose, but I wasn't ready to leave yet. "Do you mind if Allison stays at our home for a while? Say…a few weeks until Ben cools off?"

Lil scratched her head and frowned. "Let me think on that." She tripped the few feet to the kitchen, pulled open the refrigerator door, and brought out a beer.

Being the nosy person I am, I leaned over far enough so that I could peek inside. I saw lots of beer and wine bottles, some wilted lettuce, some moldy-looking cheese, but no other food.

She popped the top and was in the middle of a drink when the trailer door flew open.

A tall, thin man about thirty-five with stringy brown hair to his shoulders and a wispy goatee stopped short in the doorway when he saw me.

"Well, howdy there." He glanced at Lil. "What do we have here?"

"This here's Holly. She's asking about Alley-oop."

Lil reached back into the refrigerator and pulled out another can of beer, popped the top, and handed the drink to the man, her non-stop chatter mysteriously stilled.

"Hello. You must be Ben." I stuck out my hand.

Ben took my hand, but he didn't shake it. Just held it. And held it. And held it.

I pulled free.

He grabbed the beer and drank the whole can in one loud, noisy gulp, his Adam's apple moving up and down his wiry throat. "A man gets mighty thirsty when he's out looking for work." He slammed the empty can on the counter. "Give me another."

Lil already had the lid popped and handed it to him. She didn't say a word.

I glanced at my watch. It was 3:45. Just about time that Allison would have shown up from school…if she'd been coming.

"Oh, bother. Now look what you did. All this talking, and you made me late for work." Lil smoothed her uniform, grabbed an oversized purse from the Formica counter, and brushed past Ben on her way to the door. "Dinner's in the oven. It's warm and ready for you to dig in."

Ben headed for the kitchen and poked his head into the oven.

I put a hand on Lil's arm. "What about Allison? Do I have your permission?"

She glanced over her shoulder at Ben then back at me. Her finger to her lips was so fast, I almost missed it. "Sure. Keep her as long as you want," she whispered.

"Would you put that in writing?"

"Sure. Leave your address. I gotta go."

Then she was out the door so fast the screen slammed in my face. And I was alone with Ben.

"Well now, don't be in no hurry to leave on my account." He dropped down on the rust-colored sofa. "If you want to see Alley-baby, just sit here by me. She'll walk in that door any minute now." He kicked off his shoes, propped his stocking feet on the coffee table, and leaned back. "We got more beer."

"Uh, no thanks." I stood, sidled to the door, and put one hand on the handle. "So you know Chuck Eggleston?"

"Sure. His oldest brother was in my class in high school. Him and me, we're buddies."

"Are you a wrestler too?" I couldn't picture this scarecrow-looking man in tights or a tux.

"Naw. I'm more what you might call their manager. I get them gigs now and again."

"Did you get them the gig at the Sheraton Hotel on February

fourteenth?"

"Hmm. Let me think." He patted a cushion on the couch next to him. "No need for you to stand there. Come sit down."

I wasn't budging. "I'm leaving. I have an appointment." As stealthily as I could I slid one of my brand-new Holly Garden, Private Investigator business cards from my purse and tucked a corner of it under the toaster on the counter. Then I turned toward Ben, blocking my card with my back.

"Do you recall the Valentine Meet-A-Thon?"

"Sure. That was a highfaluting gig. All the bros went."

"Did you set up the medics too?"

"Right on, sister." He smiled. If the odor from his clothes hadn't already clued me in, his yellow teeth answered where the stale cigarette smell that permeated the place came from.

"I need to get in touch with them about their pay. Do you have addresses?" I wasn't lying. I needed to find out exactly who had paid them.

"I take care of all the pay. You hand it over; I'll see they get it."

Did this moron take me for stupid? "I have to talk with them personally. How about a phone number?"

"Here's a number for you." He leered and scribbled on a piece of paper. "It's mine." He rose and came toward me.

CHAPTER NINETEEN

Tires screeching, I laid rubber leaving the trailer park.

As long as Ben lived there, I could never, never return Allison to that place.

I so wanted to be a light in the dark underbelly of society. Well, I was trying, and that's all God asked of me. Just to let my light shine. But I hadn't done a lot of good in that pathetic situation. After I received that written permission to keep Allison, I'd contact Lil again and ask her if I could go through the court system and gain legal guardianship. Lil appeared to think the girl a burden and might appreciate getting her off her hands. If that didn't work, I'd call in CPS myself.

That evening after dinner, I walked Allison up the wide, curved staircase to her room. She plunked stomach-first on the bed, and I slid down next to her. I put my hand on her arm and told her about Chuck. She burrowed into me like a stray puppy looking for shelter from the rain and cried herself to sleep. I lowered her gently against the pink pillowcase and tucked the rainbow spread under her chin. I stood there staring down at her sweet face, wishing I could have told her Chuck was with the Lord in a better place. But I as far as I knew, he wasn't.

So I tiptoed out and called Temple. I needed to hear her lilting voice.

She answered on the first ring.

She asked about Matt, and I brought her up to speed. Then I told her about Chuck and updated her on Allison.

"Hey, girlfriend, sounds like you need cheering up. My friend called me about the airplane hangar he converted into apartments. He invited us to drop over to Addison and take a look. Now a good time for you?"

"Couldn't be better. I'll pick you up in ten minutes."

Temple lived with her mom and two brothers just this side of North Park Shopping Center in an enclave of large ranch-type homes with manicured lawns. She and I had recently talked of taking an apartment together. She'd discovered the converted hanger that bordered Addison Airport through one of her scores of male admirers. We'd been waiting for the conversion to be completed before deciding if we could afford to take the big leap. Recent events with P.J. convinced me I had to move out on my own. However, my paltry paycheck wouldn't cover much. Sharing rent with Temple and taking advantage of whatever arrangement her friend offered might allow us to swing the deal.

My headlights swept over her waiting on the front porch. Almost before I braked, she ran down to duck into the car. As I backed out of her long drive, I warned her that sharing an apartment with me might expose her to danger.

She tossed back her sleek shoulder-blade length hair and laughed. "Danger doesn't even begin to compare to torturing brothers and a high-pressure mom."

I laughed and entered the ramp to 75, then headed north toward Belt Line Road. When I briefed her on Chuck's murder, tears streamed down my face before I knew they were coming.

"I'm so sorry, Holly. But seriously, I think you should back off and let the police search for Matt. Murder isn't your field."

"If Matt hadn't been kidnapped, I'd agree. But he's my friend." I gripped the steering wheel tighter. "Besides, the police and Jake Henderson are also looking for him."

"I think Matt would be the first to warn you to stay safe and let the police find him."

"You're right. He's always been *over*-protective."

She gripped my arm so I almost drove over the lane line into a white van. "You're not going to quit, are you?" Her eyes were wide with fear for me. "You're so stubborn."

"I'll be careful."

"Sure, like you always are. That's how you earned your nickname—Hazardous Holly."

I giggled. Even though she was bullheaded about wanting me to quit the investigation, being with Temple always made me feel better. "Girl, I earned that nickname way back in grade school."

"Middle school."

"But I'm all grown up now."

"Haven't changed."

"Anyway, you better think hard about us rooming together." I took the right turn from Beltline Road into Airport Drive as I repeated PJ's threats.

"No worries. Hoku lives downstairs in one of the apartments. He'll make it a point to be home at night whenever I am. You remember Hoku?"

I grinned, feeling easy for the first time since P.J. released me. "Yeah, the guy with all the muscles that's half-Polynesian. No way could I forget him."

Temple showed her dimples. "And remember, nothing happens to us that God doesn't allow." Her faith in God's care morphed over to me and I relaxed. "So we've got God and our own private bodyguard watching over us."

I grinned. "Ditto for me with this investigation."

"Holly, it's not the same thing. Going after Matt is dangerous…."

"Same God."

"Okay, where's your bodyguard?"

I glanced again in my rearview, sure Stryker couldn't be far behind. "I don't see him. He's too good at tailing to let me on to him if he doesn't want me to know he's back there."

Temple snorted. "You're talking about that PI, Stryker Black." As I drove close to the apartment, she pulled out her compact and refreshed her lip gloss. The strawberry scent wafted over to pleasantly tease my nose. "He's got his work cut out for him."

Addison Municipal Airport squats in the middle of the city. A popular string of restaurants make piles of money just across the street from the runway. Airline Drive, a wide two-lane boulevard, intersects Beltline Road, circles the airport, and exits back on Beltline Road.

I cruised slowly past the door of the last hangar. The building was a big steel affair that looked like it could house the Concord. A red Mazda RX8 parked in the first slot of four, right next to the building. I slid the SUV in the second slot and wondered when I'd get my Jeep back from the crime scene.

"Hoku's here. That's his car." Temple slid out from the passenger side and smoothed her denim mini-skirt down over her slender thighs. Her expensive snake-skin cowboy boots crunched on the graveled drive.

"That skirt and those gray boots are bound to help our case," I joked.

"That's the plan."

Before we made our way up the short walk, Hoku opened the door and stepped out onto the concrete block that served as a porch. He gave us a wide grin. Or I should say, he bathed Temple in the grin. He barely noticed me.

Where did Temple find these guys? I'd met him one night at a candlelit restaurant, but he'd been seated, and I hadn't been able to see just how big he was. Hot didn't even come close to describing this male. Hoku stood at least six-four with shoulders wide enough to play linebacker for the Dallas Cowboys. His dark hair had just the right wave and length to make a woman want to run her hands through the thick softness. Brown eyes sparkled and smoldered above chiseled cheekbones and wide, sensuous lips. He smelled of Nautica. I suddenly felt sorry for Frank McCoy.

Hoku waved a brown, very capable-looking hand toward a side door of the hangar. "After you, ladies."

Temple led the way. The door opened into a cavernous interior large enough to house three private airplanes. Tonight only a bright red plane parked there, with Cessna 150 painted on the side. Further in, a polished propeller blade serving as modern art was planted in front of a partitioned area near the rear of the hangar.

Hoku opened a door in the brick partition. We walked in to face a paneled wall with two doors spaced equal-distance apart.

"You prefer up or down?"

Temple and I locked glances. We both shrugged and said together, "Up."

He grinned like he'd known we'd choose up. "Okay. All four apartments are identical. I'll show you the one just above mine." He opened the door to the right, and we entered a small hall that held another door and a long flight of stairs.

"This door leads to my apartment and the stairs to yours. The other two apartments have their own entrance on the opposite side."

I figured if Hoku were home, he could hear us or anyone else climb those stairs to the upstairs apartment. The knowledge sent a warm hand of comfort around me. "Are there back doors?"

As if he'd just now noticed Temple wasn't alone, Hoku glanced at me. "Nope, just the front ones. Is that a problem?"

From the tone of his voice and the appeal in his posture, I gathered if a back door had been needed, Hoku would have carved one out on the spot.

"No. No. One door is great." Would I someday wish for a back exit?

Temple smiled and motioned for me to go first. I knew she'd undulate up those rather steep stairs in front of Hoku, taking total advantage of her short skirt and long legs.

Whatever it took. Neither of us earned much money, and Temple's two brothers drove her wild with their loud, intrusive personalities. Plus her mother was as bossy as mine and kept talking about ticking clocks and grandbabies.

With the key Hoku handed me, I opened the steel door at the top of the stairs. The scent of fresh vanilla welcomed us.

We entered a tiny foyer that led to a small living room furnished with a white overstuffed sofa and two inviting taupe chairs. A coffee table with matching end tables rested on a white faux fur rug. I knelt and ran my fingers through the soft fur. The whole décor was white and taupe with spots of red color on cushions and—I gaped—a vase of live, long-stemmed scarlet roses. A sweet scent wafted from the vase on the counter between the kitchen and living room. I eased my attention from that romantic touch to the wide-planked cherry hardwood floors, polished to high gloss. The galley-type kitchen was finished in stainless steel with black appliances.

I dragged in a long breath. No way could we manage the rent for a dream place like this.

But Temple let her dimples play and looked confident.

The small bathroom had a glassed-in shower and modern toilet. In an alcove in front, a vanity table with lighted mirrors held two sinks. I ran my fingers over the lovely marble counter...space for all things girly.

The apartment had two bedrooms as promised. A double bed, chest of drawers, and a dresser overflowed each one. But a new pillow-top mattress had me daydreaming about what comforter and pillow set I would add. The place was small, but the well-utilized space made it seem larger.

Temple merely glanced at the bedrooms and focused her attention on Hoku.

"Pets are allowed, of course?"

Hoku wore his heart on his face. Confusion turned to dismay, which morphed into compliance. "Very small ones. What do you have in mind?"

"Just a bird."

Oh, no! Temple wasn't really thinking of carting over the famous Macaw? The blue and gold giant had a cage big enough for two large huskies and a voice clamorous enough to wake Hoku in his downstairs bedroom from a dead sleep.

Then again, Cha Cha would make a good watchdog.

"A bird." Hoku's Adam's apple traveled up and down his throat. "Oh, yeah. A pet as small as a bird would work."

I'm sure if Temple had asked to bring a full-grown elephant, Hoku would have found room.

After we both wrote checks, we went down to Hoku's apartment to celebrate with sodas. The decorator apparently hadn't peeked inside his pad. Though his apartment had an identical floor plan, his was strictly male—Spartan and utilitarian. Did he have the upstairs one professionally decorated to entice Temple?

I'd had a hard day, so we didn't stay long. I dropped off Temple at her home after firming plans to move into our new place that weekend. I must have had my foot hard on the pedal because I made it home in record time. I was super-jazzed to be making the big move. Now I would really be on my own. This was a good end to a really, really bad day.

When I pulled up to Mom's, my headlights beamed on my Jeep parked in front of the veranda.

I squealed and did a fist pump.

Screeching to a stop behind Bunny, I jumped out and ran to inspect her injured front bumper.

Perfect. Couldn't even tell the metal had been crumpled.

I glanced up at the picture window in the living room and glimpsed Mom handing something to Stryker.

My emotions jumped track as I ignited into Spook Mode.

Obviously they heard me drive up because Stryker stashed whatever was in his hand into his inside jacket pocket and stepped back to within conventionally accepted speaking distance from my mom. She touched a finger to her lips and edged further from him.

I stood rooted to the spot. Why would Stryker be with Mom? From the moment they'd met at the Valentine Meet-a-Thon, she'd shown him open hostility. I'd seen her pay him for the Valentine job. Why was he here?

Sure, he must have delivered my Jeep, but that didn't explain why they both looked so guilty when they realized I'd seen them. What had Stryker hidden in his suit pocket? Why hadn't he told me when I saw him earlier today that he planned to see Mom? A memory I hadn't had time to explore flashed to the surface of my mind. When Mom realized Stryker and I had been together the day Chuck's loaner car crashed, she'd said something odd. I'd wanted to ask her about that.

I replayed the words in my mind. Mom had said, "Were you on the job when you were with Holly?" And Stryker had answered, "Yes." He emphasized, "I *was* on the job." Then Mom looked relieved and went on with dinner without trying harder to get rid of Stryker.

A lightbulb exploded in my mind. An epiphany. The missing piece of the puzzle.

I stampeded up the steps, thundered across the veranda, and slammed the door open.

They stood in the hall. Mom's arms were crossed, ready to do battle. Stryker, to-die-for hair mussed like he'd run his hand through the strands one too many times, fists hidden in his pants pockets, looked like a kid caught red-handed at his school locker with drugs inside.

My anger turned to a lump twisting my stomach.

"You thought I wouldn't find out!" I knew my voice was on the shrill side, but I didn't care.

"Now, Holly, it's not that I didn't trust you." Mom wasn't backing down a millimeter.

"Trust! You talk about trust. It's not like I can put a dollar in a vending machine and pull the lever for a bottle of trust." I looked wildly around the hallway, thinking I might throw something at Stryker. "How can I ever trust either of you again?"

For once the smooth-talking Stryker had his mouth clamped shut.

His silence confirmed his guilt.

"So that's why you skulked around Dolly's Donuts the day Frank and I were shot at." I shook my head. "That's why you were angel-on-the-spot when the loaner car's brakes failed—and driving an ice cream truck at that!" I thought back to the times I'd tried to get an answer from him about why he'd be driving an ice cream truck. He'd alluded to being "on the job" and changed the subject. I jammed my hands on my hips, but hot tears pricked my eyes. "So that's why you followed me to the Lone Star Grill to meet Chuck."

"It's not like that, Princess."

Both Mom and I stared at Stryker like he'd really overstepped boundaries.

"Don't call me Princess." I gazed at Mom, so mad I could spit. "And Mom, I'm moving out."

I hadn't meant to break the news so callously and immediately felt awful.

Her face paled and she reached for support, Stryker's strong right arm being handy.

"I'm sorry, Mom." I turned my glare to Stryker. "You should have told me Mom paid you to…to what? Follow me and keep me out of trouble? To make sure that when I found Matt you'd step in and take the credit for your firm?" I frowned at Stryker and turned back to Mom. "You *want* Dad's firm to go under. You want me out of the PI business. You want me in some safe, boring job…" I sputtered. "You want me married to a lawyer and pregnant."

I pushed past them and aimed for the stairs.

Stryker caught my arm and wouldn't let me go, his sandalwood scent wrapping around me.

"It's not like that. Your Mom wanted me to protect you. To follow you at a distance and make sure you didn't get hurt." He scowled. "There's no stepping-in-and-taking-credit thing going on."

I pulled back and withered him with a look. "You're fired. Get out."

Jerking my arm free before either of them could see the tears spilling over, I ran up the stairs and into my room.

Mom still expected me to fail.

Then all those lonely nights after being left at the altar plugged into me like so many electric sockets and emitted painful shock after painful shock.

Angel was such a disappointment.

He couldn't be trusted. Only paid.

What a jerk. I've had it with men! Especially guys with dangerous jobs. Okay, from this moment on I'll only let myself get interested in men who don't carry weapons. Yep, that'll be my motto....

CHAPTER TWENTY

The heavenly scent of hazelnut coffee forced my eyes open.

Granny set the tray of coffee on the night stand and sank down on the edge of my bed. I held my hands over my ears because yesterday had been the second worst day of my life. I couldn't take any more bad news this morning.

Granny was never one to speak softly, and her penetrating voice and Available scent filtered through my defense.

"Putting criminals behind bars isn't listed in 1 Corinthians 12 as a spiritual gift, but that's your gift. God wouldn't put you in the middle of Matt's kidnapping if He didn't expect you to rescue your friend."

I caught my breath, lowered my hands, and turned toward her wrinkled face.

Her lidded eyes blinked fast, and a worry line cut deeply into her corrugated forehead. "Remember, God Himself goes before you. He'll be with you."

"Oh, Granny, maybe I should leave Matt's kidnapping to the police. What have I really discovered?"

"Maybe you just need to brainstorm what you know a little. So far the kidnapper's been giving you the slip with all his feints and turns and double-backs." She handed me a cup of coffee.

I gave her a weak smile. I'd taught Granny all about dodging tails in a car, and she used that as a metaphor for solving a crime. Well, so criminals did work that way…but I didn't feel up to brainstorming. After Chuck's murder, Mom's lack of trust, and Stryker's turning out to be a paid protector, I'd decided I was in the wrong profession. I set the coffee on the end table to cool.

Granny ignored my pathetic head-shaking. "Okay, here's what we got. Sit up and write this down." She handed me a yellow pad and pencil.

"Matt was kidnapped at a Valentine party for millionaires, and he was definitely *not* bank-rolled."

Despite my self-pity, my brain perked up. "That's right. Why would a kidnapper ignore so much wealth and snatch a working guy?" Pretty dumb of me not to follow up this angle myself.

I straightened, fluffed up my pillows, reached for the steamy hot coffee Granny had brought, and settled back against my red Egyptian cotton pillowcases to work my brain.

"What would motivate someone to kidnap a private investigator?" I sipped the fragrant, strong java. "I thought at first the motive was unrequited love. What do you think?"

"Not with Matt, Peach Tree. He's been *gaga* over you for years."

"You knew?" Was it the coffee making me feel so hot all over?

"Everybody who doesn't need magnifying eyeglasses knows."

My weak tummy took a further tumble. The back of my eyelids pricked. What was wrong with me? My chin trembled. I shook my head. That's not me. I'm not a crier. I pulled in a deep breath. "Romance aside, why kidnap Matt?"

"Bejiggers, if anyone besides you could miss that he's young, buff, and looks like a million dollars. Don't throw romance out the door so fast."

"Maybe I missed that in Matt, but so is Frank…and Stryker…and maybe one or two other men who attended. So why Matt?"

"Granted, he wasn't the only beefcake there. What about his moonlighting?"

I ran my mind over the cases he'd worked with Frank that the police detective had left on my voice mail and the two I discovered at Matt's house. "Obstruction of justice, tampering with evidence, perjury, convicted felon—none worth kidnapping except the last, and that convict is still in jail. I do have two leads from Matt's moonlighting jobs to follow up."

Granny's hazel eyes sparkled. "How 'bout that stuff you call paper-hanging?"

"Lifting credit cards and forging checks? No. Matt didn't have any of those cases."

"Hookers? Dope Dealers? Skip trace? Registered sex offender?"

I couldn't help a grin. "Granny, I've taught you too much about private investigating. You should work cases."

"Darn tootin'."

"The kidnapper's motive isn't money. Thus the ransom note without a ransom demand. And it doesn't appear to be revenge. Do you think Matt's kidnapping is connected with Dad's murder?"

"Hard to tell on that one."

"Matt started to work for Dad about the time Dad was shot, but Matt had nothing to do with the case Dad and I worked. I don't see any connection." I bit my lip. "Besides, the cops want me to back away from re-opening Dad's case...and they didn't say anything about Matt."

Granny gave me a funny look, and I realized I hadn't told her about P.J.

Fortunately Granny let my slip go. "Well, let's table that one for now." She cupped her coffee in one hand and rustled around, making herself comfortable moving from my bed to the nearby lounge chair.

We sat in silence for a few minutes while I did a mental re-enactment of Matt's kidnapping. Once again I was on the floor under the table next to Stryker's unconscious body.

As if she read my mind, Granny chuckled. "That Stryker's a real beef-cake. Women of all ages would set their cap for him. Even if I used a walker, I'd still chase him down." Eyes twinkling, she set her empty coffee cup on the night stand.

A thought nagged my brain, but I couldn't get the nebulous thing into focus. "Uh huh." I was certain the answer was vital. But the more I tried to capture the thought, the faster it flashed away.

"I got the hunk's picture off his Facebook and took it into the Pet Spa. Even Sally Smith *oohed* and *aahed* over him. And you know Sally's tighter-laced than June Cleaver."

I shot up in bed, slid the covers off, and grabbed Granny's thin frame, pulling her right off the lounge. I twirled with her 'round and 'round my bedroom until I was dizzy. "That's it! That's it!"

Granny giggled. "Well, I'm glad to see you're over that depression."

"That's the answer!" I kissed Granny on both soft, wrinkled cheeks, then dashed into the business of dressing as if an ax murderer chased me.

"Aren't you going to finish your breakfast, Peach Tree?"

"No time. Don't tell Mom, but Matt's kidnapping was her fault. I'll be on my cell if you need me. Bye."

Investigator Rule #7: When You Know Motive, the Crime's Solved.

I jammed on the brakes in front of Ace Investigations just as a big Harley rocketed out of their parking garage.

Hair on the back of my neck synchronized with hair on my arms. Both bristled like brushes from a bottle-bush. The black helmet visor hid the driver's face, but something about his bigness and the way he sat on the powerful machine told me Stryker rode that hog.

Without even thinking, I morphed into tail mode. I fumbled inside my shoulder bag to make certain I'd brought my Glock.

After following discreetly for several miles, I had second thoughts and started looking for a place to make a U-turn. Suddenly the Harley swerved into the ramp leading to 635 west-bound toward Forth Worth. My blood electro-stated through my veins. Stryker was about to pull off something stupid. I just knew it. And I had a good idea what he planned. Executing that scheme would get him killed.

With traffic bumper-to-bumper and doing dodge-cars, I dared not remain too far to the rear. Stryker cut into the HOV lane, so I stuck close behind him but in the middle lane.

Reminding myself of Investigator Rule #4, I speed-dialed Uncle Robert and told him my epiphany about the kidnapper's motive and where I was going.

"Right, Holly. You're brilliant. I'm sending Jake as back-up."

Wanting to solve this case before Jake arrived to take over, I called Frank.

"I'm right behind you, Bloodhound."

"Thank, Flash."

I didn't know where Stryker headed, but I had a good idea. And his motive was bad. If I was right, I had to stop him. As we raced toward Fort Worth, I went over my hypothesis.

A Valentine public kidnaping...a hot man kidnapped...a woman paid off Chuck then someone killed him to keep the woman's identity secret. I had a description—tall woman with red hair to her waist, beautiful, confident, big rings. Where had I heard that sketch mentioned before?

Stryker exited 635, taking a direct route to Fort Worth. Blood zipped through my veins. My hands trembled and sweated. If I was right, both men I cared about were in grave danger. But if I stopped Stryker, I wouldn't find Matt. I had to hang back, or Stryker would sight me tailing him.

Then in Ft. Worth, I lost Angel. Couldn't even pick up the manly sound of that Harley's engine I so loved.

I prowled the streets, retraced my route, and found myself driving past the Lone Star Grill. Just down the street next to the train tracks, the still-working stockyard with its corrals and cattle chutes waited for the next stock show. The roof-covered stalls in the stockyards were only used weekends to show cattle at cattle auctions. Otherwise they stood empty. Occasionally during summer, a few corrals opened to the public so people could visit them and get a taste of the Old West.

There, parked in the shadow of the two-story wooden building next to the corral, was Stryker's Harley.

I drove as close to the yards as I could, called in my position to Uncle Robert and to Frank, then hopped out. I couldn't wait for back-up, but they'd see my Jeep.

Today no longhorns milled around inside the empty corrals. The lonely fenced areas looked to have been unoccupied for a while. But manure, straw, and cow smell hung heavy in the air. Dust motes rose lazily from the straw.

My high-tops thudded on the steps as I ran up to the wooden passageways above the corrals. I followed one as far back into the maze of corrals as the walkway went. Then I jumped down inside a corral, stirring up more dust and hay. I bent and climbed through the rough bottom slats between corrals until I worked my way to the end of the last cattle-holding pen. From here I couldn't even see the street.

Nothing but stack after stack of empty pens under a wooden roof.

It was dark under the roof. The pungent odor of longhorns and old straw clogged my airways. Dust tickled my nose and made me want to sneeze. I hoped I hadn't called Frank and Jake on a wild-goose chase. Silently as possible, I trod through the ankle-high straw, picking my way through the shadows. Where was Stryker?

I'd about given up and held my cell, ready to punch in the numbers to call off my back-up, when I heard muffled voices.

A tall fence of compact bales blocked the rear of the last corral. The voices came from the other side.

I crept closer. I had no hiding place but the stacked bales and the dim light. My muffled steps kicked up dusty hay. Careful not to stir up rats, I tiptoed to where I could hear.

"I came alone. Let Murdock go."

As I recognized Stryker's voice, my stomach jumped then tightened. Chills made my hair stand on end. Just this once, I wished my gut had been wrong. There could be no good outcome to what Stryker was doing. Would he and Matt both die?

For a long, dark moment my heart stopped. My hands and feet turned icy.

A woman's voice sneered, "Maybe I'll keep both of you."

"Maybe not. You said him for me."

I stood on tiptoes and peeked over the shortest stack. A stray spike of hay scratched my cheek. Stryker stood with his hands in the air facing a woman almost as tall as he. Her back was toward me.

This was exactly what I'd hoped wouldn't happen. The woman's curvy body partially hid Stryker. A cascade of red hair fell to her waist. In the gloom of the covered corral, I could barely see the big gun she held in both hands, pointed at Stryker's chest. But the weapon was too long, so I knew she had a silencer attached to the barrel. She could shoot Stryker where he stood, and no one but me would even hear.

But Stryker was armed. His pistol inside a holster under his arm showed in plain view. He'd rolled up the sleeves of his white shirt three-quarters. His hands were empty and held above his head, fingers spread. But I knew he carried another gun in an ankle holster and maybe one stuffed into his belt behind his back.

My knees wavered. Yet she could shoot him before he even got his hand around the grip of his gun. For a second, I wished he were Flash. With his lightning reflex, Frank might draw a gun before she could shoot him. But Stryker was bigger and slower.

Had I arrived just in time to see him die?

"Cut him loose." Stryker's deep voice sounded as sure as if the whole Dallas Police Force backed him up. He nodded toward something lying in the straw a short distance from them.

I took another look at what had appeared to be a couple of hay mounds. My heart somersaulted. Matt! Hog-tied like a steer about to be branded and lying on his side. A sliver of light filtered through the shingle roof and landed on his face. His eyes and mouth were taped, his cheeks covered with blond stubble, his clothes dirty and torn. He'd been so covered with straw, I hadn't seen him.

Joy billowed through me, and I almost called his name. He squirmed, kicking up dust and hay as he tried to get his hands loose. He was alive! But even from where I stood, I could see someone had done a bang-up job with rope, and no way could he break free.

Stryker repeated, "Cut him loose."

Oh, God, she could kill them both before Stryker could get his gun out of his holster. What was he thinking?

I slipped my own gun out of my shoulder bag.

"I don't think so. Toss your shoulder holster over here, or I'll shoot him." The redhead kicked Matt's shoulder.

One of those micro-expressions that are instantaneous and completely involuntary flitted across Stryker's face. He intended to tackle the woman…and I knew he'd get shot.

I froze. Blackness took my sight. I was back with Dad. Gunshots cracked. My father crumpled at my feet, blood streaming from his head, his chest, his legs. I couldn't move. Stryker would die as my father had. At my feet. Then the woman would kill Matt. And I'd be as useless here as I'd been when my father was murdered.

I couldn't see. The blackness started spinning.

"You, drop your gun!" My voice rang out and surprised me. The blackness evaporated.

The redhead jumped like she'd been snake-bit.

Stryker grabbed his weapon, dropped to one knee, trained the gun on her, then slipped a knife from his biker boot and duck-walked to Matt, his gun still on the woman. "Good work, Bloodhound." With his free hand, he started cutting Matt free.

I dragged in a breath and realized I hadn't been breathing. Staying put behind the bales and keeping my gun steady on the woman, I wiggled my nose and fought not to sneeze from all the mites being stirred up.

In a matter of minutes, Matt was unbound. He pulled off his blindfold and gag then tried to stand. He staggered back down into the straw.

"Holly?" Matt's voice sounded rusty. "I knew you'd come."

"Hey, buddy. I was here first."

"Yeah, thanks Stryk."

"Not so fast you three. Drop your pistol, Black. You too, Garden," a deep voice behind me ordered.

I whirled. "Jake. I'm so glad to see you. You don't understand. That woman's the kidnapper." I waved my gun at her.

"Garden, *you* don't get it. Drop your gun!"

Jake slammed the hard edge of his flattened hand against my arm. Pain rocketed up my arm and I dropped my Glock. My stomach plummeted into the hay, along with my weapon. Jake scooped up my gun and stuck my weapon into his belt.

"Black, you stay where you are on your knees. Drop those weapons or I'll spatter Garden's blood all over this corral."

Stryker obeyed.

I stood there with my mouth gaping. Jake? I'd never had a clue.

He was still ordering Stryker, but his gun pointed at me.

"That's right. Now, hero, crawl over next to Matt." Jake's ordinary face didn't appear run- of-the-mill now. He looked lethal. His nondescript eyes were as cold as his gun barrel.

"Don't try anything stupid, or your girlfriend gets holes plugged into her head."

The steel in Jake's voice froze Stryker's posture into a statue. On his knees, he moved a few feet back from the dropped weapons, hands in the air.

I sneezed.

"Garden, line up over there next to your boyfriend."

I gazed at Uncle Robert's right-hand investigator and finally remembered to shut my mouth.

"Move." Jake grabbed me, cold barrel of his gun at my temple, his iron grip around my neck, and lugged me over beside Stryker. "Now you…" He nodded at Stryker. "…lie face down."

Stryker's eyes met mine, and as he watched Jake choking me, I saw the desperation he tried to hide. I wanted to tell him not to sacrifice himself for my sake, but he'd already done that for Matt. Besides, Jake had my neck in a stranglehold, and I could barely breathe.

Face drained of color, Stryker dropped flat, arms spread. I still hadn't gotten a glimpse of the woman's face. Still sitting where he'd been tied, Matt wouldn't be any help. He looked drugged. Face in the hay, Stryker didn't move. Between his shoulder blades, sweat stained his white shirt.

"Don't try anything dumb," Jake ordered again.

I would have warned Stryker that Jake was going to kill us all now that we knew he was a bad guy, but I couldn't talk. I fought for air, my mouth open like a hooked flounder on dry land. Jake tightened his hold on my throat, and my feet dangled in the air. Besides, I was sure Stryker and Matt, even in his drugged state, already knew the score. I kicked backward, hitting Jake's shins hard.

He tightened his hold on my neck, lifting me higher. I saw stars. So this was how I would die.

Above the rattling in my ears, I vaguely heard Jake ask the redhead, "What now? You still want Black?"

"More than you'll ever know. Stryker, you handsome stack of male DNA, put your hands behind your back." She held a long length of wire and twisted it tight around Stryker's wrists.

"This marvel of male rugged photogenics wouldn't give me what I want the easy way." She laughed, apparently unafraid she'd be heard in that lonely, remote corral. "So he *will* give it to me the hard way."

Her tinkling laugh got mixed up with the roaring in my ears. No air. The stars twinkled into blackness.

That's when I passed out.

CHAPTER TWENTY ONE

I regained consciousness slowly. My face was buried in straw, and the prickly strands hurt my cheeks. Dust tickled my nose. I couldn't have been out long because Stryker lay on his stomach, hands bound behind him. The redhead was putting the final twist to the wire binding his ankles together.

I didn't move, hoping the two unlikely kidnappers thought Jake strangled me.

From where I lay, I couldn't see Matt.

Still kneeling beside Stryker, the tall woman murmured, "You are so fine." She caressed Stryker's beard-rough cheek—the side with the healing eye. "You *will* give me what I want." She showed her gun to him and smiled. "This won't hurt your perfect genes at all. Here's a sample of what you'll get for sending Antonio to jail." She smashed the gun barrel into his face.

Stryker's head snapped to the side. His head dropped and he lay motionless.

That thud of metal against bone sickened me. I gagged. *Who's Antonio?*

The redhead glanced at me. "Get rid of these other two. I don't need them." She spoke as casually as if she set up a dinner date. The woman's absolute lack of concern about life screamed psychopath.

Jake stepped over and towered above me. "The girl might come in handy. Looked to me like the PI you're crazy about will do anything to keep me from hurting her."

The redhead's face darkened. "Crazy about? I hate him. And I don't need the girl. I want to enjoy all the time it takes to get what I want from Stryker. No shortcuts. I may need a week or two, maybe more. I hope he holds out that long. I expect to enjoy his pain."

She kicked Stryker's motionless body in the side. The dull thump made me cringe. I prayed no more ribs cracked.

"When I'm done, you can dispose of what's left of him."

I fought not to puke again. The hay below me was already a smelly mess. But I wasn't going down without a fight. Mentally I went over how best to take out an opponent. Use my natural body weapons— heels, elbows, fists, knees—against his vital targets—eyes, groin, top of the foot, pinky, thumb. I raised myself up on my forearms.

Both Jake and the woman were bent over Stryker. I still couldn't see Matt. My veins iced, leaving me clutching straws in both fists. Had they killed him?

They'd already murdered Chuck. They had nothing to lose killing Matt and me…and Stryker.

Why had they kept Matt alive this long? Like a frontal lobotomy, the answer hit me between the eyes.

Stryker lay bound with wire in front of the two criminals. The wrestlers had kidnapped the *wrong* man. The redhead hadn't wanted Matt at all. But since she had him, she used Matt to lure Stryker. For some reason, she wanted Stryker. Something to do with Valentine's day and gorgeous men, as well as somebody named Antonio. I could bet the motive was revenge. Somehow Stryker had crossed the psychopath.

And Stryker, being the hero he was, gave himself up in trade for Matt. He'd thought he could take the woman by himself. And maybe he would have if I hadn't shown up. But neither of us expected Jake. Or at least, not me. I hadn't figured Stryker's trade-out fast enough to stop him. And now we were both in this mess.

Why did the man insist on being noble? When he told me he knew Matt was alive, he must have received word from the woman, and he'd planned to rescue Matt himself. Didn't the man have sense enough to give himself some backup?

A lightning thought hit me. Stryker knew I tailed him. He saw me when he roared out of Ace Investigations' parking garage on his Harley. I was his backup. *He trusted me.*

With Jake and the redhead still bent over Stryker, I had to make my move.

I gathered my returning strength, jumped up, and smashed my whole body weight down on Jake's Arnold Swartzanegger back.

I grabbed his neck with one hand and jammed the fingers of my other hand into his eyes.

He cursed and jerked back and forth, trying to shake me off.

The woman leaped up and limped toward him but stumbled at Jake's feet. From where he lay in the straw, Matt had both hands wrapped around her ankles. Then he grabbed her wrists and held her down. Eyes wide, face white, Matt resembled a zombie. But he pinned the athletic-looking woman on the hay-strewn floor.

I had a harder time with Jake. He jumped and cursed and waved his gun around. Trying to relieve him of that gun, I wrestled his arm with all my strength. The gun went off.

Someone moaned.

Jake flipped me off his back. As I flew off, I raked my nails down his face and managed to land on my feet.

Eyes streaming tears, he came for me. I karate-chopped his Adam's apple. He stepped back, regrouped, then grabbed me in a bear hug. I twisted in his grip and elbowed him with everything I had above that six-pack abdomen. He dropped his hold on me and folded forward, arms hugging his gut. I gave him my best drop-kick to his jaw. He fell backward but still held on to the gun. I landed on his chest with both knees. His breath whooshed out like Old Faithful.

Jake lay flat on his back, arms outstretched, fighting for air. I wrestled the gun from his clenched fist and wrenched my gun from his belt.

"It's all over." My voice whistled through my teeth.

"Good job, Bloodhound."

Even late, Frank's voice sounded more than welcome. The gun he held on Jake ramrodded steel back into my tottering knees.

I looked over at Matt, lying on his side in the straw. Had Jake's shot hit him? I glanced around the shadowy, cavernous corral.

"The redhead's gone." I couldn't keep the sound of defeat out of my voice.

"I never saw a woman." Frank kept his gun trained on Jake.

"She's the boss."

While Frank pulled Jake's arms behind his back, I ran to Matt and wrestled him over onto his back. His eyes were open, startlingly sapphire in his dirty face, and he smiled at me. My already galloping pulse hitched. I checked him over for blood but found none.

"I knew you'd come for me. I love you, Holly." His voice sounded funny, slurred, and off-kilter.

"He's drugged." Frank looked up from the handcuffs he was snapping on Jake's wrists. "How's Stryk?" He patted Jake down for hidden weapons.

I'd been so rocked to my heels by Matt's words that I'd forgotten

Stryker. I moved from Matt to Stryker and found him unconscious. Blood dripped under his cheek where he'd been pistol-whipped. I was trying to unwind the wire from his lacerated wrists when I noticed a crimson stain seeping through the back of his white shirt.

CHAPTER TWENTY TWO

"I told you Cupid rhymes with stupid."

"But, Holly, you were talking about Preston." Temple raised slender, perfectly arched brows at me.

"No, I was actually talking about myself falling for Preston and believing his lies."

I gazed around the stark hospital waiting room where Temple and I had been wringing our hands for some three hours. I propped my elbows on my knees and dropped my head into my hands. The last word I'd gotten about Stryker was that he hung in there, and the doctors were doing a lot of surgery patching him up.

"But this time I'm speaking of Stryker. I think I'm getting too interested in him. And he might be dying as we speak."

Temple put her arms around me and held me in a hug. "Of course you're grateful to the big guy. After all, he did save your life several times. But I'd say you're even now." She jerked her head up as a doctor entered from the operating room, bringing with him the nauseating odor of disinfectant. The harried man in blue surgical scrubs passed us and went to speak low-voiced to a couple huddled across the waiting room from us.

As if my gawking could bring the right surgeon with the right news, I turned and stared once again at the double swinging doors that led into the operating rooms.

"No, my feelings have gone beyond grateful. I'm really into him. And I'm so scared he won't make it." I couldn't admit to myself, much less tell Temple, the eagerness I felt to see Angel whenever he wasn't near, or the feeling of safety when he was. "Okay, so I was angry at first. I was shocked to discover he tailed me because Mom paid him. But when Jake held us at gunpoint, I couldn't help but notice how protective he tried to be."

And I couldn't forget the warm touch of his thumb or his electric lips on mine. I still felt the fire. But I had to be honest with myself. It wasn't the sizzling attraction I felt for Stryker that opened my heart to him. His always being there for me had softened my heart. Still, much as I didn't want to admit it, Mom's money *could* account for his being there each time I needed him.

Stryker being there meant so much more to me since Preston had so publicly not been there at the altar on our wedding day.

I must have had stars in my eyes because Temple said, "Take care, girlfriend. As far as I can tell, the man's not a Christian."

"Just showing up to keep a commitment tops my list of things I look for in a man, and Stryker's halfway there."

"He has issues."

"I know. Like I said, Cupid is stupid."

"And what about Matt? You told me he loves you."

"Yeah." I shook my head again. "But that was the drugs talking."

"Drugs cause a person to blurt out the truth. People lose their inhibitions." She put a hand on my arm. "So what are your feelings for Matt?"

I jumped up to pace the tile floor. "Oh, I'm so confused. I don't know. I mean, I've loved Matt like a brother for years." I ran my hands through my messy hair. "But finding him after I feared he was dead and seeing him with new eyes… I guess I haven't really looked at him for years. He really is a…um, hunk, as Granny would say. And he's so sweet, and he's a Christian, but he—" I stopped short, grabbed my hair, and pulled. My eye twitched like a crazy woman's. "He's got a dangerous job," I mumbled.

"I hate to point out the obvious, but so does Stryker."

I slumped back into the hard hospital chair. "I know. I know. So that does it. Both men are officially off-limits." I massaged the knotted muscles that erupted into granite rocks on the back of my neck. "So I don't have to figure out which—"

"Thought I'd find you here."

My mouth dropped open as I gazed up at the tall athletic man with the wide shoulders and flashing grin.

"Matt! You're supposed to be in a private room sleeping off the drugs." Long, well-muscled legs extended from beneath the dark blue robe. Why hadn't I noticed how attractive he'd grown? Where were his pimples, his air of diffidence, his too-long hair, his slumped shoulders? Who was this self-confident stranger?

"Heard anything about Stryker?"

"No. Doctor's still in surgery."

He lowered himself into the chair next to me and reached over to pull a tiny straw from my hair. I caught a whiff of his clean masculine scent and remembered I hadn't even taken time to shower or change since my near-death experience in the hay. I'd followed the ambulance to the hospital and waited since then to hear if Stryker still hung on to life. I shifted in my seat away from Matt, hoping he wouldn't notice my smell.

"Hi, Matt," Temple said brightly. "I was just leaving to get a soda. See you two in a few."

I barely noticed her leave.

Matt took my hand, and I jumped at the electricity arcing between us. What was wrong with me? Had I become super-sensitive because I'd made it through alive?

"Look, Holly, I think I might have said some things…you know… when you rescued me."

I nodded. Here came bad news. I clenched the chair arm with both hands.

"Well, um…yeah. People say funny things when they're on drugs. I'd been drugged for days and hardly knew what I was doing. So, um…if I said anything really dumb, would you just forget it? Actually, forget anything I might have said." His blue eyes wouldn't quite meet mine. "I don't want you to feel pressured so soon after your experience with…you know. Your other romance."

I swallowed. What could I say? I knew now that he loved me. Everybody else seemed to have known it forever. But if he wanted to give me time to heal and wasn't ready to tell me, that was more than okay with me. I sure wasn't ready for love again—not with Matt…and definitely not with Stryker.

"You're right. People say weird things when they're drugged." I squeezed his hand. "You said you knew I'd find you. Thanks for having confidence in me. That means the world to me. I treasure your trust."

"You're the most competent person I know…and the smartest. I knew you'd turn out to be a great investigator."

Warmth flooded my body as if I just drank a caffeé macchiato dribbled with caramel while sitting in an overstuffed chair at my favorite coffee shop, laughing with all my friends. Delicious knowing Matt believed in me. How could I have taken him so for granted? I felt like kissing him, but my unwashed condition held me back.

Impulsively I decided he'd just have to take me as I was. I leaned over to go for first base, when a short, round doctor burst through the double-doors and scanned the few people still sitting in the waiting room. "Miss Garden? I have news of Mr. Black."

I jumped up and ran to face the rotund surgeon. "Yes. How is he? Is he okay?"

With my peripheral vision, I saw the shudder that caused Matt's hands to tremble. So he'd already figured the lay of the land. Maybe Stryker was the reason he didn't want to tell me of his love.

But at the moment I was intent on hearing about Stryker.

"Miss Garden, Mr. Black will live. It was touch-and-go there for a while." With a sleeve of his blue scrubs, he swiped at sweat on his forehead. "But he's a strong young man with a mighty will to live, and he's on the way to recovery. The bullet lodged between his shoulder and his heart. It missed his lungs. We'll keep him in ICU for a while before we move him to a private room."

"Can I see him?"

"He won't be conscious for several hours. Then I hope he'll sleep." The doctor looked me up and down, and I could have sworn he wrinkled his nose.

Okay, so I needed a shower.

"Why don't you go on home and rest? Give him a few hours."

With Stryker safe, my mind sprang to full alert, and suddenly I realized what had nibbled at the back of my mind all the while I'd been sitting in the hospital waiting room. I knew where to find the kidnapper. I walked Matt back to his room, and then Temple and I dashed to Bunny. As I sped out of the hospital driveway, I made a quick phone call to Granny.

After we talked, I signed off on my Blue Tooth then speed-dialed Frank.

"Get a judge to sign a Felony Arrest Warrant and meet me at 727 Greenhill Place. It's just off Legacy and Preston Roads. It's Monica Fairweather's home. She's our kidnapper."

"Hold on, Bloodhound. How do you know that?"

"First, I found her name on Samantha Parker's Facebook. Monica is a second cousin."

"And?"

"Jake must have told Monica that you and Stryker would handle security at the Meet-A-Thon. I don't think Jake knew that Mom first gave that job to Matt and me. Monica sent Samantha to the party to ID Stryker to the wrestlers as the PI in charge of security…and the man she wanted kidnapped. Samantha got sidetracked by Matt's attention, saw he was working security, and assumed he was in charge. She mistakenly I.D.'d Matt to the wrestlers as the PI Monica wanted kidnapped. When I visited Samantha at her apartment, she feared Monica had come to retaliate because she fingered the wrong PI."

"Pretty far-fetched. Anything else?"

"I remembered I'd heard Monica's description somewhere—tall, beautiful, red-haired, big rock on her index finger."

"Could be a thousand women in Dallas with that description."

"But she's the only one with a bad limp."

"Where'd you get her address?"

"Granny described a woman just like that who regularly took her dogs to Paradise Pet Spa."

"The Paradise *what*?"

"It's an upscale boarding and grooming spa where the rich and famous take their pets. Anyway, the redhead took her two poodles there to be groomed. Granny's never met a stranger and wandered over to talk with her. The woman froze her out. But Granny's not put off by snubs, so she kept at her chat. To make a long story short, Granny lifted the woman's pant leg to see what made her limp. Granny said Monica's feet were deformed."

"So?"

"While I was lying in the straw after Jake throttled me, I had a close-up look at the kidnapper's feet. She wears sandals because her feet are so misshapen. Believe me, Frank, this woman is the kidnapper. I called Granny at Paradise Pets, and she gave me Monica's address."

"Okay, we got a go. That's enough evidence for a judge to sign a warrant. I'll meet you there with back-up. Do you know why she wanted Stryker?"

"I can only make a wild guess. Some sort of revenge. Stryker must have dumped her on Valentine's or something. They seemed to know each other fairly well."

"Makes sense."

"Then trust me, Frank. And hurry. She's probably going to run."

Still wearing my dirty black jeans and t-shirt, with my hair messy and my body reeking, I put the pedal to the metal.

"Don't forget back-up. Bye, Frank."

Her eyes shining, Temple wanted to go with me, but I dropped her off at her house. She was too precious a friend to put in danger.

Frank would take some time to get the warrant, but I didn't want the hen to fly the coop, so in fifteen minutes I was outside the address. I parked behind some bushes where I could watch the gate, but no one driving out could see my Jeep.

Wide iron security gates and a guard station with a call button on a mounted keypad protected the estate. A camera attached to the top of one stone pillar pointed at the entrance. I didn't have to wonder how to get inside because the gates gaped wide open. A bad feeling crept down my spine that our kidnapper had already fled the castle.

Finally—but in less time than I thought possible—Frank drove up, and I rolled through the gates. Frank, in an unmarked car, screeched in right behind me. A black-and-white convoyed in behind him. Our little parade motored up a long drive, passing a rolling green lawn to stop in front of the triple-story mansion so pink the building might have belonged to Mary Kay, one of Dallas' many self-made millionaires.

Car doors slammed.

I had to run up the long flight of steps leading to the porch to keep up with Frank and the other officer, who happened to be Frank's partner, Greg Benson.

My nemesis.

I avoided Greg whenever possible because his taunts about my dad bit at me with more venom than a giant mass of fire ants.

As he pounded on the front door, Greg threw me a dirty look. "Get back in your car and wait there."

Two more officers ran around the corner of the mammoth turreted castle to cover the rear entrance.

"Whoa! I fed Frank the information for this takedown. You're not going to elbow me out." My annoyance spilled over into my tone.

Before Frank could say a word, a tall, solemn butler pulled open one of the ornate double mahogany doors.

He lifted his brows at me and addressed Frank. "Yes, officer. How might I help you?"

I spoke up from my position behind the two male backs. "We're here to see Monica Fairweather."

As if I hadn't even spoken, the butler stared at Frank and Greg, both semi-blocking me.

"Monica Fairweather, please," Frank said in that deep

commanding voice of his. He and Greg flashed their badges. My far less authoritative badge was buried deep inside my red bag somewhere, and I didn't want to take the time to dig it out, so I pushed in close to the two cops.

"Certainly, sir. I'll announce you." The butler turned and walked up a marble hall. Frank and Greg burst inside the door and started to close it. I slammed a shoulder against the hard wood and forced my way inside. I didn't sell Girl Scout cookies as a kid for nothing.

"What's going on, Frank? You're not leaving me out. You've got this takedown because of me."

Frank's superman face reddened. "Yeah, Bloodhound. But this might get sticky."

When I pulled my gun from my bag, my hand was so sweaty I almost dropped my weapon. "I can handle sticky. Watch me handle sticky. I've faced this crazy woman before—"

"Don't bicker, you two. Here she comes," Greg hissed.

Tall, elegantly dressed in a full-length red Chinese sheath with gold-braid frogs, red hair in an unruffled upsweep, glossed lips smiling as if she were welcoming expected friends, Monica limped toward us. The scent of expensive perfume reached us before she did.

"You may go, Thomas," she said to the butler.

Acting as if the woman she ordered killed only a few hours past wasn't standing there facing her, she said coolly, "May I see your badges, gentlemen?" She held out a slender hand with a huge diamond sparkling on her index finger.

Frank flashed his. Greg, ears blazing, fumbled for his. I could read his thoughts from a mile. He figured we'd all made the mistake of our careers trying to arrest a woman of this obvious influence. While she examined the badges, he threw me another dirty look.

But Frank wasn't fooled. "I'm here to arrest you for the

kidnapping of Matthew A. Murdock." He began reciting her Miranda rights.

Monica tossed me a scorching look that made my toes curl. I've been on the receiving end of many a put-down. After all, I survived Middle School and High School. But her look blistered.

"You're making a very big mistake." Monica turned her I'll-kill-you-where-you-stand gaze on the least certain of us. Greg wilted under her scorn. He dropped the police hat he'd tucked between his arm and his side, knelt and fumbled for it, the back of his neck brick red and slick with sweat.

Why does the guy who's the worst hazer turn out to be the biggest coward? Insecurity, I'm thinking.

Frank was having none of Monica's bull. He stepped forward, pulled her hands behind her back, and snapped on the cuffs.

Looking over her shoulder, she cooed, "You'll hear from the Texas Governor for this, Officer McCoy. You do know he's my dear friend." She parted those luscious lips with just enough gloss to make a man lose his sense of direction and gave Frank a pouty smile.

She was so convincing that if I hadn't recognized that husky voice, even I would've thought we were making a fatal career mistake.

The other officers, who'd entered the back door, must have heard Monica's threat because they crept up the hall behind her on silent cat's paws, chins down, hats tipped low over their eyes.

I could have kissed Frank when he continued with the arrest with absolutely no show of awe or self-doubt.

He trusted me.

I heard Stryker was awake, so I bee-lined it back to the ICU. They let me in and told me he was resting.

At the sight of his dark head lying on the white hospital pillow, my heart almost stopped. For several heartbeats I stood perfectly still, too stunned to move.

Dark hair fell across his high forehead. Thick lashes lay against pale cheeks. His big frame filled the narrow bed, feet touching the iron rail. His chest, smothered in bandages, barely rose and fell. The left side of his face was black and blue from forehead to chin. His arms lay by his side, wrists bandaged.

I'd expected him to look bad. But this—

"Princess." The deep voice sounded weak. His eyes opened slowly, slightly unfocused.

"Yeah. How did you know it was me?"

"Smelled you." His mouth turned up at the edges.

He had to see the red painting my embarrassment from head to toe. "Well, I've been busy."

"Good smell. Working-PI smell." His lips turned up more. "You arrested her?"

"Yeah."

"Good work."

"Thanks. You helped." My smile didn't even begin to reflect the satisfaction spreading through my veins.

"Me? I was hogtied."

"You know what I mean. You were always there when I needed you."

"You too…for me."

I could see he was exhausted. His lids closed, and he struggled to open them, then lost the battle and drifted into a drugged sleep.

Since I felt pretty unsteady, I balanced by grasping the back of the hospital chair for support.

I don't know how long I stood there as the sun picked out walnut highlights in his wavy hair. I thought about how when sometimes something happens to you, you know your life will never be the same, even when you don't want it to change. Like how, out of the blue, you're chosen Homecoming Queen. Or how your father is murdered right in front of your eyes, and you know, for better or worse, that your world will never be the same. You can only come to grips with the reality and accept it.

I knew right then that Stryker and I shared more than friendship.

He knew it too. I saw his thoughts in his eyes.

The change happened like a fierce undertow, pulling me in, sweeping my feet off solid ground. There was nothing I could do. This couldn't be love. I was too level-headed to fall for a man every woman swooned over. A man with no family. A man with such a different background from mine. A man with a dangerous job who could be killed on the most routine day of his life. A man who probably wasn't a Christian.

I couldn't fall for him. What I felt was the same bewitching spell he cast on all women. Hadn't another woman kidnapped him because of his allure? Stryker Black was a *dark* angel. I wouldn't let myself care about him. He was temptation incarnate.

Did Eve have feelings for the beautiful fallen angel in the garden before she sinned?

CHAPTER TWENTY THREE

The next day Temple and I moved into our new apartment.

I'd keep my address as secret as possible and give my new PO Box as my address. Those I loved knew where I'd moved, but since I had a job that might prove dangerous to my loved ones, I had to protect my family. Unfortunately the police already knew my family's address. But the time had come for me to be on my own.

It took two more days before I trotted into Frank's upstairs office at the police station. Frank was out. I handed my typed statement to Frank's partner, Greg Benson.

He looked up from the desk he shared with Frank. For once, on seeing me, a scornful expression didn't spring to his rugged features.

"You did some good sleuthing, Garden. Saved Murdock's and Black's lives. Congrats."

I shifted the heavy purse on my shoulder and pretended to look inside to hide my surprise. "Thanks."

He rose from his swivel chair, rounded the desk, and clapped me on my shoulder. "Monica Fairweather wouldn't make a peep in the interrogation room."

"Oh?" Greg's earlier words of praise must be a prelude to some new form of harassment. A new way to humiliate me.

"Nope. She called in the highest-paid criminal lawyer in the nation."

My stomach fell to my toes, and a chill spread over my body. Monica would get away with kidnapping and murder.

"She did?"

"Yep."

My voice sounded small. "Did she get released on bail?"

"Nope." A big grin split Greg's up-to-that-moment-solemn expression. "Jake Henderson spilled his guts. Copped a plea-bargain by confessing all the dirty deeds he's done for that Black Widow psychopath."

I breathed again and my hands curled. I felt like wringing Greg's neck for keeping me in suspense.

"Here's Jake's statement."

I took the papers Greg offered and settled in the chair in front of his desk. I read:

I, Jake E. Henderson, do this day give my statement regarding my knowledge of the kidnapping of Matthew Murdock.

On the evening of February 13th, approximately 7:00 pm, I arrived at Monica Fairweather's residence at 727 Greenhill Place, Dallas, Texas. It was the evening before the kidnapping. We went outside on the patio, located on the south side of the house. I sat and she paced.

She had a copy of the Diagnostic & Statistical Manual of Mental Disorders *in hand and waved it around. She appeared to be in an agitated state and threw the book into the pool.*

She stated that a psychiatrist labeled her as having an antisocial personality.

She threatened to take revenge against the psychiatrist, but stated she wanted to take care of the PI first. She stated she despised shrinks and investigators, especially the private eye she wanted kidnapped the next evening at the Valentine Meet-A-Thon.

She'd get what she wanted from him. Then she'd very, very slowly kill him.

She grew more agitated and smashed the birdbath. She stated she could barely keep from tearing off her own skin, she hated the PI so. She stated she wanted payback from Stryker Black. Only payback would cool her anger and would be so easy, so simple, so satisfying.

I, Jake Henderson, hardened PI, got cold chills looking at her.

She stated that in the past she'd used poison, but she'd used poison so many times on other occasions that the thrill had died. She stated she wanted something more clever than an accident.

At that time, her butler stepped out onto the patio and announced her attorney had arrived.

She ordered the attorney shown in. Before he arrived, she stated that cool thinking kept her ahead of the death penalty's lethal injection all these years. She stated she had a few last papers to sign and everything would be transferred to her name. Her late husband would be just another closed memory. She stated that it was too bad Hubby-Number-Three had been such a pest, but she had let him irritate her longer than the other two.

She took the four-carat diamond from her left ring finger, fitted it onto her index finger, then threw the wedding band into the Koi pond.

She stated that since she'd been in fifth grade and discovered her power, no one had crossed her and not paid her price. She stated that when she finished with him, the PI would beg to give her what she wanted.

At that point, I was not acquainted with Stryker Black. Nor did I realize until much later the night of the kidnapping that the wrong man had been kidnapped. My small part in the kidnapping consisted *of informing Monica that Stryker Black from Ace Investigations would provide security for the Meet-A-Thon. I did not know that two rookies from Garden Investigations would also be providing security. I did not attend the party.*

However, after the wrestlers kidnapped the wrong man, Monica hired me to keep tabs on Holly Garden and Stryker Black and report their movements to her. She stated she still intended to kidnap Black.

My part in the whole scheme ended. I was merely in the wrong place at the wrong time when I was arrested at the Ft Worth Stockyards.

Signed Jake Henderson, PI.

Holly folded the statement and handed it back across the desk to Greg. "Jake's trying to cover his rear. I'm sure the DA will bring plenty of charges against him."

"You got that right. And it looks like Monica killed her last three husbands."

I shook off the chill reading Jake's statement had given me. "From what I saw of her, that's not surprising."

"Yep. Jake'll end up with five to twenty for Conspiracy. Monica might sway a jury and get life, but she'll never get out of the slammer. You did yourself proud."

"I didn't do it alone."

"Flash told me all about it." Greg squeezed my arm. "Say, if you ever want to work with me, I'm your cop-on-duty."

I didn't think so, but I kept my thoughts to myself. Now that I knew him better, Greg struck me as a rawer recruit than I'd been a rookie. But I smiled. "Thanks." No need to make more unnecessary enemies in the police department.

Then it hit me. *Had been.* Wow! I *had been* a rookie, but now I'd solved my first case. I really was a private investigator. I earned my badge. The realization didn't thrill me as much as I'd hoped. Matt blurting he'd expected me to find him had really sent me to the stars. Still, the kudos from Greg felt good.

As soon as I got home I'd take all those index cards down from my bulletin board, bring them up to date, stash them in a manila folder, and mark it with bold red ink: CASE CLOSED. Then I'd store my first case inside my empty file cabinet under the divider marked SOLVED CASES.

Joy spilled over, enough that I flashed my warmest smile at Greg, though still not trusting nor even liking him, but so glad to be in the place where God wanted me.

He misread my elation. His chest swelled, he adjusted his regulation tie, and squared his shoulders. "Yeah, we'd make a great team." He grinned from ear to ear. Then as an afterthought, he waved a hand. "You just missed Frank. He left for the hospital. Said if I saw you to tell you Stryk wants to see you."

Greg must have thought I was rude when I pivoted in my high-tops and bolted for the door.

CHAPTER TWENTY FOUR

Stryker had been moved from ICU to a private room. I found him cranked up in bed by the hospital window, gazing down over the second-story air-conditioning system and one of the parking lots. He looked so much better than he had after his chest surgery. His brown eyes sparkled with the old adventurous zest. His complexion looked ruddy.

He flashed me that you're-the-best-thing-I've-seen-in-years smile of his. "Glad you came. I thought you'd forgotten me."

"Not a chance."

A speculative gleam glinted in those brown-to-die-for eyes. He lifted the one dark brow not bandaged. "Is that a promise?"

"Just being friendly—co-worker to co-worker." Regardless of all the sizzling undercurrents between us, that's as far as I could envision us going. He wasn't a Christian, and I wasn't ready for any romance with Mr. Too-Hot-to-Handle.

"So you heard your Uncle Robert offered me Jake Henderson's old job?"

"And you accepted." I didn't want to admit what a difficult position that put me in, so I kept my face deadpan. "Couldn't have been for more money."

"Nope. Job was getting stale at Ace Investigations. I suspect there's going to be a lot more work at Garden now that you solved the Black Widow high-profile case and made all the headlines." He glanced at the pile of *Dallas Morning News* strewn across his bed stand.

Doing my best to keep my emotions from showing on my face, I said, "So just like that, you up and left the firm where you worked… how many years?"

"Less than one. Yep. Just like that."

"No other reason?"

"Well, there might be one more."

I was afraid to ask…but being me, of course I did. "And that is?"

"We both know the answer to that." For once his eyes looked dark and serious.

I must have frowned or registered alarm some way because his devil-may-care twinkle returned. His lips turned up, and the dimple popped out. "Someone's got to keep you out of trouble." Did he hide his real feelings behind that lighthearted charm?

Whatever the case, his words unveiled the anger hiding under my concern. "Mom's still paying you?" A hot poker jabbed my brain.

"Hasn't paid me since that first night."

"What?" I started blubbering. "How…why…?" I grabbed the iron bed railing. "But that evening I caught Mom paying you—"

"She wanted me to keep an eye on you and offered to pay, but I declined." He shifted on the bed. "Keeping an eye on you is so much fun, I do it on my own time."

My anger fizzled out as fast as a firecracker doused in water. "But I saw her pay you. What was that all about?"

"Oh, that." His dimples played in leaner cheeks. "She'd asked me to check out Romeo—you know, J.C. Hogg, her date the night of the

Valentine security-hitch. I was giving her my report and getting paid for my services."

My mouth fell open. "Mom did that? Well, good for her. And?" I leaned forward and gazed expectantly into Stryker's chocolate, unable-to-be-read eyes.

Cop face on, he just looked back.

I had to know. "Well, what did you find?"

"That's confidential information between my client and me."

The dimples playing around his mouth told me he teased.

"He's a con man, isn't he?" I prodded. "I can smell one a mile away."

"Let's just say your mom won't be seeing the silver-tongued Mr. Hogg any more. He's got a long record of bilking widows, taking them for all their money, and then dumping them."

"Awesome. I mean, I'm so glad you found him out." I grabbed both his hands to thank him. He groaned, but one strong arm pulled me forward until I was leaning over his bed, my chest touching his. Using the arm on the opposite side of his wound, he put pressure on my back and drew me closer until my lips landed softly on his.

Just a sweet caress that left me wanting more. Oh, so much more. Then he released me.

I gasped. When I regained my equilibrium, I straightened…which took a little time since the kiss left me feeling like a high-wire walker without a safety net. "What was that for?" I hadn't known my voice could sound so breathy.

"To seal our working relationship. I need backup I can depend on."

I could handle his digs so much better than his kisses. "Back-up? Back-up!" I sputtered. His kiss still had me off-balance. "Think again." I was glad for the fun taunt. There could be no romance between us. "Uncle Robert will give me my own cases and you'll get yours." I tossed him my tart smile. "Of course, I'm sure there'll be a time or two when I'll need *you* for back-up." I turned to gaze out the window at the huge air-conditioning unit on the roof. An ugly sight.

His kiss threw me harder than I wanted him to see. Harder than I wanted to feel. I didn't want to be affected by anything this man did. I felt behind me for my shoulder bag and was about to wave a saucy goodbye and stalk out of the room when his next words stopped me dead.

"Don't you want to know why Monica wanted to kidnap me?"

Seconds earlier, torture wouldn't have forced me to stay in that room. Now I slammed my purse on his bedside table, jerked up the visitor chair to face him, and plunked myself down. My hands were sweaty, my knees shaky, but I had to find out if my hypothesis was right.

"Shoot."

"Two reasons. First, there was the revenge thing. When I was a cop, I put away a potential husband for the spider woman. Antonio DeCanaro's in jail for years, yet he won't spill where he hid the drug money. When she couldn't get to that money, Monica contacted me online. I didn't know who she was, and she lured me into cyber-dating." Stryker rubbed a hand lightly over the bandage completely hiding his chest. "Guess I should have known any woman that hot for a date had an ulterior motive."

I shrugged. Did the guy not know how attractive he was? Impossible.

"Yeah, well, we cyber-dated about a year ago. Then sometime in January, we had a few real dates. That was my first and last dive into the raging current of online dating."

"She's a Cougar." Hard to believe Stryker had been that desperate. "Were you undercover investigating her?"

"No."

"Let me guess. You broke up on Valentine's?"

"Good guess. After she found out I didn't know where the drug money was, she started pressuring me into fathering her baby." His brown eyes turned wary, and his whole demeanor stiffened. "I'm not going to have kids. Never. And she wanted a kid bad. She's past forty."

"You don't want kids?"

"No. No matter how hard a person tries not to follow what his parents did, abuse runs in families."

Slivers like glass bit into my heart. I'd never seen a grown man look so wounded. My thoughts jumped to Allison and her bruises. Puzzle pieces snapped into place. So that's why he and Allison clicked from the start. That's why they were on the same wave-length. I should have deduced as much.

"You were abused?"

"Beaten. Whenever the old man got drunk and could catch me, he beat me. Then a few days later, he'd go to church and get forgiven. Then he'd get drunk again and beat me again. And then back to church to get absolved."

"So that's why you won't go to church."

"Any church that forgives a man who's beating his kid week after week can't be good."

Father, I won't let this man die without telling him of Your great gift of salvation. One untold man on my conscious is more than enough. I'm so very sorry, Chuck. And Lord, please give me a good chance to talk with Stryker. He so needs Your healing, saving power. Please tell me when he's receptive.

From out of nowhere, I blurted, "Would you at least come speak to my fourth-grade Sunday-school class about what to do if they get caught in a situation like you had?"

"I'll think about it."

I guessed from his stony look that was all the answer I was going to get. I waited a few minutes, hoping my expression would encourage him to tell me more. But from his set mouth and narrowed eyes, I quickly realized he wasn't going to say anything else about his personal life. I figured if he hadn't been on painkillers, he'd never have told me that much.

Finally I ended the silence. "So you broke up with Monica on Valentine's Day because she wanted to have a baby with you." Unfortunately I'd been right about why she wanted to kidnap Stryker. After all, I'd heard the redhead say Stryker was a handsome stack of male DNA. I had an urge to take out a pipe, light it, and say, "Elementary, my dear Watson."

"Yeah."

"Did you give her a reason you didn't want to have a baby?"

"She insisted."

"And?"

He scowled. "We both knew she wasn't talking marriage." He sighed and muttered. "I don't want any children of mine out there in the world without my protection and guidance. Especially not with a woman I didn't trust."

Wow.

"That, and because I checked her out and discovered she was already married."

"Oh, the husband she murdered just before she kidnapped Matt. Wow, lethal woman."

I thought over Monica's motive, but it still didn't add up. "So why you of all men? When she ended up with Matt, why not have his baby? What makes you so special?"

"Yeah. Crazy, isn't it? On the surface." His mouth turned down at the corners. "She could have had a lot of other guys father her baby. But she wanted mine."

"Couldn't be because you're six-foot-three, have a really good build, a face like Michelangelo's David, and always show up when you're needed?" I smiled, hoping I looked as inscrutable as Mona Lisa. "And you dumped her. She couldn't handle that and wanted revenge."

Stryker wrapped his battered face into a swollen grin. "Is that the way you see me?"

"How?"

"Irresistible?"

Ouch. That was the question, wasn't it?

"Well, do you?"

"What?" I searched for a truthful answer that wasn't a resounding yes.

"Find me irresistible?"

"I have to work with you. If Uncle Robert doesn't have a rule against employees dating, he should. Let's leave it at that."

A slow, satisfied smile that ended up crooked because of the swollen left side of his face traveled all the way to his dark eyes, making them sparkle like chocolate bonbons.

"Okay. Back to why Monica wanted my baby in particular then. You noticed she's a beautiful woman with her violet eyes and creamy skin. The red hair's natural."

I nodded, irritated Stryker thought the criminal beautiful, and hating my instant mental vision of his running that shining, waist-length hair through his fingers.

"She explained some of the reasons. The others I deduced with my great investigative intellect."

I couldn't help grinning at his poking fun of himself.

"Yep. I'm a legend in my own mind. So she liked my looks. But that was only part of it. She wanted my murder to be clean. Nothing that could be traced to her. She knows I have no family, no one who'll keep searching to find me if I disappear. She's close to my old boss at Ace Investigations, and if necessary, planned to blackmail him to keep him from looking for my murderer. She knows I sometimes go on trips for months at a time, and no one knows where I am, so no one would start looking for me when I didn't show up for work. I might not be missed for months."

My heart squeezed. Here was a man who was really alone. If anyone needed to meet the Lord, he did. And here I was, painfully weak in my ability to tell him about my beautiful Healer of all wounds.

But I would tell him. When the time was right. I wouldn't let Stryker down like I had Chuck.

His cough brought me back to what he was saying. "You do want to know why she didn't just use Matt for the father, right?"

I sat up straight, folded my hands, and gazed right into Stryker's gorgeous eyes. "Absolutely."

"For starters, Matt's got a family. He'd be missed. He's also steady and lets people know what's going on with him." Stryker began speaking more slowly. "And Matt's dad isn't athletic. His mom's got poor hearing. Monica's really into genetics. Besides, Matt wears contacts. Monica wanted her baby to be perfect."

I frowned. "But you had an alcoholic father. What about your mother? Wasn't Monica afraid to take an awful chance with genetics?"

"I've tried to track my mother down for years. I know she went from husband to husband after she abandoned my father and me when I was a baby. But after husband-number-four, I lost her." His jaw twitched. "And Monica knows where she is." He looked down at his bandaged chest. "All I can say is, Mother must have darn good genes for Monica to still be interested."

He gazed back out the window, and a shadow fell across his face.

"That's the kicker," he said, his eyes still focused on the outside. "Monica knows my mother." He spoke as if the words were torn from somewhere deep inside.

Silence grew thick between us as I mulled that over. "And?"

"She wouldn't tell me where my mother is or what she's doing. Before Monica and I parted ways, she promised if I gave her that baby, she'd tell me."

All I could manage was a weak, "Oh." *Dear God, please help this tortured man.* "I'm so sorry, I added."

"My father hadn't been a drinker before my mother left us, so Monica wasn't worried about alcoholic genes." Eyes on the blanket covering his knees, Stryker shook his head. "So there you have it. Apparently I was the perfect candidate."

"Yeah." A sigh heaved up from deep inside my chest. But I still wasn't satisfied. "Why not just use a sperm bank?"

"Good question. I asked her that. Two reasons. She had friends who'd used a Cryobank, and their children had genetic problems— autism and early kidney disease. She said that more than fifty-thousand children are born each year using sperm banks. And they don't know their father's name. How many will end up marrying half-siblings? She had a point."

"Oh."

"So she wanted a donor she knew. My mother gave her all the background information she needed about me. I have no idea if my mother was in on her scheme, or if Monica got the information from her without Mother suspecting why Monica wanted it."

"And Monica's other reason?"

"Pure hate. I take it her dad looked much like me. She had in mind a long, slow, torturous death for me. She planned to kill Matt then keep me barely alive for a few months before she finished me off."

269

I swallowed. I didn't know what to say. I was so thankful Monica was safely behind bars and couldn't touch Stryker. He was a strong man. But she was deadly.

Matt pulled the chair out from the candlelit table by the window. We were high above Dallas in the revolving restaurant inside Reunion Tower. Our table was in a private alcove by itself. We ordered—me, lobster tail with drawn butter sauce, and Matt, a Texas-size T-bone steak, his all-time favorite. I was still thinking about Stryker's life story that kept the pit of my stomach knotted…and Matt noticed.

As soon as the waitress left, he put his hand on mine. "Did Stryker tell you why Monica has such a bad limp?"

I swallowed. "No, we didn't get around to that."

"Funny. That's the first thing he told me. I couldn't get her limp out of my mind."

"Shoot."

"It's not a pretty story." Matt gazed out the window.

Five hundred and sixty feet below us, yellow headlights from heavy traffic on Interstate 35 cast darting patterns in the darkness.

"When she was a teen, her father kept her locked in a room so she wouldn't run away. He gambled. Cards. Mostly Texas Hold-'Em. When the stakes got high, he called Monica in to distract the other players. Even as a young girl he forced her to wear clothes that would divert a man's thoughts from his game."

My eyebrows shot up. "Yeah?"

"If she didn't go overboard and make the men really mess up their game so her father could win money, he went after her. But he didn't want to get caught by CPS or ruin her beauty, so he'd tie her to the bed and lacerate the bottom of her feet with a whip. After a while her feet didn't heal so well. He must've lost big now and then and broken some bones because he left her with a bad limp." Matt swallowed. "And he left her with an enormous hate for men. All men. Especially tall, dark, handsome ones."

Though my tears blurred the slowly revolving vision of Dallas's famous skyline, I said, "You almost sound like you fell in love with your kidnapper."

Matt grunted. "Hardly. But I do feel sorry for the girl she'd been before her father did such a number on her."

"Where's her father now? He should be locked up."

"Dead. Died of some mysterious stomach ailment. There was suspicion of foul play, but nothing was ever confirmed. I suspect she murdered her father."

A dart of compassion flitted through me for the girl Monica had been twenty years ago. When I could trust my voice, I asked, "Did she hurt you?"

"Some. At first, when she was angry that the kidnappers snatched the wrong victim. After that, she made sure I was drugged out of my mind. She didn't want me to look too beat-up when she sent my picture over the cellphone to Stryker." Matt rubbed his square chin. "Got to hand it to the guy. I never thought he'd trade himself for me."

Something near the region of my heart did somersaults. I wasn't sure if the tumbles were for Matt or for Stryker…or for both the men in my life.

Matt scooted his chair next to mine. "Hey, I know you like that guy, but let me warn you: he comes with a lot of baggage." Matt's baritone voice held all the love he refused to declare. "And he's a lady-killer. Stories of broken hearts follow him like fleas after a dog."

I sniffed. After hearing Stryker's story and Monica's and feeling

Matt's unspoken love, somehow I needed to blow my nose. "I know."

Matt handed me his handkerchief. "He *likes* danger."

"And *you* don't thrive on it?" I blew my nose.

"I'm not talking about me here. He's been abused."

"Does everyone know about that?"

"I'm an investigator, remember?"

"You checked Stryker out?"

He leaned close, his sapphire eyes clear, full of trust, and sparkling with… I didn't want to face it, but I now recognized love. In his own blond way, he was as fine-looking as Stryker. And I hadn't even noticed. Me, a private investigator.

"Guy with a background like that could go off the deep-end anytime. You might not want to hang with him."

"I don't intend to. But I might have to work with him from time to time."

"I talked with your uncle about that."

I'd been playing with the swanky silverware and picking at my salad and had the knife in my hand. I jammed it down on an extra butterfly-folded napkin and spun the white fabric into a messy pancake. Why did Matt's protectiveness make me so angry? Maybe he verged on controlling.

"And?"

"He said we have so many new cases now, thanks to you, that I probably wouldn't have to worry about you and Stryker working the same one."

"Oh." I lowered my eyes, hoping my disappointment wouldn't communicate to Matt. I couldn't lie to myself. I liked Stryker having my back.

"Hey, kid, we came to celebrate. Cheer up."

"Yeah. Case closed. Everyone's safe. Let's celebrate." I smiled, really happy except for my deep confusion about the two men in my life. And I felt very, very sure I'd actually found the place the Lord wanted me to be—taking care of Garden Investigations' business.

But then Matt raised his water glass and saluted me. "You know you have a talent for pushing a guy to the limits."

"What—?"

Making no sound on the thickly carpeted floor, Matt scooted his chair closer.

I took a deep breath, inhaling his woodsy fragrance and letting it linger inside my senses. He leaned over, cupped my face with both hands, and kissed me like a man who'd had a lifetime of experience. My heart raced, and my body tingled.

I leaned into the kiss and wanted more. All thoughts of Stryker fled. Well, almost all. Visions of *his* kiss flitted through my consciousness.

But where had Matt learned to kiss like this?

This was the boy who'd spent equal time fascinating me and terrorizing me as we grew up next door to one another. This was the nerd who'd seldom had a date I hadn't fixed up for him. This was my best guy-friend.

He moved his lips away and smiled. "Don't go getting any ideas. That's for saving my life. Doesn't mean anything else."

I knew without a shadow of doubt that Matt loved me, and my world shifted again. I stood in yet another new place.

A really confusing new place, torn squarely between two equally desirable and eligible males. And as far as I was concerned, off-limit signs blinked like neon lights above both heads. My awakened feelings hadn't happened like an easy glide through the tunnel of love; they hit me like a ride on the scariest rollercoaster imaginable.

What a catch-22. Two fascinating men. One wasn't ready to

declare his love and had a tendency toward controlling, and the other didn't want kids and hated church. And I had to work with both. And I admired both. My heart gave a funny little twist that made me gasp. I was susceptible to both. I tossed my hair back over my shoulder. I did *not* want to get entangled with either. I in *no way* wanted romance. Romance simply meant pain that ripped out my heart.

And who said Cupid doesn't rhyme with stupid?

I had no time nor desire for love. I had a career to build. I had leads now on my father's murder—a dirty cop and a dirty PI to question. Jake could easily have been involved in Dad's murder. He'd been on the scene. He'd gone into the drug house by the front door when Dad had gone in by the back. Yet no one accused Jake. Oh, yes, I had a lot of questions for him.

And I had a new mission. I would track down Stryker's mother. Plus Uncle Robert waited to talk with me about a missing girl who'd been kidnapped by a cartel who used girls as sex slaves. So I was well on my way as a PI.

But what do You want me to do, God? How can I work with two such distracting men? Didn't You teach me with Preston not to trust men, not to trust my own feelings? Are these temptations to see if I've really learned my lessons?

I suspected that might be my answer.

So could a girl be attracted to two men at once? Apparently the answer to that heart-pounding question was yes. Could I work with both men? I didn't have a clue.

Still, I did know God wanted me just where I was. He'd shown me I have what it takes to be a good PI. He'd given me leads to solve Dad's murder. He'd made it possible for me to live an independent life and earn my own way. He'd brought prosperity back to Garden Investigations so we didn't have to close our doors. He'd given me a renewed spiritual journey and let me be a light in a dark place. He'd even given me friends in the Dallas Police Department, though there were still many officers who lived to see me fail. So I was happy. I was in the center of God's will for my life.

Sure, He'd called me to a big job. But I'd discovered I was a big girl. And I had a big God. He would have to take care of the men in my life.

All I had to do was let go, trust Him… and let my light shine.

ANNE GREENE